PEOPLE PERSONNEL

By
CELIA HOLUP

Grosvenor House
Publishing Limited

The right of Celia Holup to be identified as the author of this
work has been asserted in accordance with Section 78
of the Copyright, Designs and Patents Act 1988

This book is published by
Grosvenor House Publishing Ltd
Link House
140 The Broadway, Tolworth, Surrey, KT6 7HT.
www.grosvenorhousepublishing.co.uk

This book is a work of fiction. Any resemblance to
people or events, past or present, is purely coincidental.

A CIP record for this book
is available from the British Library

Paperback ISBN 978-1-83615-218-7
eBook ISBN 978-1-83615-219-4

For
HR professionals
everywhere

1

She quickened her pace. Her first candidate would have already arrived, and she hated keeping people waiting.

She was trying to recall the first candidate's name as she crossed the road at the lights and entered Smithfield Market's Grand Avenue. The men were packing up for the day, sweeping the ripped polythene and palette chips from the sticky pavement. *Sandip*, she remembered. His name was Sandip. She glanced at the imposing train station-style clock suspended from the wrought iron and glass ceiling and skidded in a puddle of stale blood. She checked the side of her shoe. It would do. She crossed over Charterhouse Street, then Cowcross Street and within a couple of minutes she'd be at work.

The Trethendar Welfare Annuity Trust was a Victorian, three-storey wedge of a building, ugly beyond belief. The heavy, blue double doors were already open and, as she approached, illuminated by the half-light through the grubby windows, she saw him sitting there in the archive; baggy suit, as if he'd lost three stone, just sitting there.

"You must be Sandip," she said as she put her hand out. He stood, wiping his palms on his trouser pockets, lanky and sweaty. She took his hand. It was boneless, limper than a filleted lettuce leaf, and clammy. "I'm Janice Mead, HR. I'll be with you in just one moment."

"OK, thank you, Janice." He noticed her hands too. She wore gloves. So thin you could almost see her skin through them.

"Excuse me wearing these," she said, "I have Raynaud's." She didn't intend explaining further. *He's hopeless*, she thought as she started up the narrow stairs, unbuttoning her coat. *No chance.*

"Morning, Janice," piped Hazel.

"Morning, Hazel... Stuart..." she said as she headed to her desk, taking her coat off as she went.

"Your first interviewee is here," Stuart said.

Stuart really is a total arsehole, she thought. How could she have possibly missed him? She picked up the papers from her desk where she'd left them the night before in preparation, and hurried back to the stairs, tapping the side of her flat hair with the heel of her hand.

"Sorry to keep you waiting, Sandip," she called down. "Would you like to come up now?"

She watched him appear at the bottom of the stairs. She turned and started up the next flight to 'the flat' on the second floor.

It was called 'the flat' because that's exactly what it had been when the charity was in more buoyant form. In fact, Trethendar used to own the whole block, but had gradually sold off parts to the neighbouring hospital, until it found itself with few fixed assets left and painted into a literal corner. Janice headed for the large round table in the far corner of the wedge. It overlooked the Y-shaped split in the Clerkenwell roads, and the July sun streamed through the tall, dusty windows. *What a shitty way to spend your birthday,* she thought. "Please take a seat," she said.

"Do you mind if I take my jacket off?" His voice was thin and pipey, like a leaking wind instrument. Asthmatic bellows.

"Go ahead," she said. He took it off. Her cat Bimbo had broader shoulders. His suit was too shiny, his shirt was dolphin grey and his tie slate grey. His shoes were patent leather, plastic, the socks, white. "Would you like some water?" White socks.

"No thank you, Janice."

Why was it so irritating when he called her that? It seemed inappropriate. They weren't even close to first name terms yet; nor would they ever be. She was a year from retirement, and he must be about twenty, looking twelve. He had bumfluff on his chin. Her dear father had shaved every day of his life. She never saw him with a five o'clock shadow, let alone a stubble and this little eel looked like he just rolled out of bed that day, expecting to get a job, entitled, like most of his generation. She was beginning her sixty-first year with this, her last working year.

"So, let's start by asking you what you know about the Trethendar."

"Well, I've been to your website and what you basically do here – it's a charity, isn't it?"

"That's right, a very old and distinguished charity." She was conscious of his eyes falling on the tiny, silver crucifix around her neck. She wondered if he would think her biased against him, her being a Christian and his being a Muslim or Hindu or something probably. She tucked it inside her blouse.

"1919 it was set up, wasn't it?" he went on. "You have members. It's a ladies-only organisation and they pay £6 a year and get a quarterly newsletter about health and wellbeing, cookery and making things like cushions and Christmas decorations. And if they're hard up, for whatever reason, they can apply to you to get a grant, called an annuity, to help them out of the sticky patch they're in. You give up to £6,000 per year. I read the website, which could do with some updating, if I can say that without sounding too cheeky." He stopped. "I didn't know what a spinster was before. I did web development at uni. so that's something I could help you with. I work well on my own but am also a good team member—"

"Thank you, Sandip."

"Sorry," he said laughing a little. "I'm a bit nervous. I always talk too much when I'm nervous." She warmed to him a little.

4

"Let me tell you about the role the agency has recommended you for. We're looking for a temp to start off with but with a view to go temp to perm for the right candidate. I say 'perm', it's a maternity cover post, so a twelve-month contract. Jenny, our office administrator, is on maternity leave. OK?" Sandip nodded. "So, tell me about your admin experience."

He started to talk ten to the dozen about his uni. course and how he'd prioritised and met deadlines but maintained an excellent attention to detail and every other buzzword he thought an interviewer would want to hear, but without any substance, without any examples. She glazed over. He was quite sweet really. Thinking she needed to be seen to write something, wrote *Honeybee Buns* and tilted the top of her pad so he couldn't see. She didn't know what they were yet, but they sounded yummy. He stopped talking.

"And tell me about your experience of working with databases."

"Databases. I haven't actually used any databases in the workplace. We didn't have no databases to use at the Heathrow Dixons, but it's something I'm really interested in, and I'd relish the opportunity to learn."

And there it was, that God-awful word, *relish*. Why does anyone think that it belongs in a job application form or interview? You never use it in any sentence other than perhaps, 'can I have some relish with this, please?' and that was only when one was eating a burger, and this, for her, was never. Her internal rant did not express itself on her cheerful, kind face. The only thing worse than 'relish' was someone describing themselves a 'people person'. People calling themselves a 'people person' needed birching.

"That's fine. A tricky question for you now."

"Oh no," he laughed, rocking from one bony arse-cheek to the other, and back again.

"If I had your colleagues from Dixons here with me now and I asked them to tell me what Sandip was really like to work with, what would they say?"

"Probably that I can be quite lazy at times, especially if I don't see the point of doing something." Her eyes twinkled at him. "But I get on really well with everyone and when we took on a new person recently my manager asked me to show him the ropes. Actually, this is teamwork, isn't it? I brought something with me." He reached into his bag and pulled out an envelope. In the envelope, was a card, *sorry you're leaving*.

"But this is personal," she said as she took the card from him.

"It shows you I'm a team player," he defended.

"Well, if you're sure." She opened the card and in an attempt to stifle a snigger, snorted. "I'm terribly sorry," she said, "the first thing my eyes fell on was, 'Good riddance and don't come back'."

"Ah that was a joke. They all loved me there."

"Thank you for sharing that with me, Sandip. I think that's all I need to ask you for now. Have you got any questions you'd like to ask me?"

"Yes." He pulled out a piece of paper with three questions on it. "You've already answered that one," he muttered. "How long have you worked here at Trethendar Trust and what do you like about it most?"

"I've been here nearly thirty-five years."

"Wow. Two years younger than my Mum."

"We're a small team. Only four of us now. There's only me in HR, facilities and office management. Then there's Jenny, Hazel the membership manager and Stuart who is director of finance and acting chief executive." Those last three words stuck in her throat. "We work hard, and we deliver a top-notch service to our membership and that's what motivates us and keeps us going." She ran out of steam. "Anything else to ask me?"

"When are you looking for the successful candidate to start and is there anything that would hold you back from offering me the job at this point in time?"

"We're looking for someone to start straight away. We thought we had someone, but she rather let us down at the last minute, so that's why we needed to start interviewing again. Regarding your second question," a question she hated with a passion, always refused to answer and one that no successful candidate ever asks, "nothing springs to mind, but I need to see all the candidates first and then have a think. We're seeing people all day today and hope to make a decision very quickly, but I always tell people we'll come back to them within five working days. If it's going to be any longer, I'll get back to Tina at In-a-Jiffy and let her know. The interview process is always a comparative one, however, and a candidate may present very well but be pipped at the post on the day by another who demonstrates they meet the person specification criteria to a greater extent."

"I understand."

"Well, thank you so much for coming, Sandip." She stood, so did he, they shook hands. "It was nice to meet you."

"You too, Janice. Thank you. Can I use your toilet before I go?"

"Of course. You passed it on the way up." *But you need to flush hard*, she mused to herself, *the pipes are old and it's a long way to Margate.*

"Any joy?" Stuart asked as she returned to her desk.

"Unfortunately not." She fired up her PC. "The agency's sending another along at 12. New Zealander just arrived in the UK. Tina said she was great. Anyway…" She'd be the judge.

Another morning drifted on aimlessly. She was counting down to her retirement in days now rather than years, increasingly impatient. Two hundred and twenty-two working days if you deducted the eight bank holidays, her basic entitlement of twenty-five days' annual leave and the additional five days in respect of her five-plus years' continuous employment.

Retirement: it seemed so far away once, now here it was, within reach, burning on the horizon like a beacon. On that same horizon was her dream cottage, honey-coloured, in Burford.

She'd started at Trethendar as Ben Westrell's PA and office manager. Her role then morphed into personnel manager. She qualified in human resources after completing her two-year, BA-equivalent course, flexible learning, self-funded. She then became a chartered member of the CIPD and after *still* being in HR and not broken down or dead ten years later, was rewarded by the profession with the rank of fellow. She changed her job title to HR and premises manager, but Stuart still referred to her as personnel. A tea and sympathy title she'd grown to loathe. She didn't correct him though, she just seethed. She had grown to hate finance people like Stuart. The older you get, the more things you loathe. Why was HR and finance always lumped together anyway? Like gay men and lesbians, they couldn't really have less in common. It made no sense that a bean counter should oversee HR when finance clearly demonstrated little to no understanding of, or interest in, HR. People don't line up and act predictably like numbers do. Yet finance were frequently given seniority and higher pay over her profession. Could it be perhaps because finance was traditionally, and still predominantly is, a male occupation and HR was female? Though in Stuart's case she used the word 'male' in its loosest form. He was as boneless as that boy Sandip. Although married, he had some issue with his masculinity and so, to her great, inner amusement, she'd frequently query it, but in a covert way that he couldn't quite be certain of.

She had missed Ben terribly after he'd been ousted in a bloody coup led by Vera Freers and Ben's trusted deputy, Irene Hartley. Janice and Ben had been such a great team. She'd thought Irene and Vera would want to hasten her own exit in some trumped-up way, but it would have been tricky to get one over on an HR manager. Vera had tentatively questioned the necessity for an HR manager when they only had thirty-five or so staff at the time. She knew they needed her as premises, office and facilities, especially once they'd started to scale down and needed to sell the building bequeathed to the charity by Lady Trethendar.

They probably considered her harmless enough, cheerful and kind; she served a function and, besides, considering her age and years' service, she'd be due a hefty redundancy package. Trethendar was one of the last few employers with a final salary pension scheme, though that had been closed to new members for years. She was the only current employee in the scheme. So, Vera and Irene decided, if she wasn't going to leave of her own volition and if redundancy was too costly a proposition, to sideline her instead. They kept out of her way, and she kept out of theirs; as far as they all could with the ever-shrinking floor space. Easier by far to let Janice whither on the vine, growing bitter, rather than prune her.

Then Vera died. Peter Miller, Stuart's predecessor, joined as finance director from the commercial sector. Irene was acting chief executive until she retired. Peter left after twelve years and then Stuart joined and took over finance; becoming acting chief executive after Irene left. The board had tried to recruit to the chief executive role, but without any success, so they just carried the vacancy. Anyone with half a brain could see the Trethendar Welfare Annuity Trust's downward trajectory. No up-and-coming professional would want to try to steer that sinking ship, and so the poisoned chalice continued to drift, with its doomed crew, into a setting sun.

Her hump-day birthday at work passed as non-eventfully as any other day. The New Zealand girl was lovely. Tina at In-a-Jiffy said she'd been over the moon to accept the maternity cover position. She had given poor Sandip his feedback, which he took well. Tina said he had another interview lined up already, UK Border Control at Heathrow.

The boiler man came and condemned it. He said she could possibly get another year out of it but, worryingly, that 'it might fall over at any point'. He gave a ballpark quote. She'd inform the board meeting that evening.

They met on the first Wednesday of every month, except August, at 7pm. Janice was required to present her report of staff statistics, building and maintenance costs, get revised policies approved and so on. She was normally only needed for the first thirty minutes. Stuart told her she didn't need to attend as it was her birthday. She thanked him, but said she'd be there, despite it already being a long and irritating day.

"Good evening, Janice." Cath was chair of the board. There were only six members now. The meeting required a quorum of four. The last meeting had been cancelled when only three showed up.

"Hello, Cath. How are you?"

"Very well thank you. You?"

"Mustn't grumble."

"Card."

"That's very kind," she said as she took the birthday envelope. She'd set up the table in the window corner of the flat. It took less than a minute. The streets outside quietened abruptly in the evening, except Fridays, when many of the office workers could be found quaffing pints outside the pubs that proliferate in that part of London. Cath never forgot birthdays.

Next to arrive was Marjory, then David, Susan and finally Meredith. Stuart was there too. He presented his report. Membership now stood at just under 14,000 and continued to decline. Annual income from membership subs was likely to fall short of the budgeted figure by about 6.8%. The charity had come to rely on a large legacy landing each year but had not benefitted from anyone's death for a number of years. Interest rates had never been in worse shape. He droned on as his gloom filled the room.

When it came to her turn she gave her quarterly staff stats; a pointless exercise now as there were now only four of them.

"It says here there are no male employees," said Stuart.

"Really?" she said with pained surprise. "I wonder how that happened. I must have entered you as a woman." His head snapped up and looked at her as she turned the page of the paper slightly and moved her finger across the line of numbers. "I do apologise." She smiled sweetly.

"On the facilities side, I have a bit of rather bad news," she said. "Our boiler, it appears, could conk out at any time. It's fine now, but we've been strongly advised to replace it in the next twelve months. I suggest around spring next year."

"Cost, Janice, please?" Cath asked, blowing vapour from her coffee into Janice's face.

"Well, the model that's been recommended is a Gloucester high efficiency, external oil combi boiler,

£2,388.50 plus VAT. Labour would be about another £1,200."

"£4,000," said Cath. Stuart looked a little put-out he hadn't been made aware prior to the meeting. "Well, I suppose if we need a new boiler, we'll have to buy one, but I think we should get some alternative quotes. £4,000 seems a lot for a fairly small building."

"Of course." Janice nodded. Her contribution to that evening's board meeting was concluded.

She couldn't get the train from Cannon Street as the last train left at 6:45pm, so she took the tube from Farringdon to Victoria for the 7:52pm, arriving at Whitstable at 9:21. She'd be home by about 9:30.

Victoria was full of the normal noise and grime and mess of people not looking where they're going. She passed through like an irritable ghost. A head-down little woman, invisible and pointless.

She got on the waiting train and passed through the carriages looking for a seat. She avoided all the ones with people eating McDonalds. She found one up near the front and sat down by the toilet, looking out of the window, down at the track. She'd thought it was a plastic bag blowing about at first. It was a pigeon, sooty, hopping with a broken wing. She closed her eyes and pulled her bag a little closer. *Only two-hundred and nineteen more days of this drudgery and then it'll be over. No more work, no more obsolete boilers, no more arseholes*. Just her and her honey-coloured cottage in Burford.

It was dark as she walked up the road towards her home. She loved the clear, sea air after London. Her house was on a T-junction looking down the length of the road. This had made it look very prominent, conspicuous, overbearing.

She'd planted leylandii all around it. They'd got out of hand, but she didn't care. The dark trees formed an ugly and almost impenetrable wall around the east-facing house. It was less Sleeping Beauty and more Miss Havisham. The only part still visible from the road were two bedroom windows. She'd had them boarded over to stop the morning light flooding in and waking her. All natural light was blocked out. The sightless eyesore of a house stared through the leylandii, at the neat houses before it. They, in return, pretended not to see the blind mess in their up-and-coming midst.

The leylandii was as drab and obscuring as her name, Janice. But Janice was her middle name. There was only one person who called her by her first name.

"Mother," she called. "Mother."

"Is that you, Myra?" called Mother from upstairs.

"Who else would it be?" she muttered under her breath. She heard Mother venturing out of her room. "Yes, it's me."

"They're keeping you too late these days," she said as she tentatively descended the stairs in her bathrobe.

"It was the board meeting. I did tell you. Did you have your tea?"

"What tea?"

"The crispy pancakes. In the freezer? You just need to pop them under the grill for a bit."

"I didn't know. I wish you'd tell me when you're going to be late. I was worried."

"You forget, Mother." She took off her coat. Mother always used to remember birthdays but hadn't said a word about anyone's for years now, not even her own.

"Are they the cheese ones or the mince ones?"

"Cheese, I think."

"Are those my gloves, Myra?"

"No, Mother, these are my gloves."

"Well, where are mine then?"

"I don't know. Where you left them."

"I don't know why you have them anyway. I'm the one with the what's-his-name, circulation, not you."

"I know, Mother. I like to wear them too though. You know I do." She paused, then for the ten-thousandth time, "It's called Raynaud's."

She put all four crispy pancakes under the grill and the cardboard packaging in the recycling. She wondered what the bloody point was, when America and China and most other places pumped chemical waste into the water and plastic and oil into the seas; mountains of landfill no longer filling the land, but spilling into the oceans, turning into artificial islands. She'd heard there were mountains of old computers now, too as well as of old white goods. What difference would recycling her crispy pancake packet make when the whole toxic world was fast going to buggery in a handbasket?

She watched the news with Bimbo on her lap, stroking his head as he purred contentedly. She felt secure with little Bimbo, so warm and safe, rattling, his eyes smiled shut. The news was shocking. She didn't know why she watched it anymore. All the horrible things people did to each other. The same vicious tit-for-tat wars in the same old parts of the world, violence in the name of religion, child missing, a horrible murder, another natural humanitarian disaster, interest rates up, skyrocketing cost of living and in the background, the politics; the politicians meticulously maintaining the whole vile mess. It had been this way for every one of her sixty years and nothing looked set to change any time soon. Even as what one might call a moderately devout Christian, she could see a very clear answer. All religions should unilaterally extricate themselves from politics and affairs of state. There should be no preferential treatment given to any one religion over another or over no religion. But she'd also learnt that, so long as there was profit to be made, the mess must continue; the greed of a handful of egos over the common sense of the masses. Everyone was out for themselves, with little to no thought for anyone else. She'd never been that way. None of her generation had. She'd read a report in one of her HR magazines that 68% of millennials would sacrifice a friendship with a work colleague for a promotion when 62% of baby boomers would never consider it. Also, that the younger ones believed socialising at work would help them up the career ladder, compared with only 5% of the older ones. She'd seen this cut-throated, grabby, two-faced attitude develop over several years and didn't like it. There were seemingly no exceptions, except perhaps for that New Zealand girl, Melissa. The agency temp. She seemed genuinely pleasant.

She also knew that elbowing your way up the ladder was not all it was cracked up to be. You may get a better view from up there and a better salary, but the shit coming down gets warmer the higher you climb, and if there's no shit coming down, then you're the grubby arsehole teetering at the top trying not to topple onto the shitty staff below.

She'd been irritable all day. It wasn't like her. She normally concealed it well, but her internal grizzling had become an incessant rant. Her head ranted on. Fears, doubts, details, plans, fear, anger. The young are given a disproportionate amount of help, she felt.

That, coupled with their greed and selfishness, was grotesque.

People went on and on about what a wonderful moment it is to be present at the birth of a new life. But in her heart, she knew it was more profound to be present at the end. Her thinking swung to Ben Westrell for the second time that day. She was looking forward to seeing him again, despite each visit being a little harder than the last.

She gazed at the top of Bimbo's head and stroked his velvety nose. Was that dried blood on the side of her shoe? She'd need to give it a wipe. She tilted her head back and closed her eyes as the TV said, 'And now for the news where you are'. She wanted to hear the weather, to see if she'd need a brolly in the morning. It had been the wettest July since records began, apparently, but was also unseasonably warm. Rumbles of thunder came out of nowhere and rolled out of sync with the rain, torrential.

The past kept replaying itself as if time too was in some kind of erratic and fragmented retrograde state. She'd had a headache for about three weeks.

She pushed the button on the TV remote. The room suddenly went a little darker and she heard silence for the first time that day.

"Come on, best-beloved. Bedtime." Bimbo moved off her lap to his nighttime place at the other end of the settee. She switched off the light and started up the stairs.

In her room, she laid out her clothes for tomorrow. She was taking it as a day's TOIL for the hours she'd racked up attending board meetings. She knew she didn't quite have enough hours for a whole day. She didn't care anymore. She brushed her teeth, trying not to catch her eye in the mirror.

She lay in bed, reading for a while. She'd bought this book for her mother, but she hadn't seemed interested. She read to the end of the chapter.

She checked her alarm was set, then reached a little further and turned out the bedside light. It was going to be a difficult day. She manoeuvred her body under the covers and lay still.

She was tired before. Wide awake now. She blinked. She listened to the silence of cold earth. Then, downstairs, Bimbo was crunching his biscuits in the kitchen. She loved that cat and loved the sound of him enjoying his biscuits. She turned to lay on her side.

"Myra?" Mother suddenly called out. She lay still, not breathing for a moment. Mother sometimes called out. If she ignored her long enough, she'd soon forget what she'd called out for, unless it was an emergency in which case she'd call out again.

"Myra?"

"What? It's late."

"I just remembered. I wanted to ask you…"

It didn't sound like an emergency. "What?"

"By the back door…"

"I know, Mother. Look, I told you this morning. I hope you left it alone, like I asked?"

"But I didn't know what it was."

"You didn't open it, did you?"

"No. You said not to."

"Good. Sleep well then." There was a silence. "By the way, I'm leaving early in the morning, but I'll be home a bit earlier. So, we can have a bit of the afternoon together if you like." No answer came. "Night, then."

"Night-night, Myra."

A warm wave of drowsiness came to her rescue. She closed her eyes.

"Myra?"

"Please go to sleep."

"What are the bees for?"

2

At 4am her alarm beeped. She had to move to catch the 5:06. She threw the covers back. By 4:50 she was dressed and buttoning her coat. She didn't need a coat. It was more habit than need. It had extra pockets; she could quickly get to her phone and season ticket without having to rummage in her bag.

The backdoor was in the kitchen. It took you into a petite, square, inner porch with another door to the left to the garden; purposeless and extensive. It wasn't really a garden anymore; being in constant shadow thanks to the thick, dark and towering leylandii surrounding and encroaching upon it. She collected the thick cardboard box, inside of which was a Dundee cake tin, six inches square. Also, inside was an old camera film container with a hole punched into the rubbery lid. About fifteen feet of string was tightly wrapped around the film container. She loosely taped the box shut.

It had been dark outside when she'd got up, but as she made her way towards the station, bag over her shoulder, box under her arm, dawn was breaking.

She scurried down Nelson Road, which the house on Whitman Road faced, then a left onto Castle Road and the first right into Station Approach. She was thinking of her friend, Martin. They'd arranged to meet on Saturday for a potter round the Whitstable shops, lunch, then some surprise he'd arranged for her birthday. She'd known him since university. They'd drifted apart but become reacquainted shortly after he moved to the Kent coastal town, to take a care worker job.

She arrived on the platform with five minutes or so to spare. She was surprised to see as many as there were. Even when she got her normal 7:16 train there were fewer people on a Thursday than on the preceding days and fewer still by Friday. A short while later and the train pulled in. She pulled the box tighter under her arm.

She went to her normal seat; the one facing the wall, travelling backwards and in a row of three. The middle seat was normally the last in the carriage to be filled; unoccupied for the first forty minutes, until the Medway towns. She would put in her ear plugs and close her eyes and wake up at Cannon Street, but today, she was on the Victoria train, so needed to be awake to change at Bromley South. She should arrive at 6:12 but probably wouldn't; then that horrible rush along the platform, up and over the bridge to the other side, just in time to get the train from there to Hempstead. She should arrive at 6:34 and be at the hospice for about 6:50.

She pulled on her Raynaud's gloves, stretched out her legs. She glanced up at the cardboard box, nestling against her bag on the rack. The cardboard was thick and its contents, subdued. Most people blasted their ears through headphones and those who didn't wouldn't hear much; even if they did, they wouldn't care.

Hempstead: it was strange how things turned out. That small, Victorian terraced house had been the family home up to her early teens. Her father's premature death had led to them moving to her grandmother's, in Whitstable. She'd never returned to the old house. The memories of her father would be unbearable; and she needed to be present today.

Just before the entrance to the drive for the hospice was a bus stop. She slowed her brisk, uphill pace. As she approached, her eyes covertly glanced through the trees and shrubbery at the building, positioning herself so she could watch without being obvious or seen. It was 6:47.

Then, from inside, she heard the bar of the ground-floor fire escape door open. Turning her head towards the road, a lighter flicked. She got a waft of cigarette smoke. Without moving her head, her eyes flashed right, then a fraction further. There she was. In her soiled care worker smock, leaning against the wall, back to the road, skiving off for a sneaky fag while some poor soul was left lying there in a pool of their own filth calling for help. Her head turned to see if anyone was watching. Myra's eyes were back on the road.

About five weeks' earlier, Myra had taken a snap, with her phone, of the rota hung just behind the reception desk, where visitors signed in. She knew this care worker would be on that morning. She moved the patients too roughly and she'd served Ben the most disgusting food. It was bad at the best of times, but this plate had obviously been left to go cold then reheated several times before it got to him. There was a scoop of orange watery stuff that could have been liquidised carrot and/or swede, a scoop of white watery stuff with green flecks (possibly potato with grated cabbage?) and a brown scoop; presumably meat. It was all sitting in a dried-out gravy slick that shellacked the plate, with thumbprint smears.

She'd heard one frail resident whimpering with frustration or fear as the care worker wheeled her towards the bathroom, "Not by you, not you." Myra had seen her be sweetness and light to the residents' relatives but, when she didn't think anyone was watching, she was rude and rough. Ben deserved better than that. They all did. There was no need.

Ben had been a tower of a man, a man's man. He'd been a teacher; moved to the UK years before to be with his British wife. They regularly visited the US. His parents had a place in Florida apparently. He had a delicious, deep-south drawl, full of warm, wet sunshine. His pale blue eyes flashed wickedly, and he'd melt your heart with a flash of those perfect, pearly whites. He was fiercely intelligent, cultured and extremely well-read. He was a gentleman, old school, just like her father had been, just like Jim Reeves.

There was something of the cowboy about big Ben. When he smiled at you, it was like being scooped up onto his piebald horse, with a tip of his hat and a 'Howdy, Ma'am' and galloping off into the sunset, the baked air filling your nostrils. For such a man, who had lived such a life and been so loved and respected by so many, to now be at the mercy of this uncaring sloucher was too much to bear. The others, the Thai and Filipino carers, were sweet and kind, but not this one. She'd complained about her. It had been the last straw. She snatched the plate out of her hand.

"Would you eat this? Tell me honestly; would you...?" She rasped as she closed the door to Ben's room.

"No," she'd replied as she glanced away from the plate held under her nose, and distractedly down the corridor.

"Would you give it to your family? Would you give it to them to eat?"

"No."

"So, if you wouldn't eat it and you wouldn't give it to your family to eat, what makes you think it's good enough to give to someone else to eat; for him? It's disgusting. It's inedible. He deserves better than this."

Incensed by how little she cared, she continued, "And another thing; every time you're on, I go in there and the window is open, and he asks me to close it. You know he feels the cold. I happen to know he's asked you multiple times to please not open it, but still you do. I need to speak to the manager..." Myra had said this as she walked to the reception area, and the duty manager's office. She'd been livid. She stood there at the desk with that disgusting plate in her hand, holding back tears of rage and complained, bitterly, about the care worker. "I don't know if it's a training issue and she needs to go on a course or something, but it's just not good enough. This is horrible; and why would she always throw the window open even though he specifically asks for her not to? Why?"

Her anger rose anew as she recalled this. She knew the rota. This one would be finishing at 7:30am, just before the residents' tea. She also knew the care worker would leave the fire escape door open; and even if she didn't this time, there was a contingency. No box was ever left unchecked.

She turned her head and looked across. The care worker took a final drag and stubbed it out in the sand-filled fire bucket. She smoothed down her smock and went back in, leaving the door ajar. Myra took a deep breath. No one else was at the bus stop. There wasn't a car or pedestrian in sight. It was time.

She turned and stepped over the tiny wall. She bent over, close to the ground, so her head almost touched her knees, and shoved her way through the bushes and plants like a wildebeest, being careful not to lose her grip on the box, emerging on the other side, on the narrow path that circumvented the hospice. She scurried towards the open fire door. It would be impossible to explain herself at this point if caught.

She passed several residents' windows before she came to Ben's. He was staring blankly out. He lifted his hand weakly when he recognised her. Holding the box with both hands, she raised an elbow at him with a cheery smile and a nod as she flew by. When she got to the door, she stopped and peered round the side. The care worker was walking down the wide corridor towards reception. No one else was there. She hurried through, turned left and in a few steps was at Ben's door. The place was silent. She opened his door and slid in, closing the door silently behind her.

"Janice, hello." She was Janice for work and Myra at home.

"Hello, Ben. How are you?"

"Still in pain. Still hanging on and trying not to get too fucked off with it all. You?"

"I'm fine. I'm fine." She walked around his bed and opened the window. She took the cake tin out of the box and put it on the ledge. She set the camera film container on the tin. She hoped the string would be long enough to reach. She opened the window as wide as it would go, only about five inches, and shoved the cardboard box out through the narrow gap. It fell onto the pathway. Ben said there was a catch to the side and that if she slid it down, she'd be able to open the window the whole way. It worked.

"It's today then?"

"Yes," she said, turning to him.

"Thank Christ."

She took a deep breath and slowed; less need to rush now. She sat by his bed and unbuttoned her coat. "Are you still sure?"

The sound of footsteps and a trolley or something coming down the corridor outside the room froze them. They stared at each other in silence. The sound passed slowly by and, eventually, away.

"Yes. No doubt at all. You have time for a quick chat first, though?"

"Yes of course. We have all the time in the world." She touched his hand. His hand closed around hers. His eyes closed.

The room was empty. Some residents had some residual items from a normal life in their rooms. He had no family and just a handful of friends who couldn't or wouldn't visit anymore. When he went, there'd be nothing to clear.

By his bed was the oxygen in its shoulder carry case and mask, so he could help himself if he felt the need.

There was a glass of water at his bedside that he'd sipped his medication down with the night before; a TV on the wall in the corner, a mirror and the remote within easy reach, next to his EpiPen.

Each time she saw him he'd deteriorated further, but he lingered on regardless in this state of slow wasting. He was completely riddled with it now. The cancer had first struck him four years earlier. The only part that it hadn't attacked was his lungs, which was strange, considering he'd been a forty-a-day man his whole adult life. He hated both having to give up and the resulting weight gain. His face had grown jowly. He wouldn't have bothered stopping if he'd known it was already too late, but that his life would linger, painfully, on; with no quality, no smokes and the constant pill-popping and visiting do-gooders who told him through their friendless, halitosis breath, what a friend he had in Jesus.

He liked the young man who'd visited with his gorgeous collie though. The dog had jumped up, tongue lolling and all waggy-tailed. He'd roughed up the silky hair on that good boy's head and held his silken paws. He was a patient care dog or something. He told the young man of his love of dogs and was moved remembering all the dogs he'd loved, way back to Buster. The best friend a boy could have had. He'd been inconsolable when Buster died. He was a great dog. Suddenly, it was no longer Buster and Ben. He never let anyone get as close to him after that. With, perhaps, the one notable exception sitting next to him as he lay there in his relentless pain. Now, he wanted his own life to end.

"How's Trethendar?"

"Same as ever. We had the board last night. It's never been the same since you."

"Kind of you to say."

"I mean it."

"How much longer have you got to go now?"

"Three hundred and sixty-four days."

He thought for a moment, "Happy birthday for yesterday."

"Thank you."

"I'm so sorry, I would have gotten you a card."

"Forgiven," she said.

"Doing anything nice?"

"I'm meeting my friend Martin for lunch on Saturday. He has something planned. It should be fun."

"He works in a nursing home, doesn't he?"

"Yes. He loves it. He doesn't need to work."

"Good for him," he said and meant it. Martin sounded to Ben like a good man. Janice didn't give much away, but there was a big, loyal heart there. Although it would technically be frowned upon, she was capable of this great act of love and think nothing of it, because it came so naturally to her. He smiled at her. She smiled back.

"And your mother?"

"Oh, same as ever, I'm afraid. Thank you for asking," she said. Small talk didn't get much smaller. "She's on medication for her heart now. Her circulation isn't good, and her memory is not what it was. But she's still the same person. We count our blessings."

"She must be getting on a bit now. She isn't short of a few bucks is she?"

"Ben, don't be awful."

"Shame most of it will go in inheritance tax when the time comes." He explained.

She hadn't thought quite so much would go in tax. Maybe a third, but not 'most of it'. *Most of it? Really?*

"They get you – they get you in the end."

"She'll out-live us all." She paused, realising what she'd just said. "She's a tough old bird."

"So are you."

"Charming," she laughed in fake offence.

"Well, you must be... to do this for me."

"...Oh, you must let me show you," she said swiftly evading with a skilled, social deftness. She rummaged in her bag and produced her new passport. "It came through surprisingly quickly," she said as she opened it to the right page.

"Good grief. Who is that? It doesn't look anything like you."

"I know," she said. "Isn't it wonderful?"

"And look here," he said.

"I know. It looks strange written down on an official document, doesn't it?" she said.

"It sure does. And that hair!" He closed it and passed it back to her. "I have something for you too." He held out a business card. "This is Frank Savile, my solicitor and financial advisor. If you need anything…" His hand dropped to the bed as he winced in a flash of hot, searing pain. She really felt for him. She slipped the card between the pages of her passport and put it back in her bag. She squeezed her eyes shut for a moment. "Well, I kept my part of the deal," he said. "I haven't changed my mind."

She needed to be sure. "No second thoughts? It's fine if you have. The decision is completely yours."

"I know. I've never been surer of anything and there's no time like the present."

"What time do they come around?" she asked, knowing the answer.

"It's normally around 7:30. What is it now?" he asked. She couldn't risk being there later than 7:20 in case they were early.

"We have a few minutes."

"Well, look," he said, "you can't stay, and I'm ready right now. Nothing is going to happen in the next few minutes to change that."

"Ben," she said looking him in those Paul Newman, steel-blue eyes, "Ben, are you sure?"

"Yes," he said emphatically. He squeezed her hand. "I'm sure. I'm sure."

"What about this?" she said nodding towards the EpiPen. He looked over at it. He let go of her hand, stretched across and knocked it to the floor, then did the same to the TV remote. The back popped off; one of the batteries sprang out and rolled across the linoleum. They waited a second to make sure no one heard and came to investigate. No one did.

"Janice, you've been a great friend to me. Thank you."

"You have too, Ben," she said awkwardly. "You have too. You were a great boss and a great friend."

"What do we do then?" he asked decisively.

She went to the window and picked up the film canister, then found the end of the string wrapped around and unwound it. She hung the end out of the window and put the tin on top of the string to keep it in place. She unravelled the rest as she walked to the bed. There was plenty of slack. The other end of the string was tied tightly round the canister. She put some of the slack on the bed and the canister in his hand.

"There's one in here?" he asked her. She nodded. She'd had a few spares too, in case this one died. He saddened, smiled. She took the transparent, plastic oxygen mask, stretched the elastic bands out and put it over his head. The mask covered his nose and mouth. Their eyes met. "Thank you," he said nervously. She leant over his bed and held his hand, the hand holding the film canister. She held it to her cheek and squeezed it.

"So," she said "once I'm out of the room, you take the lid off and shake it out inside the face mask. Do it at the top, near your nose. Try not to let it fly away."

"OK," he said, "but if it doesn't work?"

"It will," she said. "But if it doesn't, it doesn't, and no one will be any the wiser and we'll think of something else. But it will. I'm sure of it. OK?" He didn't respond. "Ben? OK?"

"OK. Yes, thank you."

"Shall I go now? Are you ready for me to go now?"

"Yes," he said. "I'm ready. Let's try this."

She let go of his hand. She touched the covers covering his chest, straightened herself up, rebuttoned her coat and went to the door. She looked at him. He had one hand on the transparent oxygen mask covering his mouth and nose and the other hand holding the canister to his cheek.

"I won't look back. So, if you change your mind, I won't know. Are you still sure, Ben?"

"Yes, Janice. Thank you for this," he said weakly. "Thank you."

She opened the door an inch and listened. There wasn't a sound or a soul in sight. She glanced back and smiled. Hands full, he lifted his little finger to her. She hurried out along to the main corridor and peeked around the corner. The care worker was heading into one of the resident rooms near reception with the tea and medication trolley. She left by the same fire door, along the narrow path, pausing to grab the end of the string dangling from Ben's window, wrapping it tightly round her finger.

Ben had both arms stretched out into the air above him. His eyes were screwed shut. The bee, buzzing inside the mask, settled on his upper lip before slowly crawling up his nose. He let out a moan. She pulled the string back and retrieved the canister tied to the end of it, stuffing it all into her coat pocket - then she saw it. The lid of the canister still lying on his bed. She couldn't go back in. She'd have to leave it there, but they'd find it. A flush of panic. She hadn't been seen. She couldn't go back now. No one would know what it was to do with. Would they? They'd probably just throw it away.

Ben suddenly winced and let out a cry. The bee crawled out of his nose and started buzzing furiously inside the mask again. She had to go. She grabbed the cake tin from inside window and popped the lid. Keeping both lid and tin inside the room, she shook the contents into the room as hard as she could and the spare bees filled the room, swarming menacingly. If the one in the canister didn't get him, one of these would, especially with his fists now thrashing about like that and the bees, so disorientated, so infuriated. Her hands gloved, put the lid on the empty tin and, leaving the window open, grabbed the misshapen cardboard box from the path and hurried down towards the trees and shrubs between her and the road.

Just before her final push back through the undergrowth, she put the box down. Tin back inside, canister and string inside too. Folded over the cardboard flaps; up under her arm and shoved her way through the foliage and back onto the road.

Not a bus or car or pedestrian was there to see the small woman falling through the bushes and over the tiny wall onto the pavement by the bus stop. She picked herself up, brushed herself down, then slowly walked back down the hill back towards the station.

On the deserted platform, she tore the cardboard box into pieces just big enough to fit inside the tin. She had a plastic carrier in her bag. She put the tin inside and waited patiently for her return train.

She pictured the slovenly care worker knocking on Ben's door and, when there was no answer, going inside. She imagined the shock when she saw him in bed, turning blue. She'd see the bees everywhere and go to open window to get them out but see it's already open. She'll think she must have left it that way. She'd lie. She'd tell the manager the window had been closed when she went in and that she'd only opened it to let the bees out. They'd see through her lies. There'd been complaints about her. She'd deserve everything she had coming.

Myra's train arrived. She found a quiet window seat. It was almost empty. No one gave her a second look on this leg either. There'd been the occasional, muffled buzz coming from the luggage rack over her head on the way up. No commuter ever involved themselves in what any other commuter was doing, even if it was transporting a cake tin of bees into town. They were all plugged in to their iPods listening to some rubbish. She smiled to herself. She pictured the care worker noticing the EpiPen on the floor and the remote with its back off as she ran for assistance, and Ben escape his prison. She thought about the trouble that grubby, bullying liar would get into for opening the window when she'd specifically been told not to. She hoped she got fired. She really hoped so. She hoped those poor residents would now be free, once and for all, from that mean, fag-ash cow.

There was satisfaction too that she'd been able to do this for Ben. Not for any material gain, but simply to help a dear friend in his greatest moment of need. She wondered when she would get the call from the hospice; what the duty manager would say...

"We're so sorry to tell you that he passed away. We don't know quite how it happened but, despite all our careful precautions, it appears an insect may have stung him in his sleep."

She wondered what they would make of the photo film canister lid she'd left behind. The care worker would probably have thrown it away. Maybe they'd think it was something to do with the EpiPen or fell off the oxygen mask or something. They would never even know she'd been there.

At Bromley South, she crossed to the other platform. About fifteen minutes later, and she was on her way back to Whitstable. She'd be home well in time for elevenses.

Just as the train was pulling out of Faversham, the stop before Whitstable, she opened her bag and reached inside for the government envelope and her new, secret passport.

Five weeks earlier, Hazel had noticed something was up with Janice's hair, but didn't say a word about it. She'd had it done especially for the passport photo. Her normal hairstyle, if you could call it that, was a bob with a side-parting and slide, to keep it out of her face. Her hair was straight and flat, but shiny, like rain on a pavement. She'd never had it any other way. Even pictures of her as child of five or six showed the same style. But that day she had had it dyed and permed. She had bought a new top and applied make-up too. She'd wanted to look nice, different. This was the Myra she was meant to be, not the Janice she was.

But as soon as the pictures were done, she changed the top to one more familiar to her Trethendar colleagues, straightened her hair back as far as it would go and removed the colour by going a shade of brown, much darker than her natural, slate grey.

At work the next day, her hair still had a few kinks and that colour; she saw their expressions, but no one said a word. They probably thought poor old Janice was having a bit of a late-life crisis and made a catastrophic hair blunder. They pretended her hair looked just as it always did.

She devoted the rest of her day experimenting with a new recipe, created in Ben's honour. She would make honeybee buns. It was nice to take the day off work and he'd have loved these sweet treats.

She opened her new passport. He was right. It was an extraordinary transformation. It didn't look anything like her. The name too looked odd, written there on an official document.

She stared into the eyes of the stranger in the photograph, into her own eyes; Mrs Myra Westrell.

3

She led Mike, the plumber, down the stairs. The only light was at the bottom. Most of Trethendar's archive was stored in the basement, in five dusty filing cabinets against a partition wall that split the space in two but didn't reach as high as the ceiling. It was built that way so the strip light didn't have to be repositioned. Now it straddled the partition, unequally dividing the light.

On top of the cabinets were boxes, mostly containing leaflets of hurried and botched campaigns for members; historic, redundant. There were also archive copies of *Handy*, the Trethendar magazine, and grimy annual reviews. She flicked the light switch, and a heartbeat later the strip light blinked and fizzed into action.

"Here we are again," she said as she bustled past the cabinets and smell of musty cardboard, turning left at the end, U-turning towards the other end of the narrow basement. "Will I be able to leave you to do what you need to do?" she asked. "I have rather a lot on," she lied.

"No problem," said Mike. "Though I'll probably only be a minute or two." He had already recommended the best boiler for the job but needed another look so he could more accurately cost out the labour. Under his arm, he had a leather-look portfolio folder with a clipboard inside, a small calculator built in, and a pen; it contained his order pad. He'd been servicing this boiler for years. He liked an excuse to drop by and see Janice. "These paints shouldn't really be stored down here though. Fire hazard."

She wondered why he hadn't told her this last time he came to service it; or for that matter, any time in the last ten years they'd been there. "Oh," she said, "oh dear. We'd better move them then." She flattened herself against the wall as he passed her to get to the gassy old girl and her weedy, blue pilot light.

He knelt in front of the boiler and put his folder on the painted concrete floor. "Now, let's have a look at her." He removed the front and got his cheek close to the ground to see underneath. He grunted then got to his feet.

"What is it?" she asked expecting to be told about more work that would need doing and how much more it would cost. He flattened his cheek against the wall to peer down the side, to the back. He tried to get a better look. He got back on his knees, straining; his jeans and polo shirt parting to reveal the tradesman's cleavage.

"Well, that's odd," he said. He reached underneath. She heard a metal grinding sound. "Can you pass me that torch, Janice, please?" There was a narrow shelf that ran the length of the wall opposite the partition with assorted bits and bobs, a plank on wall brackets. There was a biro, a pad, various tools and a torch. She turned it on and tapped it with the heel of her hand. "It's like a manhole cover."

"Under our boiler?"

"Yes," he said. She heard another metallic sound, heavy iron on stone. She put it in his hand. "Thanks", and he shone it under the boiler. She knelt behind him.

"What is it?" she asked.

"I've no idea," he said. "Doesn't smell like a waste pipe. There's a small hole in the floor to the side and I could probably lever it up if I had a screwdriver. Not all the way off though; the boiler's in the way. It's deep, I reckon." There was a piece of chipped masonry by the foot of the boiler rumbling above him. He dropped it down the small hole. They listened for it to land. Five feet or thereabouts. "It's got to go somewhere. Maybe an old storm drain or something."

"Odd to put the boiler right over it though, isn't it? Surely you'd need to access something like that," she said.

"Unless its defunct. That's what I reckon. Didn't sound like there was any water down there so likely it's blocked at one end or other. There's no breeze or anything as far as I could tell."

"Is it a problem?"

"No, shouldn't be, if I'm careful when I come to do it," he said. "You wouldn't know it was there though, would you, unless you knew," he said looking back over his shoulder.

"As long as it's not a problem."

He reached back under with his cheek pressed against the boiler, his tongue poking out. The manhole cover was slightly bent at the corner, by the gap in the concrete floor. She was getting fed up. It smelt earthy down there. She wanted a wee. She didn't like the basement. It always made her want to wee.

"I'll probably be another ten minutes or so if you have other things to do," he said, sensing her boredom. He retrieved his folder to start working on a less ballpark quote. He'd reduce the cost as they were a charity, and for Janice.

"OK, just come back up when you're done," she said as she turned and walked back along and round to the front of the partition.

"Righto."

She hurried up the stairs to the ground floor. Some daylight made its way onto this floor through the tall windows, but they were so dusty, and the other archive cabinets so filled the room that it wasn't much lighter than the basement. She had cancelled the quarterly window cleaning contract a few years previously, after catching them breaching health and safety requirements by working at height without appropriate personal protective equipment. She thought once a year would be enough but never got around to sourcing an alternative window cleaner. On the bright side, the grime on the windows meant passers-by couldn't see in, unless it was lighter inside than out, which it never was.

The ground floor clutter and grime bothered her whenever she passed through. It reminded her of everything she hadn't done, as it fell within her remit to keep it in good order. It was overwhelming but no one commented on it, not to her face anyway. She walked back up the to the office, stopping at the tiny loo; a break from pretending to look busy.

Mike's arrival had interrupted her meeting with the new girl, Melissa. She'd just started showing her around the shared drive and the electronic filing system. After her meeting, Melissa was to spend time with Stuart and then the rest of the afternoon with Hazel, who would induct her on Trethendar's membership, membership filing and direct debit systems. The last hour would be spent on the backlog of membership data entry work that should keep her occupied for most of the following week. It was odd to have someone start on a Friday, but Janice was glad she could start as soon as possible after the last temp from In-a-Jiffy had let them down.

Melissa was all smiles and professionalism; enthusiastic and engaged. You only had to tell her something once. She made notes, without being advised to, and held good eye contact. She asked sensible questions. She had a good work ethic, arriving very punctually, exactly five minutes before her start time. New people always started at 9:30 even though the usual start time was 9:00. The later time enabled Janice to arrive, get settled and organised and so made for a slightly more relaxed start for the new person.

After her slot with Stuart, Janice showed her the local sandwich shops and treated her. Melissa had bacon and avocado in an oatmeal bap and a hazelnut latte with one sugar. Janice had her usual 'healthy option', egg and cress. She didn't see the point of buying a beverage when they supplied tea and coffee at work.

They sat by the windows of the flat upstairs and ate together. One of the windows was open a crack; a breeze made the room feel pleasantly fresh and alive. Janice normally ate at her desk, but when it was fine, she'd sometimes take a stroll and sit on a bench in the grounds of the hospital, which had rather a lovely old courtyard with grassy quads that most of the people employed locally didn't know about.

"What does the M stand for, if you don't mind my asking?"

"Pardon?" Janice asked.

"When we were going through the staff records, I noticed your first name began with an M and your middle name began with a J. It's not Melissa too, is it?"

It could stand for 'mind your own beeswax'. Not even Hazel knew what it stood for and the two of them had worked together for more than two decades. But Melissa was sweet, curious and engaging. "My first name is Myra."

The girl smiled appreciatively and nodded with her hand held over her closed mouth as she chewed. "It's lovely. Unusual," she said.

"It fell out of fashion decades ago. Janice is much more 'everyday'. Much more me."

"I couldn't help noticing your gloves too," she said. "Is it Raynaud's?"

She had an un-British directness. A New Zealand thing perhaps, or just a refreshing honesty she'd been brought up with. It deserved a direct answer; that closed the conversation down. "Yes."

"Mum has it too. A terrible thing."

After lunch, Janice and Melissa returned to their desks. Janice put her bag under her desk. It leaned and tipped and the envelope containing her passport slipped out. Hazel stood and walked across. Janice stuffed the passport back in and pinched the tops of the squashy-sided bag together. But when she let go, it leant again, and the passport slid again. Irritated, she took the envelope out, opened the lower drawer of her desk pedestal, placed the envelope on top of a pile of paperwork and slapped it shut and again when it didn't quite shut the first time.

Hazel was keen for Melissa to start on the backlog. Hazel, a Glaswegian, had been employed by Trethendar almost as long as Janice.

"Are you ready for me now?" Hazel asked.

"Yes, I think so," Melissa said, looking to Janice for approval, which she got with a kindly smile and a nod.

"Then if you'd like to come over. You may want to roll your chair across."

Janice had been distracted by thoughts of the cake tin of bees, which now contained the honeybee buns she'd brought in for her colleagues. Although her birthday had fallen on the Wednesday, it was custom and practice to celebrate such things from 4:30 on the Friday.

The previous day, she'd received the call from the hospice, much later than expected. It had been just after making the cakes. She let the answerphone take the message as she had her hands in the sink at the time. Her mobile rang next. She let it go to voicemail but called back within five minutes or so. It was Matron's tone of voice that gave her the first indication that it had worked. She was so very sorry, she'd said, but her husband passed away just before lunch. It was sudden and unexpected but very peaceful at the end. There had been no indication that he was about to pass. He had just closed his eyes for a nap and didn't wake up.

You complete and utter liar, she'd raged inside at the deceit and crocodile-tear tone. They were covering up for their incompetence, leaving the window open, allowing the bees in to sting the man, when they knew he could have a severe allergic reaction. It would have been preferable to hear they simply didn't know how it happened. But to say it was peaceful when they couldn't know, was unforgiveable. His death had been anything but peaceful.

"Thank you so much for telling me," she said after a dignified pause and slight choke of shock. She felt a sudden thrust of anxiety pump the pit of her stomach and up to her throat. She heard her own voice, pleased that her vocal emissions could equally have passed for grief. Matron went on to say that the doctor had been visiting and so was on site to register the death straight away. She explained where Mr Westrell had been taken and that, as his next of kin, she would be required to register his death. Matron said it was a very difficult time, but that she would be guided through it all by the funeral home in Hempstead nearest to the hospice, as was the instruction in his notes. Matron said Mr Westrell was in very good hands and was at peace now. She said a gentle goodbye to Matron and thanked her one more time for calling so quickly to tell her the sad news.

Ben had said something that stuck in her mind. It was replaying on a loop that day as she returned to join her mother in the lounge to test out the honeybee buns while they watched *Countdown*. She knew about some of the rules of income tax but nothing of inheritance tax. Once Hazel started inducting Melissa at the other end of the office, near Stuart, she opened Internet Explorer to research it.

Inheritance tax is 40% on an estate worth in excess of the £325,000 threshold. The revelation filled her with horror; not that Ben had anything to leave her. She obviously wouldn't benefit from the spousal exemption with her mother's estate. She started a new search. Property prices: four-bedroom, detached houses in Whitstable. Surely, she wouldn't have to sell the house, her mother's house, to cover the tax when she died? She felt panic rising but never permitted uncomfortable feelings expression. To anyone else in the office, she just looked as if she was concentrating.

Houses were between £480k and £525k. Theirs would be at the lower end, as a buyer would need to do a considerable amount of work to update the property. But the point was, her mother had a considerable 'little' nest egg sitting in a high interest account that would put the estate well in excess of the threshold. It was sitting there for that fast-approaching rainy day when she'd be unable to continue looking after her any longer and would need to find a care home where she could spend her final days.

She moved her calculator from under her screen to the side of her keyboard. The total value of the estate, if she understood it all correctly, including the house but after the deduction of inheritance tax, was £582k.

Her eyes fixated on the number, burnt her retinas. Would that be enough to buy her honey-coloured, dream cottage in Burford? Possibly, just; but there'd be nothing left for furniture, fixtures and fittings. Maybe she could aim smaller? Or look at another Cotswold town? Smaller or a newer build, maybe? Her finger still hovered over the calculator, wondering what to calculate next. She'd still have her pension of course, but... she'd planned, and Mother had saved, for a far greater level of financial security than this. This didn't feel secure or sustainable in the long-term at all and why should she be forced to compromise on what she'd dreamed for so long? She'd done everything you're meant to do. She'd done everything right. This wasn't the retirement she'd planned for since her mid-forties, not by a long chalk. Her phone rang.

"Trethendar. Janice Mead speaking."

"Janice, it's only Mike."

"Hello, Mike."

"The labour for the new boiler and removal and safe disposal of the old combi will be £1,050 plus VAT. However, as we've known each other as long as we have, and as I always try and do a good price for my charity customers, I'll do it for you for £950. So, with the VAT, labour and materials it would be £1,116.25 inclusive, plus the new boiler, the cost of which I will fix for twelve months at £2,388.50, plus the VAT on that gives you a total of £3,922.74." He paused. There was a silence. "Janice?"

She wanted to tell him to just fuck off. "Yes, thank you, Mike."

"I realise it's still a lot, but it's the best I can do. I don't think you'll find a better deal."

"No."

"So, I'll drop you a line confirming the quote and once you've had a think…?"

"Yes, thank you."

"Alright. Thanks, Janice."

"Bye, Mike." The phone was already moving away from her face as she spoke. She hung up. It was the same as his ball-park figure. Her working life, like the decrepit boiler, was now under twelve months' notice.

The rest of the afternoon dragged absently. She'd gone through her post; another notice of planning application for a neighbouring building. This time only a few doors down. It extended right up and behind Trethendar; there was a potential 'right to light' issue as the proposed demolition and development would mean some of Trethendar's windows would be obscured and overlooked by walls with aircon units.

She logged off at about 4pm and used the tail end of the day to plan her work, prioritise and diarise for the following week. At 4:25 she went upstairs and opened the tin, placing the buns on a plate, which she set on the table in the window. She put the kettle on and took the teapot from the cupboard. She stood with her hands on the work surface, her arms locked straight. She sighed. Her colleagues were on the stairs.

"Ooh lovely, Janice," Hazel cooed as she came in and saw the cakes. She made a beeline for them. "Oh, here," she said as she double backed and handed Janice her book-shaped present and card.

"Now that is unnecessary but very lovely, thank you."

"Happy birthday," said Melissa.

"Thank you. Help yourself to cake. I made separate ones this year. Saves washing a knife."

"It was actually Janice's birthday on Wednesday," Stuart chimed in.

Melissa enthused, "This has been the best first day in a new job ever!"

Janice opened her card and read the almost monosyllabic good wishes from the four of them. Hazel had managed to catch Mike on his way out and got him to sign it too. She started to tear at the paper. She didn't want a book. She resented anyone who said, 'you must read this', or 'let me lend you mine' or, even worse, buying a book to dictate what she read. It had a beautiful cover, a bright myriad of colours with gold flashing in the dusty evening sun. She opened it. A notebook.

"Well, this is perfect," she said.

"Well, you're always telling us about your recipes, we thought you could write them down in here," Hazel said as she put three of the flattish, golden sponges on her plate and began tucking in. "Or use it as a diary or journal, or whatever you like. Ooh these are yummy." A delicious honey, butter-cream treat.

"Thank you, all," Janice said. "You know, it's funny, I have post-its and scraps of paper, backs of envelopes with recipe ideas all over them. This will be just the thing."

"You make up recipes?" Melissa asked, impressed.

"Indeed, I do. In fact, these were an experiment. Do dig in."

Melissa helped herself then moved back to the work surface as the kettle boiled. She warmed the pot with a splash of water swilled around and made the tea.

"They're delicious," Melissa said. "I love honey. You must give me the recipe." *Chris would totally love these too,* she thought.

"I don't really share recipes," Janice said. Melissa glanced at her, a little stung.

"It's true, she doesn't," said Hazel. "Don't even ask."

Melissa smiled. "I'll get it out of you one way or another," she laughed as if scheming. They were just too tasty, and Chris had a sweet tooth; a sweet everything. "I love your tin too," she said picking up the lid. Then, noticing the three small holes deliberately punched through, she frowned quizzically.

"Myra?" Mother called. "Myra, do you want to play this or not?"

She came via the kitchen, having poured herself a glass of wine. She'd taken a break from Scrabble to wash up after their evening meal of crispy pancakes, frozen peas and oven-bake hash browns.

She'd forgotten Mother's plate with its neatly folded fairy cake papers on. She sighed; she'd just drained the sink of its sudsy water. She'd leave it for the morning.

She sat down and turned the television off. It had distracted her from the game and, having missed so much of the plot, she'd lost interest anyway. She'd been keeping score though and unless something extraordinary happened, Mother would lose.

"Wine, Myra?"

"Why not? It's my birthday."

"Was your birthday," Mother corrected.

"Shall we call it a night? You're tired."

"No, I want to finish this first." She had four letters left, an A, a U, an N and a C, all worth one point except for the C, which was worth two. Myra only had the X, worth eight.

She settled herself with her glass at the table. Bimbo was a tidy, curled up ball on the sofa.

"How about some music then?" she asked, having already decided. It was seeing Bimbo that suddenly made her want to listen to the dulcet tones of Gentleman Jim. The tortoiseshell tickle-puss had been named after one of her favourites. Every maudlin song sung with that Jim Reeves smile.

She wanted the game over quickly now. She didn't know where she'd use her last letter. She never decided until her mother had placed her tiles anyhow, then the best word and the next move would pop into her head in an instant. It was like the board and tiles were always conspiring to help her win. She didn't know why Mother insisted on playing. Some of her words weren't even words.

She moved the CD on a couple of places to *Adios Amigo*. Jim's terminally soporific voice took the edge off the background silence. Myra sat back down in front of the almost full Scrabble board. She looked at her mother's tired, old face as she chewed the inside of her cheek, turning a tile in her fingers. How many years did she have left? It had been a long time since her father had shuffled off. She couldn't bear dwelling on his loss, so she returned to thoughts of the loss of Mother.

At least she'd have her dysfunctionally generous final salary pension to fall back on, if Mother's savings got fingered and filched by the tax man. Rage surged again. The money had been taxed when it was earned; it was grossly unfair to tax it again. Maybe this was why successive governments seemed to wheel the elderly into draughty corridors, figuratively; there's money in death. She would just have to make every penny of her pension count.

"So, Myra, what are you doing tomorrow?"

"I'm seeing Martin. Do you remember me telling you earlier?"

"Yes, of course I do. I was just checking. How is he?"

"I haven't seen him yet."

Her mother was looking at her. "Why don't you find yourself a proper man?"

"Mother, how rotten. Martin's a very great and old friend."

"He's a very great and old fruit, more like."

"Don't you think I'm a little too old for a fancy man now?"

"I always wanted a wedding. What mother wouldn't? You're my daughter."

"Don't I know it! It's still your move, you know."

"I know. I'm thinking."

"Well think quicker. It's getting late."

"All I'm saying is, I don't know why you waste your time on basically an old poof."

"Alright, Mother."

Her mother focused back on the board again. She tapped the tile on the edge of the table. Jim started singing, *I love you because*. Bimbo sighed deeply and audibly. Mother's mouth opened in a slow, cavernous and toothy yawn as the rest of her face shrivelled into a scrunch. People always said that yawning was infectious. Myra must be immune.

An image of Ben popped into her head as Mother's warm breath touched her face. His airway slowly constricting as he gasped his last. She wondered if, when you breathe in for the last time... if you know that's the last time.

Then, it popped into her head. Framed by an almost euphoric excitement, the same feeling felt when you used all your tiles, including the high scorers, making words out of empty spaces, hitting a double or triple letter square along the way; all falling into place so elegantly. Intelligent design; the one perfect solution popping out from the zero point. She couldn't stifle her smile.

"Yes," said Mother decisively as she collected three of her four tiles and headed towards the 'triple word score' square in the corner. This would normally disappoint Myra, but not today. She knew it would work out OK. The fourth letter of Mother's word, the T, was already in place from the 'tyrant' Myra had put down. It was on a double letter square. Mother placed the C in the corner. Myra looked up and across at her. A self-satisfied smirk started to appear on Mother's mouth. She couldn't help herself. Myra's eyes narrowed;

she suspected she knew where this was heading. Mother then placed the U and finally squeezed in the N.

"There," she said triumphantly.

"Really?" Myra asked. "Really, Mother?"

"It's a word," Mother protested.

"I know it's a word. It's just not a word we want gracing Aunt June's Scrabble set." They looked at the board. The word leapt off and slapped you. "What have you got left?" Mother showed her A. "You could have put 'cant', you know."

"What's that?"

"Look it up. I bet they won't have your word in the Scrabble dictionary, not our edition. Anyway, so four... that's a double so five, and its triple word... so fifteen."

"Do I win?"

Myra looked at her own X. She could have used it to spell out that old Scrabble favourite 'Xu' (one hundredth of a dong) and, instead of just winning, wipe the floor with her mother, but instead...

"Yes, Mother," she said, "you foul-mouthed old witch, you win."

4

She made her way down one of the alleyways of Whitstable, towards the Old Neptune where she'd arranged to meet Martin at midday. The alleyway passed the back gardens and the school, overgrown with dandelions and nettles.

It had been given the name of *Stoke Newington-on-Sea* by some, because the proliferation of trendy, London types moving down and pushing house prices up. Couples dressed in black with triangular shaped prams for baby Sebastian or Jocasta. They all seemed to be designers or new media or some such made up job. The ones who were down from London for the day were known locally as DFLs. Most DFLs didn't even know the alleyways were there or, if they did, were nervous of them, as it was sometimes unclear where they would come out, or if they came out at all; some ended abruptly in overgrown dead ends. Snakes and ladders.

She cut across the high street and down Knight's Alley onto Island Wall. It was then just a short walk to the Neptune. Occasionally she liked to go down Squeeze Gut Alley, just to prove she easily could. As she approached, she noticed Martin, nursing a pint of cider outside.

"Janice, darling!" he called.

She smiled and quickened her pace. "Hello."

"How are you?" they said simultaneously.

"I'm fine, thank you, how are you?" she said.

"Wonderful. Is outside OK for you?"

"Yes, lovely," she said. They had dispensed with birthday cards over the last couple of years. It would have irritated her to have had to carry more than was essential.

"Gin and tonic?"

"Yes, please."

They ducked into the piratey pub with its slightly sloping wooden floors. It was surprisingly quiet in there. There was normally a folksy singer or skiffle arrangement. Drinks in hand, they passed the gorgeous sleeping dog with his red bandana.

They climbed the concrete steps over the sea defence wall and onto the beach, walking around to the back of the pub where the tables were. All of them were rather exposed, but there was little to no breeze, so anywhere would be fine. She could feel the shingle through her shoes. The sea was a millpond. In the evening, the sunsets from this vantage point were stunning, almost Mediterranean. Sparkles on the calm sea flecked like golden stars on the lapis lazuli ceiling of an Egyptian temple.

"Is here OK?" he asked. She told him it was fine. "Happy birthday, darling!" he said as they clunked plastic glasses.

"Can you believe that this time next year, I will be a retired lady of leisure?"

"It'll be wonderful," he said. He sighed and turned, looking over his shoulder and out to sea at the wind farm and the decrepit sea forts rusting on the horizon. "How's Linda?"

"Oh, she's fine, thank you. I think she's losing her marbles. Cantankerous as ever." She took a slurp.

"Good week?"

"So-so."

It was always lovely to see Martin, but she thought they were beyond small talk now. He always insisted upon it, until they got down to really talking and belly laughing. She didn't know what he'd planned. She guessed it would be a quick drink, then, when slightly oiled, a wander through town to wherever he had reserved for lunch. She hoped he'd booked somewhere. It only took a bit of forethought to make the phone call, but some people were so very, what they would call it; 'laid-back'? To her, these people lacked the basic good grace to make plans, were invariably unreliable and because they cheerily described themselves as 'spontaneous', despatched one as 'uptight' or boring for feeling vexed by their abdication of responsibility. They didn't care about the poor sods they left loitering on street corners, like Billy-no-mate prostitutes. The mobile phone meant people didn't have to be on time anymore, they could just text to say they were running late when they couldn't be arsed to arrive on fucking time. They were passive aggressive scum who needed to be rooted up and ripped out of the world. She diverted her thinking to sipping her G&T.

It turned out he had booked somewhere, the tapas place. Martin's treat. Then, after that, he had something else planned. They had to be somewhere at 4pm.

She sipped again and looked over his shoulder, as he chattered on, at the glassy sea. He was talking about his week at work, she was only half-listening. He didn't need to work, but he liked to give something back, he'd say. No one likes the smell of burning martyr. They were both hard workers and had both long ago decided that if they were going to work so hard, they wanted to do it for a worthy cause rather than to line some fat cat's pocket. Martin was independently wealthy after the death of his parents. Not exactly *wealthy* but, wealthy enough to live a modest life without the inconvenience of work.

A couple of years before, and in recognition of his increasing years on the clock and the onset of various aches and pains, he'd reduced his hours at the care home. He now worked twenty-one per week. He had trouble walking, too. His ankles looked swollen and sore. He reminded her of the sofa at home. She'd washed the covering once, but it never quite fitted after that. In fact, at the back, it was completely open as the ends were so far apart you couldn't zip it up anymore. He looked like that. Prick his ankle with a fork, and sausage meat would volumise out. He'd gained weight since she'd last seen him. Moved into the realm of 'portly'. Now, he had a large paunch overhanging his trousers. *Good God*, she suddenly thought, *he's wearing those same old trousers*. He'd had them decades, and that horrible belt. She tried to remember when she first saw them. She calculated they must be older than Melissa, the temp. Not to mention what lay beneath. Those vintage underpants must be historic. He'd stopped talking and tilted his head to the side.

"But you look peaky, darling."

"Do I? I don't feel it. I'm fine."

"I hope so," he said. "You'll need to be. We're going to have an absolute blast, but you'll need to have a bit of energy. Maybe a coffee after lunch." He noticed her thinly gloved hands. "Darling, don't tell me—"

"It's nothing."

"Is it Raynaud's?"

"I think so, undiagnosed. It's not definite. The gloves seem to help a little." She didn't really know why she'd started to wear her mother's gloves. Sympathy? The cobwebby elastic gloves were soft, almost see-through and comforting. She appreciated the concern people showed when she wore them. She didn't have to touch other people, or things touched by other people.

After their drink, they meandered through the town. She didn't need to buy anything and had never been a recreational shopper. Her anti-shopping tendencies, coupled with the fact that she had the maternal instincts of Herod, made her less than female in the eyes of many women and people like Martin.

They walked slower than she'd naturally walk, owing to Martin's sore ankles and soft wheezing. They passed the boutique shops and galleries. The rainbow windsock fish that normally danced in the wind hung limp outside the kite shop. She gave a wave to the ladies in the health store where she bought her St John's wort and healthy chocolate. The shop that used to be one of those old-fashioned gentlemen's outfitters, elderly men with tape around their necks and half-moon specs halfway down their faces, now a Costa. The town retained its high street of independents, when almost every other place had lost theirs. Whitstable still had its uniqueness, its gritty, working-harbour edge, but had embraced the benefits of some gentrification without swinging too far and becoming precious, anodyne, samey.

Perhaps the notebook work had given her could record not only recipes, but her thoughts too. A journal of the last year of working life. So that in years to come, she could open it up and reflect on just how miserable her tawdry working life had been.

What had been the point? Had any of that, often colossal, effort improved anyone's life in any significant way at all? The question smouldered in the back of her head. No one but hers probably; the income had led to a moderately comfortable life. It had never been hand-to-mouth. She had her final salary pension and when her mother eventually passed away, she'd have her inheritance; or what was left of it. She remembered that wicked thought that had crossed her mind the night before during their game of Scrabble. Now that it was the cold light of day, she couldn't possibly ask Martin. Could she?

Lunch was a grazing affair. They started slowly with three dishes and a carafe of sangria. Very soon the alien silences had passed, and the belly laughs were coming.

"Stop it, Martin," she laughed, "don't be so wicked."

"It's your fault," he joked, "you're a terrible influence on me. Everyone says so."

They ordered what they wanted when they wanted it. They picked at the olives and crusty bread, the patatas bravas and sizzling chorizo in wine; those lovely chipolata-things and stuffed peppers, oozing in molten cheese and every other flavoursome morsel they fancied.

The sun had come out. The number of weekenders on the street outside had picked up. The queue outside

Ossies and VC Jones, which Martin regularly described as the best fish and chip shops on the planet, were longer than ever, and the old-fashioned sweet shop was stuffed full of middle-aged men, their eyes bright, reliving their pocket money pasts.

The coffee arrived and the empty carafe, their third, was removed with the last of the terracotta dishes and plates. They could breathe again.

"Shouldn't we be going wherever we're going?" she asked.

"Yes. But we're fine. We're not going far. I checked out your shoes earlier; sensible as ever. You won't need to change them."

"You're going to have to tell me at some point, you know."

He smirked knowingly. "Well, I know how much you love country music and Jim Reeves. I remember all about the Daddy connection too and blah blah, but I thought…"

"Just tell me, Martin, please, before I slip into a coma."

Dramatic pause and uncontainable grin. "We're going line dancing." He clapped manically, flat-handed, wanting to laugh but not letting himself. She rolled her eyes.

"OK," she said, not sounding at all sure, but secretly a little excited.

"I know it's naff, but you love your country, and we've never been before; it'll be fun!"

"I'm sure it will. Thank you."

"It's only over the road at the Horsebridge too. And if we don't like it, we can stand at the back and misbehave."

The others were of all ages and all shapes and sizes. A few were seasoned line dancers, but most were first-timers too. Beth led the hour-long class; £2 per person. Mid-twenties with a black shoulder-length bob, she had a ghetto blaster, duffle bag and was dressed as you'd expect a dance instructor to dress.

Beth had a twinkle in her eye and a spring in her step. She was welcoming and, seemingly, genuinely so. The tall floor-to-ceiling windows were thrown open, the warm, sea breeze picked up and spritzed the hall.

The class of about thirty had milled about in embarrassment after paying up and completing the sign-in sheet: name, email, phone number and brief disclaimer.

"OK," Beth called. She introduced herself and said no fire drill was planned, so if the alarm sounded you had to leave or burn. Housekeeping over, she continued, "Right, let's get started. If you can get yourselves into maybe four or five lines but staggered slightly so you're not standing directly behind anyone. A few newbies today?" Most of the room's hands went up. A few at the front turned and grinned. One, a woman in a cowboy hat and with her thumbs already in the pockets of her tight Levis, said something to Beth that Janice missed. "I know you're not!" said Beth to the keen-as-mustard, mutton-dressed-as-cowgirl. The ones at the front laughed. "Well, that's great," said Beth to the rest, "we love fresh meat here." Another laugh. "Me and the ladies at the front are going to show you what you're going to be able to do like experts in about 45 minutes' time and then we'll walk you through it. So, are we ready?" There was a giggling murmur and groaning. "I'm sorry, I didn't hear y'all," she called in a dodgy American drawl, "I said, are we ready?" There was a slightly louder version of the earlier groans.

Beth pushed the play button and took her position. The seasoned line dancers at the front shifted their weight and wiggled in anticipation. The music kicked in, "Two, three, four..." and then it started. From her position at the back, she was transfixed. The line moved as one, in a casual, but efficient, way. They stepped and kicked and toe-tapped and quarter-turned and grinned. Their heads moved cheekily as if winking, and their buttocks in those tight jeans, round and pert, winked too. A smile started to manifest on her face. She turned to Martin who was studying every move. The dance looked too ambitious. Would they really be able to do this and move like that, in under an hour?

Then it was their turn, with the music off and slowly at first. Beginners' steps.

"So, weight on the left foot to start. And tap, tap with the right. Then the left, tap, tap. Kick, kick. Back tap, stepping forward; brush together and quarter-turn to the left and then the same again. So, tap, tap, tap, tap. Kick, kick, back tap, step, brush, turn. That's it; and again."

This was a *Walkin' Warzi*, which apparently cropped up in the '70s. Beth was informative on the history, from its country roots to the ballrooms of the 1950s, with dances like the *Madison* right up to today. They ran through the steps three or four times before adding the music. They'd learn the second part after the break.

"We'll stop here for now, for a five-minute stretch and comfort break. We run a class here every Wednesday evening at 7:30, so if you've left your email address, I'll send details out to you and hope to see you there." So, this was more of a recruitment drive than a class; and at £2 a pop, not much of a present. But she was enjoying herself. It was different and fun and not something she'd have signed up for in a hundred years.

She and Martin stepped out onto the narrow terrace that overlooked a wide, shingly cut-through to the beach with the Oyster Fishery restaurant opposite and the Pearson's Arms behind. You could hear the clinking of sailing boat rigging and walker's feet on pebbles; the contented warm, beery, pub chatter and smell the seaweed breeze.

"So, are you enjoying it?"

"It's great. I'm loving it," she said enthusiastically.

"I'm not sure if I'll sign up."

"No? I'm rather tempted. What a great idea of yours." Martin didn't look quite as perky as he did before. Maybe his ankles were bothering him again. Maybe he was becoming more acutely aware of his own increased limitations, brought on by age, weight and diabetes. He took his kit out. She looked away. She'd seen him do this many times but felt she could demonstrate how normal she viewed it by nonchalantly looking away and not drawing attention. He did his thing with the pinprick pen and put it away again.

"Everything OK?" she asked.

"Yes, I expect so. It's all a bit all over the place at the moment."

She wasn't totally sure what that meant but wasn't going to ask. She breathed in deeply. It would nearly be time to go back in.

"Martin," she said after a moment. He turned to her. "I have something to ask you, and you can say no…"

"What is it?"

"Well, I've… to be honest, it's about Mother."

"Oh," he said, bracing himself.

"Well, not just about her. I've been thinking a lot about retirement. It's only a year and counting now, and Mother isn't getting any younger."

"No," he said.

"OK, everyone!" called Beth from inside.

She couldn't ask.

"What is it, Janice?"

"We'd better go in. I'll ask you later."

"No, now, it sounds important."

"Later," she said with finality. Then with a sigh and a smile, "We have a line dance to master."

The second part of the dance had some tricky, but strangely satisfying, steps. Then they put it altogether, firstly without music, then with. It ended with some collective and heartfelt whoops and a spattering of clapping. No embarrassed groans and giggles at the cheesiness of it all now.

"Wow! Because you all learned that so quickly, we have time to do it once more, but this time I think we need to have a bit of that Yankee attitude." Everyone laughed. "You know what I'm saying? I want to hear some loud claps on those side-steps, I want to see some real springy quarter-turns and see you really have fun with it. I want to hear those *yee-haws* and *alrights* from all of you. So, let's make some noise, people! You ready? You ready for a bit more Billy Ray? I can't hear you. The DFLs outside can't hear you. You ready for a bit more from Miley's sexy DILF dad, ladies? Am I right?"

To a sweaty crescendo of shrieks, squeaks, laughs and claps the music started again at about three times the volume. Janice felt a chill go through her. Her hips were tingling, and Billy Ray sounded so manly yet vulnerable and sexy. It was too much. She wiggled and side-stepped and quarter-turned and brush-flicked away like the best of them, certainly as well as the fat-arsed cowgirl in that dozy hat.

But the weird thing was, it all suddenly made sense and were it not for a sensible sense of shame, she secretly wished she was wearing a cowgirl hat too. She saw herself out at a country hoedown, with those sawn-off wooden cowboy heels stamping on a straw-strewn floor, so hard the beer mats jumped in time on the tables, like Mexican jumping beans.

Of course, she knew that *Achy Breaky Heart* song from before, but she didn't really 'get it' until then. And Billy Ray, although he wasn't Jim Reeves, was great. She didn't know if she had room in her life for another country and western singer, but she certainly had space for that song. It buzzed around her head, and she couldn't help the thigh-slapping and happy humming.

Outside, onto the wide, concrete path with the shingle encroaching upon it. Instead of heading straight home, they walked along the beach away from the harbour. She bought two extra-large 99s (two flakes) from the van and they sat on an artily carved bench on the beach. She felt like she was on holiday. *This*, she thought, *is how I'll feel in twelve months' time, every day.*

Martin was dying to know what she'd wanted to say but didn't want to appear pushy. He knew she'd tell him if she wanted to and was ready to. He imagined that perhaps Linda had only a few months left. Perhaps she wanted to leave him something in her will. He had known her for years, after all.

She broke the silence by talking about Ben. She said she'd been shocked to hear of his sudden death and what a great boss he'd been. Martin had heard about Ben numerous times, but they'd never met. Janice didn't have many people in her life, and she tended to keep them compartmentalised, so their paths never crossed. Ben died of—

"What's the word?" she searched. "Not 'prophylactic'…"

"Anaphylactic shock?" Martin helped. She nodded.

Conversation began to dry up. It was time to call it a day. Martin spent time with people he could have fun with. He was friends with Janice for that very reason, because they had a laugh. He didn't much care to be around people who were down in the dumps like she suddenly seemed to be. If he wanted the dumps, he could go back home and sit in his own, empty company.

"I don't know what it is. But I suppose it's the fact that in twelve months' time I'm going to be retired and with Ben dying so unexpectedly, it's just brought a few things into sharp focus."

Why did he never feel convinced by her when she did 'emotional'? "You need time to grieve," he said. He really was utterly useless in these situations. On the plus side, he'd be the first to admit it, hence his avoidance of things heartfelt; she couldn't do heartfelt, and he hated heartfelt. He would have appeared so much more empathetic by maintaining an enigmatic silence. "Is this about your mother?" She didn't answer. "Have you got an achy, breaky heart?" She smirked, and a sniffed exhalation shot from her nose. This was as close to a belly laugh as she was going to go.

"No, I have not got an achy, breaky heart, you wretched old queer," she said still smiling. "I've had a lot on my mind lately. It's Ben and work and Mother and retirement and the whole inheritance tax thing. It's been bothering me." She looked at him, his diabetic tongue fellating the ice cream. "You're a care worker." He nodded. "Well, a solution presented itself to me…" He nodded again. There was a silence. Had he asked her a question? He wasn't sure. Had she answered. Should he answer? Should he say something funny? What was she saying?

He said, "…There's always an answer to everything if you set your mind to it, and you know I'm always here for you, darling."

"I know, we have fun together. I don't really see as much of you as I'd like, and something came to me the other day and… well, if you don't ask, you never know, do you?"

"No, you don't. What is it?"

"I have so much that I need to be getting on with right now, and that's set to continue for the foreseeable, and she's clearly getting worse. I'm just so afraid that something will happen when I'm not around," she lied.

"I can always nip over whenever and check up on her, if you like?"

"That's sweet of you, Martin, thank you."

He realised there was more. He thought it was too simple to be true.

"I need to ask you something…" she genuinely found it hard to finish. "It's such a silly idea really and you can obviously say no if you want to, and I won't think any the worse and we can forget about it."

"What?"

"An idea popped into my head last night." His ice cream was melting faster than he could lick it and the warm air caressed the sea. He tilted his head and slurped the cone. "You two have always got along so well. I was thinking that you could sell your place and live with us… in the spare room." He stopped licking and looked at her. Her eyes were small, slate-grey like her hair, and piercing. She didn't often look at him like that and it was more than a little disarming. The melting ice cream dribbled over fingers. "You'd have the money from that to do whatever you wanted," she said with a smile. "We could all live quite well and cheaply, the three of us; economy of scale and all that. Why heat two homes when you can heat one? And while I'm out working, you could do the caring bit for Mother, and

I'd avoid paying the inheritance tax when she eventually... snuffs it."

He didn't know what to say. He looked down. His shoes were all dusty from the beach. The thought was utterly ghastly. Was she insane? It couldn't possibly work. They'd end up hating each other. The resentment. The upset. He didn't think he could bear sacrificing his personal space, let alone their friendship, for that. That said, Janice's house was large and could be very nice once he'd finished putting his spin on it. Having a garden would be boon, too.

"It would mean giving up your job, Martin. Not straight away, of course, but eventually, when you were ready and when she needed more intensive care, as she will one day. You're probably getting quite close to wanting to call it a day at the care home anyway, I expect. I know it's an awfully big ask."

"Janice, just so I'm clear... I'm really confused. Are you asking me to sell my place and move in with you and provide the care for your mother...?"

"No. Well, yes and no," she said. "I want you to marry her."

5

She had no expectations that the marriage be consummated; it was more of an 'arrangement'. He liked Linda, it was true, and it made sense to heat one house rather than two. Janice's house was big, and their lives separate enough that they'd probably not see very much more of each other than they did currently. She'd be happy if he just gave it some thought. He planned to never refer to it ever, ever again.

Phase two of her proposal would be after her mother's passing, when she and Martin would marry, thereby avoiding inheritance tax. The burning question for him, which he hadn't dared ask, was, what was in it for him? Presumably, whoever outlived the other, inherited the lot. An amount not to be sniffed at. He was considering it, despite himself.

On Monday, she left work at lunchtime, marking it down as a half day's annual leave, so she could register Ben's death, at Lewisham. She'd been in a hurry to get away and take with her the new passport. She thought she'd left it at work, in her pedestal drawer, but perhaps she'd put it down at home somewhere. She'd had a fair bit on her mind lately. Luckily, she had the marriage certificate, as well as his death certificate, and a handful of utility bills as proof of address.

The registrar was a half-wit. He spilt half a bottle of ink on the desk between the last people and her. He barely said two words and typed with one finger; ball-achingly laboured. She stifled her irritation. If she was to appear short on time or vexed, it might raise an eyebrow. He was sorry for her loss.

"It's Me…" said the voice on the other end of her mobile.

"Who?" She'd been dozing on the train back to Whitstable when it had buzzed from inside her bag.

"Mel at work? I'm sorry to call you. I know you're off this afternoon, but I have Mr O'Brien here. He says it's his annual meeting? He's from BDI? It's about the pension scheme?" It was more of a statement than a question, but in her ever-so-slightly grating New Zealand accent (perky-perky-perky), everything she said sounded like a question?

"Was that today? It wasn't in my diary. I'm on the train now, halfway home."

"Shall I rearrange?" There was another voice in the background. "Actually, Stuart says he can do it, if you like?"

"No. It's fine, I'll do it. Tell him I'm very sorry, Mr O'Brien, tell him I'm sorry; I had no idea. I can do any time to suit him." Melissa stifled the phone with her hand. The voices sounded like they were talking through pillows in an adjoining room, like her ears needed irrigating. It suddenly cleared.

"He says its fine. He'll come back tomorrow at the same time. He says it's no problem at all."

"Thanks, Melissa."

"No problem. Have a lovely rest of your day off."

It didn't surprise her in the least that Stuart wanted to get his hands on the scheme. He angled for it every year, acutely aware of Janice's impending retirement. The scheme's actuary also acted as the charity's auditors, so Stuart knew Mr O'Brien, but only dealt with him on the audit.

She was on just over £39,000 gross per annum. She wasn't entitled to any automatic incremental rises since reaching the top of her pay scale thirty years ago. She'd stagnated there ever since. She was, however, entitled to any percentage 'cost of living' rise applied across the Trethendar pay scale. Any pay scale seemed ridiculous now, bearing in mind how the staff numbers had dwindled to their current level; four plus the agency maternity cover. Jenny must be due to drop any day. So, assuming Melissa, or Mel, as she wanted to be known, worked out, she'd be given a fixed-term contract of employment. This would bring the establishment count to a heady five. Pathetic, considering how great Trethendar had been in Ben's day.

She pulled out her calculator. Mr O'Brien would arrive soon, and she wanted her own position to be clear before they met. The others were getting on with whatever they normally did, playing solitaire or online shop browsing. All credit to Hazel, though, she was probably the only one who did a proper day's work anymore.

Assuming a 2% rise the following April, she'd be on £40k. One sixtieth of the final annual salary was multiplied by the number of complete years' paying into the scheme at retirement. The last few UK organisations with similar pension schemes had gone into administration because of the colossal associated deficits. Trethendar's scheme had been closed to new members for years and she was the only current employee in the scheme.

Her dream cottage in the Cotswolds had never been nearer. Honey-coloured and in the centre of village life. She'd make jam and volunteer at the local church. Perhaps her skills could be used on a committee. She'd be a quiet, well-respected new arrival.

Her mother didn't feature in this dream. She'd stay in Whitstable until Mother kicked the bucket. Martin hadn't featured either. *Probably best,* she thought, *too much like Mapp and Lucia otherwise.* She was probably more a Miss Mapp than Lucia, and Martin was far too big boned for Georgie.

She and Philip O'Brien headed upstairs to the flat and sat in the window overlooking the Farringdon street below. The blinds blinked against the open window in the breeze. There was the normal small talk of weather and how their respective organisations had faired over the past twelve months since last time. She apologised for not being available to meet him the day before. He said it was probably his fault; got the wrong day.

He sighed rather ominously, as he opened his case. He took a ratty-looking green card folder out and, putting on his glasses, opened it. Various documents and letters. On top was a page torn from a notebook with handwritten notes and calculations.

"I'm afraid I have some rather bad news," he said, "but it may not come as a total surprise, bearing in mind the current climate and what's been happening regarding schemes like Trethendar's."

"What is it? Our scheme has always been solid, sustainable, I've been led to believe."

"And so it has. I review it every year, as you know, and I remember saying last time that we had an affordability issue." This, to her, sounded like someone covering his back.

"I remember our last conversation too, and there was no mention of an issue," she said.

"Well, regardless of that, I'm afraid we have an issue now. With a scheme like yours, people in it don't have a personal 'pot' as such. There's one central fund, with everyone, including the employer, paying into it. Unfortunately, since the last crash, most investments have failed. Your own scheme has in fact... and no one, not even I, could have predicted..."

"Just tell me."

He sighed deeply. "I'm afraid there are insufficient funds to pay all the current beneficiaries much beyond the end of the next financial year."

His words hung in the air. How could it go from being solid as a rock twelve months ago, to being virtually bankrupt a year later?

"What?"

"I understand it's a lot to take in."

"All the beneficiaries?" she asked. "What do you mean 'all the beneficiaries'? How many are there?"

"We'll need to write to everyone to explain the situation."

"How many?"

"The good news is it's only three. However, all three were quite senior, so had a higher final salary, and all had long service. That, coupled with the deficit we've been running at and the investments under-performing... I notice that you're retiring next year..." His voice trailed off again. "I'm afraid this will have a rather significant impact on you personally."

"I've been paying into this scheme for thirty-four years. My employer has too. Thirty-four years, Mr O'Brien. You're telling me that there'll be nothing left for me at all?"

"No, I'm not saying that." He blinked nervously in the face of her thin, tight-lipped rage. "What I am saying... is... that there are insufficient funds in the scheme to pay all the beneficiaries, and that includes yourself, much further beyond the end of the next financial year."

"Isn't there some kind of protection, insurance, in these circumstances? Compensation?"

"Normally, yes. Trethendar opted out of that when the organisation first started to decline, presumably as a cost-saving, but people are living longer nowadays; signed by V Freers for Trethandar. I have the signed paper here somewhere." He leafed through his file. She waited.

"So that's it?"

"Janice, I'm doing my best. Our advice was correct at the time, and that's all I can say. These are challenging times for everyone, unprecedented. I know it's very hard to hear, but I... we at BDI, can't see a way out of this for you. I've reviewed the scheme and been over it many times with colleagues in recent weeks and I'm afraid that the scheme will close... in just over twelve months' time."

The shock refused to abate. She couldn't speak. So that was it?

"Who are the beneficiaries?"

He looked into his file. He sighed deeply again. What he'd had to say had been said. The rest was just detail.

"OK, so we have Mrs Miller." She frowned at him questioningly. "She was the wife of the late Peter Miller. He was finance director, I believe."

"But why's she a beneficiary?"

"Under the terms of the scheme, the partner receives a pension for the rest of their life. It's an amount equal to half the total entitlement." He waited for a reply or another question; neither came. "Then we have Mr Ben Westrell." She closed her eyes. "I am sorry," he said, "I know this is really difficult for you."

"You have no idea," she said. "Look, there's no reason why you should know what I'm about to tell you and I'd ask that you keep it strictly confidential." He nodded at her. "Ben Westrell died last week."

"On the plus side, that does mean the scheme may continue for longer than predicted."

"I was married to him."

O'Brien didn't know what to say. "Oh my God. I didn't know. I'm so, so sorry."

"But as I say, I'd prefer it not to be public knowledge."

"Of course. The third person is Irene Hartley, who I believe was..." he said referring to his notes, "marketing and campaigns director and deputy chief executive. Then yourself, obviously."

"And Vera?" Mr O'Brien looked confused. "Vera Freers; finance director before Peter Miller. She died about ten years ago."

"No dependent beneficiary. Not in the scheme," he said. "It's just the four of you. You would obviously count as both a member beneficiary and a qualifying beneficiary now, because you were married to Mr Westrell."

"Irene wasn't married, so presumably hers stops with her."

"That's correct." He nodded quickly. "She has no qualifying beneficiaries. So, just her and Peter Miller's widow and yourself."

"So, for the sake of argument, just thinking hypothetically, if I were to be hit by a bus tomorrow, would there be enough to last beyond the twelve months for the other two?"

"Oh, undoubtedly. Your share stands at one third, and even though your final salary will be less than theirs, it would definitely run longer. And, who knows, if the economy takes a positive turn, and the investment fund bears fruit, it could go on longer still, possibly indefinitely." She was silent. He slowly closed his file. He rolled his pen between his fingers, slowly retracting the ballpoint. "Is there anything else you want to ask me while I'm here?"

"No, I don't think so," she said. "I'm sure I'll have other questions, but I think I've heard enough for now. I shall have to take something to the charity's trustees and to Stuart." A smell of warm, baked pastries wafted into the room from the sandwich shop.

"I can email you a full breakdown."

"Thank you."

Meeting ends.

Margaret Miller (or Margie as Peter called her) and Irene Hartley... Irene Hartley. She'd been cheated out of all she'd been promised. You honour a promise, but she'd found out too late to be able to do anything about it; all her retirement plans, gone.

Stop. Breathe.

She'd learnt that, when you don't know what to do, probably the best thing to do is nothing for the time being, until the right response presents itself to you; just like in Scrabble.

She missed the 17:52 from Cannon Street by a minute. Her thoughts were snowballing, overthinking themselves at a rate of knots. She couldn't stop. She didn't know Margie Miller. She remembered speaking to her on the phone a couple of times yonks ago. Well-spoken; booming, but cut-glass. Intimidating. There'd been a picture of her on his desk. Well-turned-out, on holiday somewhere, smoking a cigarette. Funny what you remember. She couldn't picture the face at all, just that voice, that perfectly coiffured hair and cigarette. She couldn't forget Irene though. That complete and utter, ginger, fucking bitch from hell.

The train arrived. The doors opened. She took her normal seat near the door that, on arrival at Whitstable, was opposite the platform exit. She gazed out of the window and down onto the track. Another dead bird. This one had a light dusting of soot or oil or something.

Ben had taken three weeks' holiday, as he normally did in August. The trustees didn't meet that month or December. She remembered that dreadful meeting as if it were yesterday. He didn't know it, but deputy chief executive, Irene, had been surreptitiously lobbying key trustees for months, and she wasn't alone. It turned out Vera Freers, finance director at the time, had kicked things off by discussing the possibility of a coup with the treasurer, chair and deputy chair nearly a year earlier.

The trustees' meeting was called in his absence, with just two weeks' notice, in that first week of September, by Vera and Irene, to discuss the financial situation again. Ben offered to cancel his leave, but Irene told him she'd handle it, that he deserved a break and that she didn't foresee him being required to make any decisions at, or immediately arising from, the meeting. He'd trusted her.

Janice hadn't been required to attend either. She'd not been asked to provide any cost projections for redundancy payments or timelines, nor had Ben said anything much to her about any of it.

It was a set-up. There'd been some discussion as to whether they should stay and refurbish or sell and move. Back then, they occupied more of the building bequeathed by their founder. There were thirty-five employees then, and they had business tenants in the smaller part (the Y-shaped corner section of the property that overlooked where the road divided), with residential tenants in the second-floor flat. Janice assumed that releasing the capital through a quick sale was the most likely option.

There had been a recruitment freeze for twelve months, and the staff attrition rate was increasing steadily each quarter, leaving additional pressure on those left, and every year, the same strategy; to achieve more, better, for less. Every year the same prayer that one of the members would keel over, leaving a generous legacy on which the charity could survive for a little longer. But the charity hadn't received a legacy for a long time. Existing on a wing and a prayer.

Nearly a week after that meeting, her phone rang.

"Janice, I'm with Vera. Do you have a moment?" Irene asked.

"I'll be right there."

It had been a beautiful building. On entering through the front door, you were confronted by the long, sweeping stairway with carved, oak balustrade. The marble floors had a rather ornate design picked out in different colours, grey-blue, white and kidney. A central lozenge lay under the carpets and marked the spot, she surmised, where a three-legged table once stood for Lady Trethendar's large chinoiserie vase.

She left her office and climbed the narrow back staircase, the ones the servants would have used, up to the third floor where the three directors' offices were. Irene's door was ajar, but she knocked anyway. She was called in; invited in to take a seat. Vera, seated to the side of Irene's desk, glanced up and smiled feebly, then looked back down at the floor. There was a chair right in front of the desk that was clearly meant for her.

"Janice, thanks for coming up. I know you're busy. I asked Vera to join us because of some information she presented to the trustees the other week regarding the financial situation." She looked across to Vera. "Actually, perhaps it's better if I hand over to her at this point and she can explain." Vera looked backfooted. She cleared her throat.

"Last year, as you know, we ended in deficit, for the third year running. There are several reasons why last year was more significant; expenditure on the rebranding project, increase in marketing spend, moving the newsletter from quarterly to monthly, improving the look and feel of our materials and all against the continuing trend of falling membership. There are a lot more charities out there nowadays, and we're all competing for funds in a much smaller pond. We'd come to rely on a legacy each year and kept expecting, or hoping, to hear something, but the reality is... The long and the short of it is, if we continue the current trajectory... I informed the trustees we've been in a state of financial crisis for some time and that if immediate action is not taken to arrest the situation, the charity will fold."

"I knew things were bad," Janice said, "but... something always turns up."

"Charities can't run on faith and hope," Irene soundbit, "and I'm afraid we need to make some difficult decisions."

She went on to say that there'd been three proposals heard by the trustees. Janice's initial, unaired reaction was to wonder why on earth this was happening now and why they hadn't waited a week or two until Ben was back from leave. But it soon became clear.

The first of the three proposals was, as she'd guessed, to investigate the possibility of selling up. The second was to restructure the organisation. To ensure the long-term sustainability of the charity, cuts needed to result in at least a twenty-five percent reduction in net salary expenditure. Taking into consideration the redundancy payments to be made, and very much depending, of course, on who would go, Janice instantly guesstimated that this would mean an actual reduction in headcount of perhaps fifty percent. She couldn't see how the charity could possibly maintain current services with sixteen or seventeen people. It certainly couldn't operate as it had done.

"Your position will be quite safe of course," she said, glancing at Vera for a second. Neither one of them could be trusted an inch.

Thirdly came the reason why none of this could be revealed while Ben was around. The trustees had decided he should be exited from the organisation, through a compromise agreement rather than redundancy. Irene added, with pained expression, that she would not escape feeling the pinch. Her position of deputy chief executive was to be deleted. She would, however, be invited to stay on as acting chief executive. So, no *real* pinch at all for Irene then.

"It's not about making good decisions or bad decisions. There are no good options here to choose from," Irene said. "It's about thinking long-term and doing what we can to make the least bad decision; and, no matter what, ensure Trethendar survives."

Janice was the only one qualified to have the 'without prejudice' discussion with Ben. Irene had checked Janice's diary, she hoped she didn't mind, and had already written to Ben to say Janice would be meeting with him at his home, the day after he returned from Florida.

"This is very hard for me, Ben."

"I know, honey." He was a handsome, bronzed, oak of a man back then. So different to the frail invalid he was to become, gasping for oxygen, flailing around in a room full of bees. "But you've got to do what you're here to do. I'm not stupid, HR don't make house calls unless it's serious."

"I need to have a discussion with you, without prejudice. This means that it can't be referred to and cannot, and will not, influence or prejudice any other formal dispute resolution procedure."

"I understand."

"It's informal, off-the-record."

"I get it, Janice. When do they want me to go?"

"With immediate effect."

"Alright. It's OK," he said reassuringly. "And what's their best offer?"

"Payment in lieu of your three months' notice, which will be subject to the normal tax and national insurance deductions and an amount equivalent to three months' pay that won't be taxable."

"I see."

"There would normally be a payment in lieu of annual leave, but you've taken yours. In fact, more than you'll have accrued at the leaving date, but the charity won't be seeking to claw back any money for this. We will also pay up to £200 towards your legal expenses because you'll need to seek legal advice for the agreement to be valid."

"OK."

"I'll put it all in writing to you and then you'll need to sign to say you agree. It will be quite long, but it's basically just saying that Trethendar will make this payment to you and in turn you'll leave, resign that is, and not sue."

"That's fine."

"Ben, I'm so sorry."

"It's alright. I figured Irene was up to something."

"It's Vera too."

"You know what? I've had enough anyway. I'm not going to speak badly of either of them. I've had a good run," he said. "I made mistakes, but I gave it my best shot. If they think they can do a better job, good luck to them. I don't want to make this any harder for you either, honey. I won't push for more."

She wanted to cry. "I haven't prepared the agreement yet, but I can post it to you when I get back to the office."

"I didn't think it would end like this," he said with a gentle giant's smile, "and does it make me sad? Yes, of course it does. Can I see anyone employing me at my age? Hell, no. Could you?" She couldn't answer. The truth was too harsh to hear, and a lie, too obvious to tell. "I've had a long, mixed and interesting career. It's enough. Out of all of this, I'm glad it was someone as lovely as you who broke the news to me. And you know what? I wish Irene and Vera nothing but the best, really I do; nothing but love and light, and in my heart, I know that one day, somehow, and I don't know how, karma will come back and bite them both in the ass."

Six months later, Vera was dead. The redundancies were made, both sets of tenants were given notice and the parts of the building that could be sold, were. The much-diminished charity then backed into the wedge where the road split, the part previously occupied by the commercial tenant and the residential tenant above. Irene carried on as acting chief executive until she retired.

She looked away from the dead bird on the track and at her hands, snugly glove-wrapped, neatly holding each other in her lap. She'd call in sick tomorrow or work from home. *The Queen's gloves can't be this grey and yellowing around the fingers*, she thought. Little wonder they were grubby; Myra's gloves polished everything she touched. Wherever she went, a little of the world's shit was silently wiped away and replaced with cleanliness, and all without leaving any trace of her ever having been there.

6

"Hello?"

"Good morning, is that Mrs Miller?"

"Yes, it is. Who's this?"

"My name is Janice Lucas and I'm calling from Reeves Plaistow International. We're an independent market research agency based in London and we're conducting a lifestyle survey today. As a thank-you for taking part, you'll be entered into a free prize draw for cash prizes of up £2,000. Do you have a few minutes to spare now to answer some questions for me, please?"

"Well, er... it's not very convenient right now."

"When would be a more convenient for me to call back?"

"...er... Where did you get my number from?"

"We're given pages at random from the telephone directory."

"But I'm ex-directory."

"Sometimes the pages we're provided with are from rather old directories so it's possible your number was removed after this one's publish date."

"Oh dear. Is it selling something? I'm not really very interested, I'm afraid..."

"No, it's a legitimate, bona fide, market research survey. Not a sales call at all."

"Well…"

"Would you have a few minutes to spare? We'd really appreciate it. The results of the survey are presented as graphs and tables so it's all strictly confidential and you personally won't be identifiable in any way as having taken part."

"How long did you say it will take?"

"Just ten to twelve minutes depending upon your answers."

"Oh, yes, alright then, if you're very quick."

"That's lovely, thank you very much. Firstly, which shop do you use for your main weekly grocery shopping?"

"Marks and Spencer's." *Of course.*

And they were off.

Before she became Ben's PA, and her subsequent career change into HR, she spent six or seven years in market research, at a ropey call centre in Putney. Firstly, as a telephone interviewer, then as supervisor, and finally as recruitment and training manager.

After six months of temping, she was offered the temp-to-perm role of personal assistant to the chief executive at Trethendar. She never forgot what she'd learnt in market research, a sector that she'd helped feed at the rectum of manipulative, problem-creating, parasitic and freeloading marketeers.

She'd pulled a lifestyle survey, sent to Mother, from their paper recycling bin and completed it over the phone with her one and only respondent, the beneficiary, Margie Miller. She learnt how many times per annum she took overseas and domestic holidays, the brands she favoured, what she smoked and drank, her favourite television programmes, her internet usage, her interests and hobbies, the causes she supported, her utility providers, who she voted for in the last local election and who she was most likely to vote for in the next (general) one, and on and on.

Mrs Miller favoured spicy food because it was about the only thing she could taste nowadays. She complained of almost no sense of smell whatsoever. So she didn't wear perfume or deodorants for that matter, "Because what's the bloody point?"

Her persistent interviewer knew how strongly or slightly she 'agreed and disagreed with the following statements' and faithfully recorded her answers, probing fully for clarification and more information. She also built a rather cheery rapport with the bitter, privileged Mrs Miller, who'd relaxed considerably since the beginning of the questionnaire, becoming more comfortable with Janice Lucas; more candid. Responses delivered with a sneer rather than the snarl. She was unaware that thirty-three minutes had elapsed since she'd answered the phone.

Her life was empty, a waste of skin. She ate minimally and had little-to-no social life. "Because what's the bloody point of anything?" She had a houseful of her husband's antiques, which she loathed because of the dust his 'old clutter' gathered. She loathed all dark wood furniture.

She smoked, she drank, she read the *Daily Mail,* thought immigration was the greatest problem facing the country today and watched television until she was broken, bored or so incensed that she couldn't stomach anymore. Then she'd fall into bed for a lovely smoke and wake up marginally more objectionable than the day before, for another sorry Groundhog Day.

"It's all sodding dross on nowadays," Mrs Miller said. "Don't you think? All untalented wannabes or opinionated tossers or pompous, out-of-touch politicians gassing on about some crap or other. I mean, for Christ's sake. Not forgetting all that reality show crap. Freak shows, I call them!"

"Well, you'll be pleased to hear that we are now at the end of the survey—"

"Oh." She'd been on a roll.

"But just before I go, I have to ask you a few classification questions to ensure we've interviewed a balanced cross-section of society. So firstly, which of the following age groups do you fall into? Are you nineteen to twenty-four, twenty-five to thirty-four, thirty-five to forty-four, forty-five to fifty-four, fifty-five to sixty-four or—"

"That one – fifty-five to sixty-four. How utterly depressing."

"And are you married, single, widowed, divorced, separated or living together?" Her questions now were from memory of classification and social grading. It had probably changed considerably, but she ploughed on confidently regardless.

"I'm widowed," she answered, beginning to sound a little less comfortable.

"How many people, including yourself, live in the household?"

"Just me."

"And what was, or is, the occupation of the chief income earner in the household?"

"He was a finance director."

"And how many people did the organisation employ?"

"God, is all this really necessary? Haven't you got enough?"

"I'm nearly finished. I have some categories. Was it up to one hundred, one hundred to five hundred—"

"Under one hundred, I think. What's this for anyway?"

"I'm not really meant to say, but it helps us determine which social grade you fall into. We have to get a certain number of people of different ages, genders and so on in each of the different social grades: A, B, C1, C2, D or E."

"It's a bit of a bloody liberty, don't you think? I mean you sound normal enough but bugger me!"

"I'm only asking the questions they give me."

Lighting another cigarette, she asked, "Are you in some kind of squalid, sweatshop call centre?"

"Yes," she said in a quick whisper to give the impression she was fearful of getting into trouble.

"Rather you than me. I bet it's full of bloody foreigners, isn't it? Eastern Europeans, Nigerians. I hope you're on more than minimum wage for this."

"Did you ever work?" she asked, clearly going off-piste, even for a fake market research survey.

"God no. Why on earth should I? I was the hostess with the mostest, the trophy wife. Not much of a trophy, I'll admit, but he could have done a lot worse. You can always do worse, can't you? Well, maybe not you…"

"And what sector did he work in?"

"It was a charity."

"Not-for-profit sector," she clarified, for authenticity. "Last one, what qualifications did he have that were relevant to his job?"

"He was a member of the Chartered Institute of Bankers."

"Chartered Institute of…" she read back slowly as she wrote it down.

Mrs Miller reiterated, "That's Bankers with a 'B', not a 'W'. Though he was a lifetime member of that club too." Her lips popped on her cigarette as she checked her gold, anniversary present watch. "Are we finished now? I'm getting rather bored, I'm afraid."

"Let me just confirm the address and the number I called," she read back the address and telephone number, not from the phone book, but from a letter in Peter Miller's personnel file, photocopied.

"Yes, that's all correct," said Mrs Miller.

"Well, that is the end of the interview, but just before I go, I have to say thank you for taking part—"

"Fine."

"All the answers you have given me today will be treated in the strictest confidence and in accordance with the Market Research Society code of conduct—"

"Yes, alright."

"The results of the survey will be presented in the form of tables and statistics. Sorry, I must just finish reading you this bit before I go. And as a thank you for taking part, your name will be entered into the free, prize draw with cash prizes of up to £2,000—"

"Oh goody."

"If you have any questions about the survey, I can give you the number for Reeves Plaistow International or for the Market Research Society, which is a Freephone number, and they can confirm our status as a legitimate market research agency. Would you like either of those numbers at all?"

"No, you're alright. What was your name again?"

"...Janice..." she had to think for a moment, "Lucas."

"I don't envy you your job. You deserve a sodding medal."

"Thank you so much for taking part."

"Alright."

"Goodbye, Mrs Miller."

"Bye then." Mrs Miller, Margie, hung up.

She put her finger on the phone hook and slowly put the handset down. In the space of thirty-five minutes, she'd learnt everything she needed to know about Mrs Miller's empty life.

"Mother?" she called out of the living room at the stairs. "Mother?"

"What is it?" shouting back from the toilet seat, wiping.

"You'll be alright on your own for a couple of days, won't you?" She carefully folded the questionnaire, and the information gathered.

"I can't hear a word you're saying." She farted unexpectedly, like a balloon animal asking a question.

"I said you'll be alright for a few days on your own, won't you? I need to go to Hull in a couple of weeks... for an HR conference... Mother?"

"Yes. You go and do what you have to do. Leave me on my own. I'll probably be fine. I'll try not to fall and break a hip and die alone in my own mess."

She called Martin and asked if he had plans for lunch because, if not, she'd like to treat him to a sandwich on the beach. He wasn't working and said he'd thought a lot about the question she'd asked him.

They hadn't gone for anything fancy. She had roast beef and horseradish in a floury bap, and he had coronation chicken in a soft, oaty baguette. They sat on the benches in front of the tennis courts at the western tip of town.

"I've been thinking about what you said the other day," he said as he folded the sandwich paper and wiped the last traces of roast chicken juice and creamy, curried sauce from his lips.

She chuckled. "I was just being devilish."

"On a lot of levels, it's actually quite a bright thing to do."

She stopped chewing. "Really?" she asked with her hand covering her mouthful.

"Were you joking?"

"Not at the time, but it seems a lot to ask, don't you think?"

"Well, when weighing up the pros and cons, really the only reason I can think of for not doing it is that it seems dishonest to marry for this reason. But then,

I lived a lie for the best part of my adult life and I'm sure most people probably get married for convenience. To live under one roof seems sensible financially, and under two seems careless, and if it helps you out with the inheritance tax…?"

"I don't know what to say, Martin. I mean, I really don't. It's a bit weird, don't you think? She might say no, of course."

"I know, but if she doesn't, then I wouldn't object, on paper, just as an… arrangement. I wouldn't want a church wedding—"

"I understand!" she said. She couldn't ask the trusted local vicar to do it anyway, it would be just too peculiar; she didn't want to raise eyebrows.

"So, she and I could marry in… I think the nearest is Maidstone…" He'd clearly done his research. "And just so we're all clear, I'd sell my home, leave my job, move in with you, care for her and when she dies—"

"God forbid."

"God forbid, then you and I will…?"

"Marry," she said helpfully.

"Yes, marry. Then when I die, you get everything, avoiding inheritance tax."

"Yes."

"And if you…" He couldn't quite finish.

"If I croak before you," she leapt in, wrapping the dog-end of bap in the greaseproof paper, "…then *you* get everything."

He paused for a moment. "Well, I'm game," he said cheerily, as if agreeing to another round of whist.

She laughed. "OK. I'll ask Mother and see what she says. If, that is, she can stop pissing herself laughing long enough to reply."

Two weeks later she was on the train from Kings Cross to Hull. She mentioned the prospect of marrying Martin to Mother, who'd also been peculiarly pragmatic and receptive to the idea. She cackled like an old witch at first, but once the arrangement was explained in full, she understood the rationale and couldn't disagree that it made perfect sense. She couldn't quite see what was in it for him, despite hearing how the benefit would really kick in once one or other popped his or her respective clogs.

"What if I outlive you both?" she asked.

She thought for a moment. "Good question. Presumably the state, gets everything."

"I could leave it to the donkeys!"

Mother wondered if the house was big enough for the three of them without being under each other's feet. If it didn't work out, she said, she could always divorce him and take him for everything, citing irreconcilable differences. "I could say the marriage was never consummated," she laughed, wheezing and coughing, her eyes watering, "because he turned out to be a big, old, fat poof."

"Mother, behave. He's doing us a favour. You like Martin, don't you?"

"He's harmless enough, I suppose, even if he isn't a real man." She stopped. Her eyes lost their wicked twinkle for a moment, realising what she was saying, what she was remembering. They were both thinking the same. That poor dear man, her husband, Myra's father. There was still the mixture of difficult emotions, even if they had lost their edge with time; but still they reappeared periodically, unexpected and unannounced. The smile slid from her face. "Alright, Myra. If you think it will work. If you think it will help."

It was to be a September wedding.

It had been an eventful few weeks, she reflected as her train sped north, through the emerald green and pleasant countryside. To Ben's credit, he had tied up all his affairs long before his death. He'd sold his London flat and moved all his current and savings accounts to one place. The hospice had stopped his direct debits from the day of his death and his entire estate was in the hands of his solicitor, Mr Savile, acting as executor. Not that there'd be much left. End of life care is prohibitively expensive.

She'd made a small diversion via Hempstead to collect his ashes from the funeral directors. He was now stuffed into her overnight bag on the rack behind her seat. It seemed a long way to take him but was unavoidable; she didn't have time to make a separate journey.

She opened her Boots egg and cress lite and closed her eyes as she chewed. The train chackety-chacked. She didn't know what she'd achieve by her trip to Hull. Acceptance of reality, perhaps; peace of mind? She made the trip anyway. She wasn't even sure how she'd get to meet Margie Miller. She decided she wouldn't try and work it out, even though the train was the perfect place to plan, and planning was her 'thing'. She stared out of the window. She knew the right thing to do would come to her. It always did and until it did, she wouldn't waste time and energy trying to search her mind for it. She leafed the tiny *Collins Gem Book of Antiques* she'd picked up at WH Smiths and started to work her way through, from cover to cover.

The 12:35 from London Kings Cross should arrive in Hull at 15:11. She disliked having to change and could have made the earlier train, but she opted for the later, slower one, with no change at Doncaster. There was no hurry. She was glad of the time. Wide awake, but with eyes closed, and one gloved hand holding the other lightly in her lap, her ear was drawn to the dreadful buzzing of the inconsiderates with their iPods and iPhones.

This was a reconnaissance mission more than anything. She opened her eyes and moved her glove from her wrist to see her watch: 14:58. Her eyelids unfolded shut again. A heart leap. She still hadn't decided what, if anything, she'd do on arrival. The best she'd come up with was that she was an antiques buyer for a London store and was randomly calling to see if any residents had pieces they might be interested in selling. It had been her first idea and despite her best efforts, she'd failed to better it. She was in Hull for one night only. It had been a spontaneous move to book the train and hotel; she may as well roll with the punches. If she couldn't think of anything better, then this would be her foot in the door with Margie Miller: a London antiques buyer.

Her ticket devoured by the turnstile, she traversed the concourse towards the exit. *Ferensway had to be right here,* she thought, so the Royal Hotel had to be no more than a stone's throw from where she stood. She looked to the left and took a few steps forward, rolling her bag forward. She wanted to avoid opening the bag and disturbing Ben if she could. It was surprisingly cool; the sun only just beginning to go down. She hadn't been to Hull before. She wanted to believe it was the gloomy, arse-end of the country she'd been led to believe it was, but instead it looked rather pleasant. To the right was a Union flag sticking out from the side of a Victorian pile, which she guessed could be her hotel. She walked towards it. Her instincts proved right.

Beautiful with its honey, limestone build, arched windows and smart gold lettering over the entrance. The same honey colour that she wanted for her dream cottage. She wanted a typical Cotswolds cottage with the large bricks like souvenir, country fudge. The hotel had a rather grand lobby area, with reception to the right.

"I have a reservation; Myra Mead?" she said with a smile.

"That's lovely," said the girl, Polish accent, as she entered the name into her system. She took out the door keycard and popped it into her machine. "Just the one night, I see. And can I have the card that you booked the room with, please?"

She gave it to her. She glanced to the right. There was a man dressed as Captain Kirk putting leaflets on a desk.

"We have a sci-fi convention in the ball room this evening from 7," the receptionist said.

"I see." She looked back at Captain Kirk who, mouthed *live long and prosper* and gave her a Vulcan salute. She nodded an uncomfortable smile back at him.

"That's lovely," said the girl again. "Thank you." She handed the card back, took the keycard from the machine and folded the cover around it. "Now, you are in room 219. The easiest way to get there is to take the lift to the second floor and turn right. There are signs pointing the way. Breakfast is included and is served in the dining room here," she continued, indicating the right of the reception desk, "from 6:30 until 10." She smiled. "The lift is behind you, there."

Her room, it turned out, was in what must have been the staff quarters in days gone by. She walked around corners, upstairs, through halls, downstairs, through narrowing corridors until, eventually, in a quiet corner at the back of the hotel, at the end of a long corridor where there was only one other room, she found hers. Perfect.

She glanced her critical eye through the window, checked the bathroom, pushing down on the mattress as she passed. She put her keycard in the slot so the electricity would work and turned the bathroom lights on. Pleasant enough; warm, functional and clean, with a stack of fluffy towels on a heated rail. White towels are so unforgiving. She turned on the lights, then the TV, and unzipped her bag.

At 3:25pm, she lay on the bed, hands behind her head, legs crossed at the ankles, watching the tail end of some rubbish children's show. Ben, in his urn, sat on the dresser by the TV. She decided she'd relax until 4pm. She estimated Margie was a twenty-minute walk from the hotel. She'd go straight there. Then she'd head back and either pick something up to eat in her room or eat in the Royal's restaurant and perhaps have a nightcap at the bar before calling home to check Mother and Bimbo were still alive and kicking.

She filled the diminutive kettle and made herself a cup of tea. She opened the complimentary shortbread biscuits and crunched as the kettle boiled. She kicked off her shoes. It was nearly time to change into the clothes she'd brought. She checked herself in the bathroom mirror. She had job interview butterflies. She sat on the bed and read the questionnaire she completed with Margie. She couldn't take it with her, so last-minute revision was essential. She downed her tea and folded up the paper questionnaire. She returned to the bathroom and sloshed a mouthful of Listerine. She rinsed out the cup and put on her gloves. She looked her reflection in the eye. She put her lifeless, flat hair behind her ears and smiled. She smiled again, this time showing her tea-stained teeth. She was ready. As ready as she'd ever be. What time was it? 4:05pm.

She stepped out of the bathroom with purpose. She took her bag and double-checked she had her gem antique book. She turned off the TV and took the keycard from its holder by the door, plunging the room into darkness. Retracing her steps back through the labyrinth, she came to a sign pointing her towards the lifts and reception.

She turned left outside the hotel and walked briskly down Ferensway towards Springbank, where she'd need to turn left. She felt in her jacket pocket for the map she'd printed off, showing the best route between the Royal and the Avenues.

She walked past St Stephen's Shopping Centre on her left, then a theatre and crossed over Lombard Road. It was a strange end of town. There were some other hotels and the kinds of businesses you'd find in a business park rather than a town centre. It felt slightly depressed. There were some obviously empty buildings and businesses, possibly pop-ups. She couldn't live there. The road turned into Beverley Road. She half-saw a shop front for Hair by Donna Karan, which surprised her as it wasn't the area where you'd expect to see the designer set up shop; she didn't think she did hair. As she drew closer, she saw just how ropey it was and that the sign actually read, 'Hair by Donna & Karan'. There was a convenience store, a dental laboratory, Cupboard World, a care home, a video rental and the redbrick church. She looked back at the convenience store and nipped over the road.

"Can I have twenty Silk Cut Ultra, please?" she asked. The price was shocking. How anyone could afford to smoke nowadays, she just didn't know.

On the other side of the road, there were fast food independents doing kebabs, fish and chips, chicken in a bun, pizzas and the like. It looked like student accommodation. She continued, turning left onto Springbank. There was clearly a large immigrant population too, Kurdish restaurants and Turkish food stores. It was refreshingly and unexpectedly cosmopolitan.

After walking a distance, she turned right onto Princes Avenue. It was taking longer than she'd bargained for, but she was in no rush and enjoyed being somewhere different. It started to become less student and more urban village, with boutique shops, homey pubs, the local Thai and post office.

Soon, she was away from the shops and the residences grew grander. The road was wider and leafier and Victorian gothic mansions loomed splendidly. Enormous red and honey brick buildings with black, cream and terracotta patterned tiles leading to front doors, many glowing with stained glass. Palisades of long-established trees created an emerald canopy. She felt another flutter of nerves as she turned left into Margie Miller's avenue. She slowed her pace. Margie's would be the same side of the road she was on, so she crossed over to the other side. She could always do a quick fly-by and double back, escaping to the hotel.

She counted the houses and fixed her eyes on the one that must be it. She looked again and slowed once more. Smaller, slower steps. Someone stood in the porch of Margie's house. A woman, (retired, possibly elderly) looked at her watch, in a terrible hurry. Needing to be somewhere else, she stepped back and looked up, looked at her watch again, then scurried off down the road. Was Margie out?

She was in front of the house now. She turned and walked up the path to the front door. The house was beautiful and well cared for, but it didn't look like anyone was home. She took a deep breath as she reached to ring the bell. At her feet and to the side, she noticed a large casserole dish. She bent her knees to see if there was a note (there wasn't) and picked it up. Suddenly a light backlit the stained glass, and someone came down the stairs. She couldn't leave now, she'd already be visible. She took a step back, still holding the casserole; the shadow in the hall loomed larger as it approached the door, which flew open.

"I'm so sorry to keep you waiting," Margie said; that voice was unmistakable. "I was... indisposed, shall we say. Thanks so much for returning it so soon." She took the casserole. "I hope it was alright, I'm not much of a cook, I'm afraid."

"It was lovely," she answered.

"Anyway, you must come in. If you have time that it is, if you're not having to rush off somewhere? Cup of tea or something? Do say you will?"

"Thank you," she said, as she stepped inside.

7

"I can't stay too long, though."

"Moving is such a bore."

"Yes," she said.

"Come on through." Margie led the way down a corridor.

The first thing that struck her was that the house didn't smell of cigarette smoke. This was surprising as Margie was a heavy smoker. She suddenly had the horrible feeling that she was in the wrong house. As she followed her down the corridor she tried to remember the face in that picture on Peter's desk. She was as thin as a rake, as Peter's wife had been. She had that hair, coiffured and set like a crash-helmet, like her breed frequently had. Thatcher had thought she could put that style on and instantly become aristocracy, but this was not the kind of hair you put on lightly, this was hair that came from within.

On the right was a large sitting room. She glanced in at an exquisite cream carpet, warm cream walls, a suite of leather furniture. A monolithic mirror hung over the marble fireplace mantel; a crystal chandelier, every oversized shard dazzling with rainbows.

The stately staircase swept down to greet the wide, illumined hall corridor. The thick pile ran throughout, wall to wall, down the hall and up to the top of the house, to what promised to be a warm, calm and regal nest.

There were paintings all the way up the stairs; not prints, actual paintings. The surfaces appeared dusty, the paint beginning to crackle; an aging you cannot fabricate satisfactorily. It was caused by decades of the frame and canvas expanding and contracting with different temperatures and humidity. Oh yes, she'd done her homework.

Next there was a large dining room, also on the right, painted a lush indigo, a vibrant lapis lazuli. The ancient, dark wood dining table with eight, swirly-backed ball and claw foot chairs; the arms became heads of creatures, snakes perhaps. Another golden mirror, another chandelier, but this time the crystal was blood red, matching the ruby glassware in the glass-fronted cabinet, the most delicate rosewood woodwork, almost filigree. Dining there would be like being entertained in the eye of Tutankhamun.

At the end of the hall, the space opened into a cavernous kitchen; smart, modern, uncooked-in. Oak cabinets, work surfaces of black granite with blue star freckles. Margie filled the kettle from a water filter by the sink.

"Have you been here long?"

"Oh God, now you're asking. We've had the house fifteen or seventeen years now. We moved here after Peter retired. All so traumatic, I said the only way I'd ever leave would be in a box." She was from the home counties originally, and spoke with an affected, languid, drawing out of the vowels. "You all unpacked? Settled in?"

"Not really," she said, improvising, seeming so natural. Nothing is ever about what it seems to be about. "I can't thank you enough for our delicious dinner. It was very kind."

"I tend to leave the seasoning out and let people do it themselves. My own taste buds are shot to ribbons after years of abuse." The kettle took an age to boil. "Earl Grey or English Breakfast? I think I have some Lapsang Souchong or Darjeeling or something knocking about, if you want me to look?"

"Oh, no, please don't go to any trouble. Just normal is fine for me. White no sugar."

"I'm not sure why I did it to be honest." Margie's bony hip pressed against the granite countertop. She crossed her arms and looked straight at her.

"Did what?"

"The casserole. I'm normally frightfully antisocial, but I saw the removal lorries after that house had lain empty for almost twelve months and thought, *Come on, Margie, pull your sodding finger out and get over there and say hello, for God's sake.* I'd made double quantities anyway, so I thought I'd drop some by, as an unnaturally neighbourly act of welcome. I can do stews and things, but not much else. You can't overcook a stew."

"You can't."

The kettle boiled. She had an American-style fridge with water cooler and ice maker and everything, except, it would appear, much to keep cold. There was half a pint of semi-skimmed, an opened bottle of white wine with approximately one third missing, some eggs, something orange in a plastic container, two defrosting chicken breasts and what looked like a bag of salad in the drawer at the bottom.

"So, is it just you and your husband?" Margie asked.

"No, my mother stays with us."

"It must have been her I saw when I popped around."

"That's right." Her casual lies seemed to be fitting in with reality nicely. Mustn't say too much though. Mustn't be uncareful and be caught out.

"Anyway, poor you. I know a particularly good nursing home nearby when the time comes." She handed her the mug of tea. "And your husband? Retired?"

"I'm not married, actually."

"Oh." She paused. "Then who's the 'us'?" Her crossed arms. Her steely stare, sudden and disarming.

"…Pardon me?" She felt she should tug her forelock and call her 'ma'am'.

"You said your mother lives with 'us'…?"

"Oh, me and Sooty."

"Please tell me you're not one of those dreadful cat women?" she said with a roaring laugh.

"I am, I'm afraid. Just the one, though."

"Well as long as it doesn't shit in my garden."

"I don't think he will. He doesn't wander far nowadays, and I'm sure he'll find somewhere in his own garden when he needs to... shit."

"I don't really care anyway. It's all a bit overgrown now, so I wouldn't know even if it did. I had a great big beautiful black lab as a girl; daft as a box of frogs, but I loved him. I won't tell you his name. You certainly couldn't call a dog that nowadays, but there was nothing wrong with it back then." Actually, there was. "Political correctness gone mad. Then we had to call them 'coloured', do you remember that? Then that became inappropriate too; now it's black or BAME, which sounds to me a lot worse than... the 'N' word. I can't keep up, honestly, I can't. It's impossible to breathe nowadays without causing offence to some poor sensitive soul."

Myra was repulsed by bigotry in all its forms. Most offensive was when someone said the most appalling thing to you, assuming you were of the same mind. 'I'm not being racist but...'. What was it in her that made them think she'd share the same vile view? Under normal circumstances, she'd have challenged it, she always did, but instead, she changed the subject.

"You have a very beautiful home."

"I have a cleaner."

"Is it just you?"

"Yes. My husband, Peter, died."

"I'm sorry."

"Why? You didn't kill him, did you?" She roared again.

"No."

"Because if you had, I'd have given you a pat on the back. No. I shouldn't be horrible, should I? He was alright. He was a Yorkshire man, and he was very clever, but frightfully dull really, an accountant. Say no more. I mean, show me an interesting accountant, and I'll show you a flying pig. He looked after me, I'll say that for him. He left a substantial amount of money, a beautiful home, as you say, and the mortgage was all paid off many moons ago. I get my state pension obviously, and another from his old job too for 'pin money', so I really can't complain. I enjoy an extremely high standard of living in comparison to many."

People had always been Myra's strength. This was how she'd been so successful in the career she'd found herself in. She never dreamt of moving into the more highly paid world, an almost exclusively male world back then, of bean-counting. Maths was never a strong point, but she had no problem working it all out. Peter Miller had been earning £67,500 when he had retired after 12 years in the job. This meant his widow, Margie, was currently in receipt of nearly £600 per month, tax free. Myra knew that if it were her, she could exist quite happily on this amount alone. She also knew this 'pin money' that Margie had never earned, didn't deserve and definitely didn't need, value or seem to even want, equated to a proportion of the pension Myra had contributed to, was entitled to and would be receiving this time next year, had Margie Miller not been squandering it away.

"Children?" she asked.

"No, we… we decided not to try. Again, probably best, our offspring would have been nauseating. Either a terminal dullard like him, or a vulgar old lush like me, or, God helps us, some grotesque hybrid of the two… a chimera." It was happy hour somewhere.

"I don't think so," Myra said, feeling awkward.

"I'm sorry, I do apologise. I'm talking to you like I've known you for years, and I don't even know your name."

"Janice," Myra said.

"I'm Margaret, but please call me Margie, all my friends do… did. It's nice to meet you." They shook hands. Margie directed her to the rustic oak kitchen table. All Margie's 'friends' had either died, been permanently insulted or moved away. There were no Christmas cards now. There was no one.

"He wasn't always like that though, Peter. He was rather dashing when he was young, and charming; funny too. Frighteningly bright. When we were courting,

I remember we just laughed all the time. Then we got married, and everything that led to us getting married either quickly fizzled out or became intensely annoying. We bickered for the first twelve months. I was terribly unhappy. He must have been too. Then we settled into a routine. He worked, and I stayed at home and met up with girlfriends and so on. I'm not sure when he became quite so dull…" She glanced over at the sink, devoid of any dirty dishes or dishwater. "Or when I became… quite so loathsome. Still," she went on, "I wouldn't wish what he had, in the end, on anyone. Despite what you may think of them at the time, you don't want to watch them endure a long, undignified and painful decline and then die quite so horribly. So much better to go out like a light." She snapped her fingers. "You know, here one minute and not the next. I'm surprised it hasn't happened to me long before now to be honest. I don't really do anything. I don't contribute. I don't volunteer or anything."

"You made a casserole."

"I did. I'm a tough old bird and I can make a casserole." Margie smiled from behind her facade. "What time did you say you had to get back?"

"I'm not far, and I could always call Mum." She looked at her watch. "There's always time for another cup of tea."

"I was thinking of something a little stronger," she said with a devilish smile.

"Oh, alright."

Margie stood and left the kitchen, talking as she disappeared down the corridor. She was drawing the curtains in the front room.

"What would you like? Sherry, wine, gin, martini, vodka, brandy, port...?

"Wine would be nice, please," she called. Margie had drunk less than a third of her tea. She glanced around the kitchen and across to the back door. It was dark outside.

"Red or white?"

"Red, please."

"Red it is," Margie said. She sailed through the corridor and kitchen towards the back door. She pulled a bottle, any bottle, by its neck, from a wine rack with no empty spaces. Every month she received a new case from Wine Club. "Lovely." She pulled a corkscrew from the counter drawer and started scratching at the foil to expose the cork.

"So, do you like Hull?" Myra asked.

"I think I'm resigned to the fact that I'd be miserable wherever I was, so I may as well be here as anywhere. It's alright. The shops are nearby. You have pretty much all you need on the doorstep except jobs, but a lot of people here commute to Leeds as it's so much cheaper to live here than there. The natives are lovely on the whole. We've been rather inundated with immigrants though. There's a big Polish and Kurdish population.

I think that's what they are, anyway, Eastern European. Asylum seekers and immigrants." She uncorked the bottle and poured two large glasses. Returning to the table, she passed one across. "Cheers."

"Cheers."

"I don't mind them per se, but I don't like the strain they put on the area. They're not interested in integrating, they take jobs, fill the doctors' surgeries, fill our schools, use our libraries... do we still have libraries? To be honest, I'd like to see them all shipped back to wherever they came from, and I'm not alone. We can't do it because the sodding EU and its liberal rules, so we must take them. We take more than anywhere else and we're running out of space. I voted UKIP and I'm not ashamed. I read the *Daily Mail* too, and a bloody good read it is. Just because I think we should repatriate them, people who contribute nothing to our local community, but just sponge off the state so they can send taxpayers' money back to their families in Romania, or Syria or Ethiopia, or wherever and... I've lost my thread; and these women in their robes..."

"I've just had a thought," said Janice chirpily changing the subject. She detested Margie Miller; despised her ungrateful privileged life, her holier-than-thou attitude, her arrogance, her empty stupidity, her shrill, rampant ignorant bigotry, her hypocrisy, her spotless house, her pointless life and her draining the Trethendar pension.

"I'm sorry to go on. It's just I get so bloody angry..."

"It's alright."

"You're a good listener. I think we're going to be good buddies."

"What I was going to suggest," said Myra, "if you don't have plans, of course, is that I cook dinner."

"What?"

"Well, it would give me the opportunity to repay you for the lovely casserole and, to be honest, I'd rather be occupied when having a glass of wine."

"You would do that?"

"Of course. I could see what you have, and I'm sure I could rustle up something tasty. Then I could nip back home before Mum even notices I'm gone."

"Well, that's exceptionally kind of you. I don't think I have much in. We could always order in. That's what I'd normally do. I'll pay."

"I can have a look at what you've got and see if I get any brainwaves. It'll be fun."

"Well, if you're sure. That sounds lovely. I am beginning to feel rather peckish," she said as she stood and tapped her tummy. "I think I've piled on a few pounds since I stopped smoking. Probably won't last. I have no will power whatsoever. Back in a mo." Myra heard her walking upstairs.

She sat in silence in the kitchen. If she'd put on a few pounds, she must have been skeletal before. Margie tinkled in the loo at the top of the stairs. There was a pause, then a flush. She rinsed her hands. She must be checking herself in the mirror. The door opened and she heard her descending. She turned and smiled.

"Well, if you're absolutely sure," Margie said.

Myra stood up. "Of course. I love cooking, especially for others."

"Be my guest then. My facilities are at your disposal. Work your magic."

Myra went to the fridge. It was turned up too cold and the freezer compartment was so cold it felt hot to the touch. In the salad drawer, as well as the bag of mixed leaves, were some fresh chillies and half a chorizo. The Tupperware container had sweet potato slices in it. She took all these items out, and the chicken breasts.

"Where do you keep your other things?"

"In the cupboard, next to the fridge, are some onions and there are tins in the cupboard up there," she replied, pointing at the cupboard over the work surface by the cooker. She found tins of kidney beans and chopped tomatoes, some tomato puree, mixed herbs, garlic powder and smoked paprika. There was also a box of matches. "Feeling inspired?"

"Yes, I know exactly what I'm doing. Do you like things spicy?"

"Yes, it's about the only thing I can taste." She noticed Myra removing her gloves and reaching for a knife. "I couldn't help notice the gloves."

"Unfortunately, I don't have much sensation in my fingers anymore. They help me to get a grip."

"What a nuisance. Are you alright chopping, or do you want a hand?"

"I'll be fine." She intentionally went at a much slower rate than normal, to demonstrate the point. "So, when did you stop smoking?"

"Day before yesterday."

"Must be hard."

"It's a living hell. Did you ever smoke?"

"No. I never started."

She thought for a moment. "I know you're expecting me to say that that's marvellous, but I have zero admiration for any form of temperance. You should have tried it at least once. You don't know what you've been missing all these years. Cigarettes are bloody wonderful."

"Why are you stopping?"

"I'm not absolutely sure. Something to do. See if I can. My heart isn't really in it. Talking about it just makes me want one."

"We can change the subject."

"I suppose… the main thing is that, for some reason, it makes a hangover a gazillion times worse if you've been smoking like a bastard at the same time. I don't have the constitution for it anymore. I used to be the life and soul of the party. Now, I'm just—"

"A hollow, dried up, old husk of your former self?"

Margie roared with laughter. Myra smiled and tipped the chopped onion into a shallow pan with oil, a splosh of water and a pinch of salt. She put the lid on, turned the knob and pushed the button to ignite the gas. The onions started to sizzle.

"You're a hoot, Janice."

"I'm sorry."

"No, it was funny. The only time I laugh now is when I'm walking about the house at night, like the Phantom of the sodding Opera, and I catch a glimpse of my drunk, naked, bloodless, bony self in the mirror. It's either laughter or tears. One or the other."

"Don't you sleep well?"

"I'm alright dropping off. Normally I'm out like a light, but I wake up and can't get back to sleep. I wake up earlier and earlier. I probably sleep more than I think I do. I'm waking up at 3:30am at the moment, and I have a pee and come downstairs. Sometimes I'll have a smoke, which I know is the last thing you should do if you can't sleep, but when you can't and you've got nothing to wake up for, where's the harm? I don't have any ciggies in the house just now, so I won't be having that problem, tonight at least. Can I top you up?"

"Oh, yes please," Myra said. She'd only taken a couple of sips, but she passed her glass across. Margie's was empty. She topped up Myra's and poured herself another large one.

Myra started to slice the chorizo and tossed them into the pan with the onions and gave it a stir. Then she threw in the herbs, spices and the chicken she'd skinned and diced.

"So, is there much work to do on your place?" asked Margie.

"Not really."

"Thought not. Say what you will, those two dreadful old homos you bought it off kept it well. Not to my taste; a bit old-ladyish for me. Chintzy, with that maroon striped wallpaper, lace on the surfaces and all that Wedgwood. Those awful cameos on the walls, ghastly. Expensive, but ghastly."

"We'll probably redecorate when the time is right, but its liveable in for now."

"Oh yes. God yes, you can't do everything right away. Get settled first."

"So, did you know them well?"

"Lionel and Cedric? Fairly well. Lionel, the older one, was the antiques dealer. The younger one was a failed actor, or a failed dancer; a failed something, anyhow. Brazilian and terribly pretty when they first moved in. Brazilians will do it with anyone, you know. The only nationality with a vagina hairstyle named after them tells you everything you need to know. I think he may have caught the deadly diet. He certainly looked ravaged by something. Anyway, Peter, with his interest in antiques, got on with Lionel. I did wonder sometimes if there was something else, but then I thought, *no, this is Peter we're talking about*. A bit of drama might have helped us both feel not quite so dead below the waist. Anyway, we started to see less and less of them, then Peter got ill and eventually died. I'd see one or other of them occasionally, but we hadn't spoken for years by the time they moved. They didn't say goodbye. Something I said, probably. But I can't be held accountable for how people feel or for every little thing, especially when I'm pissed. I shouldn't really be left unsupervised. So blame Peter."

Myra transferred the contents of the pan to the casserole dish and started arranging the sliced sweet potato on top, hotpot-style. She fired up the gas oven.

"Oh, you'll need matches for that. In the cupboard. It's meant to fire up automatically, but it's never worked properly."

Myra put the pan in the sink and turned the taps.

"Leave it, darling. I'll wash up in the morning."

"It's no trouble. I'm used to washing up as I go."

"How very efficient of you. Were you a girl guide too?

"No, but I was in the choir."

"You are a good sort. You really are. Why didn't you move here years ago?" Myra rinsed her hands under the tap, then picked up the casserole with a tea towel and took it to the kitchen table.

"I forgot something. Can you pour a large glug of wine in there for me please, Margaret?"

"With the greatest of pleasure. Looks lovely. Aren't you clever; and it's *Margie,* for goodness sake. Is that enough?"

"That should do it."

She took it back to the oven, now roaring away like a crematorium furnace.

"It's funny. I do that." Myra looked at her quizzically as she slammed the glass-fronted cooker door, designed more for a catering school than for one emaciated old drunk who never cooked. "You know, use a tea towel or oven glove to put something in the oven before it's been in and got hot."

Myra smiled. She washed the pan in hot, soapy water. She washed the knife, tin opener and chopping board. She drained the sink and ended by wiping the aluminium sink and taps, wiping down all the work surfaces. She dried her hands then put her gloves back on. No prints. She put the spices back in the cupboard.

"You are good."

"Where did they move to?" Myra asked.

"London, I think I heard, to be nearer Lionel's elderly parents. I don't know if the idea was for him to be near them, so he could look after them, or whether they were going to be looking after Cedric. His face was so gaunt last time I saw him, and he had that look in his eye."

"Look?"

Margie thought then. "You know those photographs of young men in the trenches? That look. The look of someone who knows their death is imminent, unavoidable. Empty and resigned." Myra looked at her. "I can't be sure. None of my business. All I do know is that he started wearing one of those little embroidered Aids hats that people stopped wearing after 1989."

Myra sat at the table.

"All done?"

"All done."

"That was bloody quick. You are a marvel."

"It'll be ready in about twenty minutes."

"Top up, darling?"

"I shouldn't really."

"We can always go onto another bottle. There's plenty more and I'm not counting." She paused for a moment, then stood to rescue another bottle from the rack. She opened it, let it breathe, and threw the cork away. She wouldn't be needing that again.

Just over an hour later, and Myra had finished eating. Margie had not stopped talking, so had some way to go. Much of her diatribe was liberally sprinkled with the offensive remarks that came so easily, whether it was racist, homophobic, or anti-Islamic. There was something wrong with everyone and everything. She kept saying, "I can't complain," but wouldn't stop. She said she'd read that over ninety percent of disabled people weren't really disabled at all but could get back to work if they really wanted to. She hated trade unions, religion, Eastern Europeans, any party that wasn't the Conservatives or UKIP, sports fans, what's happened to Covent Garden, the EU, Nigerians, the French, the Portuguese... There wasn't much she didn't have a distorted view of and had no qualms about sharing. She was full of anger and hate; much of it aimed at herself just as much as everyone else. It couldn't be supressed.

Myra didn't challenge or disagree. She just listened. She nodded, she smiled.

"Well, that was delicious," Margie said as she collected the plates and took them to the sink. Her eyes drooping, her head lolling, she'd be sound asleep within an hour or so. Myra wanted to keep her awake if she could. "And did you truly just make that from what I had lying about?"

"I did. I hope it wasn't too hot."

"No, it was perfect. I don't have much of a sense of taste, or smell, for that matter. It was just hot enough so as not to blow your head off. Now, what can I offer you?" She said turning and slurring as she spoke. "More wine, or a short perhaps? What would you say to a little nightcap?"

"I'd say, 'hello little nightcap'!"

"Hah!" Margie laughed and bent over, her face distorted with the hilariousness of it all. "God, you make me laugh. You really do. But seriously, something to drink?"

"That would be lovely," Myra said.

"You don't look pissed at all," Margie said as she went for bottle number three.

"Oh, I am, believe me. I can go for quite a long time not looking drunk and then suddenly I keel over. But that hasn't happened for ages. In fact..." she said looking at her watch.

"Oh, come on, Janice. Don't be a party pooper. Mum'll be fine. Have a small one, for the road. Then stagger the two or three doors down and... and... we'll call it quits."

They went through to the plush lounge. More like an embassy room than a home, it was just so perfect with its cream and gold and so snug and secure with the heavy cream drapes drawn. Margie planted herself on the couch and pulled her legs up beside her, nursing her red wine.

"Where's your toilet please?"

"Have you not been yet? Haven't you? You must have the bladder of a camel, or a vagina made of girders. Top of the stairs on the left." Myra stood to leave. "I'm sorry. I didn't mean to sound horrible. I really am awful."

"You're alright," she said as she left.

Myra had a quick wee upstairs. She didn't take her gloves off. She turned off the light and went downstairs. On re-entering, she saw Margie's eyes had closed, her mouth hung open and her head was so far back that her Adam's apple pointed sharply at the beautifully architraved ceiling, exquisite plaster-cast friezes, cornices and rosettes.

She stood in the doorway for a moment. Margie snored a little. Myra collected her glass. She took it to the kitchen and washed it in the sink. Lots of hot, soapy water. She dried it off. She took her plate from the dishwasher and a knife and fork and washed them also. She dried them up and put them away, wiping down the sink and taps again. She put her gloves back on and went to the lounge and to Margie, who hadn't moved.

"Margie? …Margie?"

"What? God, how very rude of me. I must have dropped off."

"Don't worry. Look, I should be going."

"So soon? Are you sure?"

"It's Mum, I need to get back."

"And Sooty. Don't forget Sooty." Margie stood and picked up her wine. "I suppose I really ought to be turning in too. Thank you, darling. It's been so, so lovely." She opened her arms wide, and Myra embraced the pointy, boozy, stick.

"I think you should go to bed," said Myra as she walked Margie into the hall and pointed her at the stairs. "I can see myself out."

"Are you sure? Truly? Thank you." She walked heavily up the stairs, still holding her glass of wine and dribbling a few spots on those perfect carpets along the way. At the top of the stairs, she drifted around a corner to her room.

"Good night, Margie," Myra said as she walked quickly back to the kitchen. She grabbed her bag from beside the chair at the kitchen table. She left the packet of cigarettes she'd bought on the corner of the work surface at an inviting angle, clearly visible from the door. She took the matches from the cupboard and put these next to the cigarettes. She left the door to the cooker ajar and turned the gas up full. It hissed a sigh. The windows were closed. Gas began to fill the room. She could smell it. She switched off the lights in the kitchen and left, closing the door behind her, turning off the lights in the lounge and hall. She opened the front door an inch and turned, wondering whether she should say goodbye again or not. There was a light from a room somewhere upstairs, but not a sound. She stepped outside, not a soul in sight, all was dark, quiet. She pulled the door to behind her with a soft click.

She didn't look back, walking briskly back the way she'd come. An intense thrill of schoolgirl naughtiness pushed up from the pit of her stomach into her throat; warming the place where the neck meets the sternum, with a delicious, nervous aching. It was difficult to tell how much she had drunk as her glass kept getting topped up without ever being emptied. It was probably not more than two glasses over the whole evening, and it was still relatively early. A discernible smile broke on her face; like she'd just pranked the most hated bully, without being sure the prank would work, but knowing no one would ever know it was her if it did.

Back at the Royal, all manner of sci-fi characters in tacky, homemade costumes filled the reception area. She bypassed them all and went straight to her room. She turned on all the lights and closed the curtains, stripping down to her bra and knickers. The room was cosy with a marmalade glow. She went to the bathroom and brushed her teeth. Washed her face.

Back in the bedroom, she grabbed the remote. She stood in front of the TV, her tummy overhanging pant elastic, like bread dough, proved but before you've knocked the air out. She aimed and pushed the button; the light flicked on the TV and after a second's warm-up, there was sound. She gasped, her favourite Bond theme of all time, instantly recognisable, the opening bars. Everything was working out just perfectly. The universe was truly on her side.

With no prying eyes, there was space enough in the room to do whatever she wanted. Carly's beautiful voice swept in like warm syrup hitting a stack of buttered pancakes, and Ben's urn illuminated with the copper of a Floridian sunset. She swayed about with the remote in hand.

"Nobody does it better…" She lifted her arms over her head, then a quick, quarter-turn spin on her heel as the remote became her microphone. She goose-stepped into bliss. It was true, nobody did do it half as good as her. Myra swung round again, sexily holding the remote, now a Luger, as she fell backwards, slo-mo, onto the trampoline bed as Carly's multiple echoing voices, backing herself, built with every throb. "Baby, you're the best…"

8

She rarely slept in, but she awoke bright-eyed and bushy tailed shortly after 8am. She had a steaming, hot soapy shower and was still dripping when she stepped, naked, into the bedroom rubbing her hair between two towelled palms. What did she care if she dripped? It wasn't her carpet.

She turned on the TV. The news had just ended. She had time to stop by Margie's just to see if... anything had happened. If it had, though, it would not be wise to return. And if nothing had happened; well, it wouldn't matter anyhow. Margie was certainly drunk enough to sleep through the whole of the following day. She may have seen the cooker door open and closed it and turned the gas off. She may have resisted the temptation to have a cigarette. She may have thrown the windows open and given the whole house a good airing, if she smelt gas. She may have turned over a new leaf, smokeless and sober.

Myra wondered if she'd have heard the explosion. It was quite a walk, but urban and it had been a still night, so it may have reverberated and reached her at the hotel. Her room was situated at the back. So, more likely to have heard it or less? She didn't know. Maybe there wasn't an explosion at all, just a fireball. She switched channels.

There was nothing about it on the other side either. Chances were, she'd heard nothing because there had been nothing to hear. Margie would probably go around to her neighbours later that day, meet the old mother she'd given the casserole to and then the daughter and think, *well, if you're the daughter, then who the bloody hell did I have in my house last night?* like a rambling drunk.

She couldn't remember if breakfast was served until 9am or 10, so she hurriedly got dressed and turned the TV off. She would brush her teeth before checking out. She put the last of her things into her bag and stuffed the *Collins Gem book of Antiques* into her case, leaving space for her sponge bag at the bottom rather than the top, in case anything leaked.

Funny, after all her homework, that she hadn't had her knowledge of antiques tested at all. It just went to show that sometimes preparation really is a total waste of time. Often best to act on the fly. But then there's always the possibility that it could have been a lifesaver, or that if she hadn't done all her reading up and market research, then perhaps she wouldn't have felt so confident to improvise as she had. Her overthinking started slipping into overdrive again.

Maybe there had been an explosion, but Margie had survived it somehow. She pictured her in her hospital bed, bandaged from head to foot with severe burns, giving a statement to the police, smelling like a bonfire after the rain. The police. She suddenly felt a rush of panic. Or was it excitement again? One thing was clear, if Margie Miller had been blown to smithereens, it would be a kindness to her, a service to the world and, to Myra herself, a small favour. Because now the Trethendar pension fund would have one less beneficiary draining it. In fact, there were two less people to draw on it now if you counted Ben.

For the first time, the realisation hit that she'd killed Ben, for sure, and that she'd attempted to kill Margie Miller. The jury was still out on murder number two. Murder. That word filtered its way into her consciousness, another first. Was two enough to make her a serial killer? *No*, she thought, *you'd need to do at least three*. It was the same kind of reasoning that made 'a few' three or more. A 'few' was clearly more than a 'pair'. She reasoned that, assuming she really had successfully killed two people, it probably didn't fully qualify as a 'spree' either. A 'spree' sounded more about randomness and having fun.

She stepped out of her room and walked the corridors towards the lift. Surely a 'spree' had to consist of more than two done in one go or in quick succession; for example, five random people killed in a day could be reasonably classed as a spree. Perhaps there's a journalist's thesaurus with the most appropriate phrases to be used in the reporting of circumstances like these. She had noted long ago that whereas a man could be easily labelled a killer, women were more often described as 'driven to kill'. She considered this sexist. She called a spade a spade.

The lift doors opened, and she stepped inside. Captain Kirk was in there, but he was in his day clothes now, so it took a moment to recognise him. She nodded at him, a half-smile.

"Did it go well yesterday, your convention?"

"Not bad," he said. There was a pause. Yes, there was nothing else to say. Or ask. That was it. The door opened and he gestured for her to step out first. It would have seemed gallant if she'd not been nearest the exit anyway.

She selected her table and put her bag on the spare chair. It looked like most people had already been and gone. There was fruit, yoghurt and cereal. There were fruit juices to drink and tea and coffee. There were croissants and cinnamon swirls for those who liked to have a continental breakfast. She, however, needed to know that she'd got her money's worth, so once she'd fetched her tea and grapefruit juice, she headed straight back to the hot buffet for the full English.

She helped herself to crispy bacon, two Lincolnshire sausages, scrambled eggs, grilled tomato, hash browns, black pudding, mushrooms and some fried bread. She sat back down at her table, napkin on her lap. She and

Kirk were the only ones in there, except for the girl who'd ticked their names off the breakfast list after having had to wait in silence at the 'please wait to be seated' lectern.

She swiftly crunched her way through breakfast. She sipped her tea and glanced up to see that, on one of several TV screens dotted around the dining room, the 9am news was about to start. She dabbed her mouth with her napkin. She called across to the girl.

"Excuse me? Would you mind turning up the sound a little? Just for a moment so I can hear the headlines. You don't mind, do you?" she asked Kirk at his table across the way. "For the weather...?"

He said, "I'd quite like to hear it myself."

With a smile but without a word, the girl went to the sound system behind the bar and turned it up. She stepped back around to the front and watched on the screen nearest her. There was the usual international and national news, until...

"And now for the news where you are," the announcer said. Myra looked up. She put her knife and fork together and dabbed her mouth again with her napkin. She moved her plate to the side slightly and lifted her teacup to her mouth, comfortingly holding it in both hands.

There was a local news item about a factory that was just about to go into liquidation, laying off nearly eighteen hundred full- and part-time local people; then another story about something else and in a flash the image behind the newscaster changed to an avenue like Margie's. Myra's stomach flipped and her breathing stopped. They panned to their correspondent, broadcasting live.

"Shortly before 4am this morning," she said, "the residents of this quiet corner of Hull were awoken by a loud explosion coming from one of the houses just behind me here. We believe it was caused by gas and it has been confirmed that there has sadly been one fatality. It appears that no other houses were damaged, or people injured. I spoke to the local police this morning, and this is what they said." The film cut to a piece of footage shot an hour or so earlier. The correspondent was holding her microphone up to a stern-faced, lady police officer.

"It's early days obviously, but the area has been made safe and we're not treating the incident as suspicious at this stage," she said. Myra watched the screen; unmoving, unflinching.

"Has the family of the person who died been informed yet?" the correspondent asked.

"Not at this stage. We haven't released the name yet. There will be a full and thorough investigation, conducted with the fire services."

"Thank you very much," said the correspondent, thinking the police statement had concluded.

"There is one other thing," said the police officer. "A woman was seen—" Myra's stomach lurched to the side and churned, but no trace of emotion flicked across her face. Her eyes shot to Kirk who wasn't watching, he was taking a bite of toast, and then to the girl at the bar. She was watching. The girl's eyes closed sleepily in a long, slow blink. Myra's eyes darted back to the screen. "outside the house late yesterday afternoon. As we say, we don't believe there are any suspicious circumstances, but we would like to speak to this woman as she may have been the last person to see the victim alive. She is described as elderly, of slight build. She was seen outside the house, holding what the witness described as a casserole."

"Back to the studio," the correspondent said.

Myra took the last sip from her teacup and put it down with both hands, so it didn't rattle when it reached the saucer. One witness. Did she say 'one' witness or 'a' witness?

She had her confirmation. She had murdered two people. *Well, not exactly murdered,* she reasoned to herself. A bee had killed Ben, that and his severe allergic reaction. He had been begging to die. And Margie's need for a cigarette had killed her, not Myra. If the bony witch had one ounce of willpower, she'd be wasting life today just as she'd wasted every other day of her life. Myra had simply provided the circumstances that meant Margie's nocturnal craving for a smoke would kill her.

It was not like she had pointed a gun at her then pulled the trigger. She had merely loaded the gun and left it for her. She was, at worst, an enabler, she reasoned.

There was not a single link to her, not a single fingerprint. She was just an unnoticed little lady. Drab, but polite. A person who keeps herself to herself. No one would be able to provide a recognisable description, not even the people in this room. She was that innocuous. It would never be found out. You only ever hear about these things when it's so blindingly obvious or the person is caught. But for every one of them, there must be ten like her that go completely undiscovered. There must be hundreds, thousands maybe, of normal people like her killing people every year and it all goes on completely unnoticed. She didn't want to think about it anymore. She didn't want to think about anything, but she couldn't stop. Her focus was in and out, her thinking over-thought, fragmented.

She stood and slowly walked past the restaurant lectern.

"Was everything alright for you today?" called the girl at the bar, trying not to sound quite as exhausted as she was.

"Very nice, thank you," Myra said with a calm, benign, grateful smile. "Very nice indeed."

The summer passed without anything dramatic to report. As the months rolled on without any mention, by anyone, of anything, what had happened took on an air of unreality. Work had been quiet. People had taken their long-talked-of holidays in the Canaries (Hazel) and Santorini (Stuart). Mel had settled in well. She hadn't been back to New Zealand, which had helped ensure continuity of service. Hazel was delegating more and more to her. Although they all sat in the same room, they sat with their backs to the walls so no one could see what anyone else was working on. Nobody knew, nobody asked.

Jenny had had her baby, and a picture of mother and child (a boy, Toby) and demi-husband (he hadn't fitted into the frame) was circulated, snapped by the midwife with no time to take a quality picture.

Myra tended not to take long holidays anymore. She had taken her mother to the Cotswolds a few years in a row, but nothing substantial for about five years. She tended to take days here and there, to extend a weekend or break up a week; to take her mother to a doctor's appointment or stay in so the gas meter could be read. The only other holiday she'd taken since her trip to Hull to coordinate the self-immolation of Margie Miller, had been on the day after the August bank holiday when Martin drove her and her mother to Maidstone, the Archbishop's Palace, to give notice of marriage.

Martin and Mother had to take their passports. They also needed two documents showing evidence of address. In August, Martin had given the care home his one month's notice and put his two-bedroom flat on the market. He'd had little interest shown other than a few nosey timewasters. No serious buyers. If worst came to the worst, they could always rent it out, she'd helpfully suggested. There were a lot of students in Canterbury. This got Martin's creative juices flowing. He wondered if weekend visitors may be interested in having it for a few nights here or there. She pulled a face. She didn't think it had quite the style or finish for the demanding, trendy types, down from London. She had only been there a few times. It had been an unsettling mix of that grey, dull pink and chrome from the eighties but with touches of Edwardian chintz, and of course that peculiar aroma hanging in the air, reaching for your nose; the scent of old man's colon. So, they'd taken their passports, proof of address (they had put Martin's name on a few of the bills) and her father's death certificate.

"Will I need this, do you think, Myra?" Mother called, holding it out to her, as Martin went to bring the car closer. "You know, to show I'm available and not a bigamist."

"I don't know, really," she said taking the certificate. She'd never seen it before. She never particularly wanted to. She didn't know why she'd taken it or glanced at it. Her eyes fell on the one thing she'd never wanted to see: 'immediate cause of death…'. Her eyes saw peripherally what followed on the line below. She handed it straight back. "Take it with you anyway, then if you need it, you'll have it."

"Shall I take my cheque book too?"

"No, Mother. It's alright. I have a cheque ready for you. Martin is paying his £35 himself."

"Do I need a blood test?"

"What?"

"You need a blood test when you get married, don't you?"

"I think you'll be quite safe not having one."

The date had been set for late September. Ray, a local independent cab driver, had been booked to drive the party to and from Maidstone and act as a witness. Ray was retired so had nothing better to do that day. Myra, or, to be more precise, her mother, was possibly Ray's last regular client. He did the odd driving job from time to time to get him out of the house and give him some income to spend on whatever he did in his spare time.

Martin, Myra, her mother and Ray arrived at the Archbishop's Palace at 10:30 for their 11am ceremony. The Palace was formally a fourteenth century residence of the archbishops of Canterbury. The car crunched along the gravel drive towards the grey, stone pile basking in the rays of an extended summer. He parked and they all stepped out, squinting in the sun, each hoping someone knew what the next step was and where they'd need to go. They'd gone for a midweek date to avoid the crowds. There were no guests. The working population of Maidstone was already hard at it behind closed doors and the kids had all gone back to school. Late bees buzzed round the apothecary's garden, and the Medway swam in the near distance.

Once inside, Martin and his frail, elderly bride were directed to a private room to meet with the registrar. This was to check the right details would be entered into the register. She had an anxious moment alone, outside the door, waiting for them, but they were finished quickly and came out, all smiles.

She looked at her mother then at Martin. She couldn't decide whether they looked sweet together or obscene. She was old enough to be his mother too and he was obviously gay. Any reasonable third party would conclude he was a gold digger. Why else would he want to marry a decrepit, old woman with poor circulation, borderline dementia and smelling of lavender and wee? She wondered if the smell of Martin's flat would move with him to their home. She hoped not. Perhaps the two smells would cancel each other out and the house would smell clear and fresh like a mountain spring. But everyone seemed to think they looked sweet. Maybe they said this for her benefit. Her presence obviously indicated that she not only condoned their coupling but supported it. And if someone so close to the happy couple supported it, then who were they to judge? *To be honest*, she thought, *no one else needed to know what their arrangements were.* It would just be three people living together, supporting each other.

Before they knew it, they were in a small office with a mahogany table and French windows into the aromatic gardens. It would have been horrible if they'd been rattling around one of the larger function rooms, row upon row of unoccupied chairs.

The registrar seemed nice enough, dumpy with glasses; wide, black rims. If she had taken her glasses off, she'd probably be unrecognisable as the same person; one's attention was so drawn to them. The kind of glasses that would normally have a moustache and false nose attached.

"Welcome," she smiled. Martin seemed to be genuinely happy. He was beaming like a little girl who'd always dreamt of being a princess, distracted from *whom* he was marrying by the fact he was getting married at all. "As part of the ceremony," Groucho, as Myra had now christened her, the registrar went on, "I'll be asking Martin and Linda to repeat after me some statements and to answer some questions. Saying 'I do' or 'I will' in front of family and friends can be nerve-wracking, but I'm here to help every step of the way. There's only me and your daughter and...?"

"Ray," said Ray.

"...Ray, and I will guide you through everything you need to do and say, so there's no need to worry about forgetting your lines or doing things in the wrong order or anything. OK?"

Martin and Linda giggled and nodded without looking at each other. All eyes were on Groucho.

"May I begin by welcoming you all here today to the lovely setting of the Archbishop's Palace," She opened, as if she were talking to twenty people rather than four, "our beautiful Garden Room, and the marriage of Martin and Linda. Today marks a new beginning in their lives together, and it means a lot to both that you, their family and... friend, are here to witness their wedding vows and celebrate their marriage. Today, Myra shows her love for her mother, Linda, and therefore I ask her, who presents this woman to be married to this man?"

"I do," Myra said brusquely.

"Marriage is a desire by two people to share themselves and their experiences with each other, and a willingness to accept each other for who they are. It is making a commitment to friendship and mutual respect and calls for honesty," a silent collective gulp from all but Ray and registrar, "patience, courage and of course, humour. Marriage is where each partner is there to support the other in all that they do. Marriage requires closeness and distance; the closeness of a couple growing together and enough distance to allow each partner to be an individual. A good partner in such a marriage will be loving, caring and above all, a best friend.

"It is one of my duties to inform you that this room in which we are now met has been duly sanctioned, according to law, for the celebration of marriages. You are here to witness the joining in marriage of Martin Ian Blair and Linda Ann Mead. If any person present knows of any lawful impediment why these two people may not be joined in marriage, he or she should declare it now." Nothing unexpected about this uneasy silence. "Then could I ask you both to stand, please, and hold hands."

"Do it, Mother, hold hands."

They did so, Mother with a bit of a wobble, as the chair was too heavy for her to move backwards, but managing not to fall, face first, into the registrar's paperwork. Martin almost leapt to his feet. He was getting married, at last!

"Before you are joined in matrimony here today, I must remind you both of the solemn and binding character of the vows you are about to make. Marriage in this country means the union of two people, *voluntarily* entered into, for life, to the exclusion of all others." Another collective gulp. "These vows, which unite you, constitute a formal and public pledge of your love for one another. I am now going to ask each of you in turn to declare that you do not know of any legal reason why you should not be joined in marriage to each other."

She turned to Martin first and he repeated after her, "I do solemnly declare, that I know not of any lawful impediment why I, Martin Ian Blair, may not be joined in matrimony to Linda Ann Mead."

She turned to Mother, and she repeated the same after the registrar.

"Now, the solemn moment has come for Martin and Linda to contract their marriage before you, their witnesses, families and... friend, so can I ask you both to stand please and join together for the celebration of their marriage." Myra and Ray stood. "Martin, will you take Linda to be your wedded wife, to share your life with her, to love, support and comfort her, whatever the future may bring?"

Myra took two of the cheapest bands she could find on the high street from her purse. She leant across behind the backs of the happy couple, and poked Ray's jacketed arm just above the elbow. He turned and looked at her, then down at her hand. She dropped the two rings into his.

"I will."

"Linda, will you take Martin to be your wedded husband, to share your life with him, to love, support and comfort, him whatever the future may bring?"

"I will."

"It is an ancient tradition for a bride and groom to exchange rings. This giving and receiving of rings symbolises the continuity of their relationship and the sharing of their lives together. A wedding ring is an unbroken circle that symbolises an unending and everlasting love, and we would ask you to wear your wedding rings as an outward sign of lifelong vows and promises that you have both made to each other today."

Martin put one of the rings on Linda's finger and repeated after Groucho, "I give you this ring as a symbol of our marriage and as a token of my love, trust and commitment. I promise to care for you above all others, to give you my love, friendship and support, and to respect and cherish you throughout our lives together."

Linda put her ring on Martin's finger, as complicit as he and her daughter in their deception. She repeated the words after the bespectacled registrar, who then continued, "Martin and Linda, you have both made the declarations prescribed by law and have made a solemn and binding contract with each other in the presence of the witnesses here assembled. It therefore gives me the greatest honour and privilege to announce that you are now husband and wife." She turned to Martin with a celestial and encouraging smile. "You may kiss your bride."

He looked down at the frail old woman smiling up at him toothily. He'd forgotten about this bit. She closed her eyes and puckered up. He kissed her quickly, in the region of the corner of her mouth. Close enough to her mouth to look as if he was kissing her on the lips and yet far enough towards her cheek to make it marginally less flesh-creepingly grotesque.

"There now. Please be seated while Martin and Linda sign the register." A process that took almost as long as the ceremony itself. As they finished, she wrapped up the proceedings. "To conclude the ceremony, I will now present you both with your marriage certificate. Can I be the first to congratulate you both on your marriage. May I wish you both a wonderful day today, a very long and happy marriage and all the very best for your future lives together. Congratulations Mr and Mrs Blair." The congregation clapped.

Ray took three or four photographs of Mr and Mrs Blair and Mrs Blair's daughter in the apothecary's garden, on some steps. They waited for the sun to come back out, but it refused and none of them wanted to wait. The pictures all had an overcast look.

As soon as they were in the car, Mother, in the front seat, started giggling. At first, a throaty chortle, but quickly graduating to a full-blown, maniacal cackle. Myra and Martin chuckled uncontrollably too. Myra saw his tears of hilarity baste his bloated, pink-veined cheeks.

"Don't think..." said Mother to Martin eventually, "that you're getting any action tonight," she rasped. Myra howled. "I'm not that kind of girl."

"Nothing to fear in that department," he said. "You're not my type."

Mother, through her giggles, continued, "It would be like being trapped under a wardrobe that's fallen over, but with the little key still stuck in the door."

The hilarity petered out and, before long, they were sitting in silence, all looking from their respective windows as the leaden skies appeared more autumnal and stormier. Everything had gone as it should without any hiccups or awkward questions. There were no judgements or sideways glances. There was no question, no suspicion, but the skies darkened, nevertheless. It was strange how life seemed to conspire to her benefit. Was hers a charmed life? *It certainly seems that someone is looking out for me,* she thought.

It was one of those days when it was alright not to go out, and loll about inside instead, listening to music. Her father had loved Jim Reeves. On a Sunday, the house had been full of Gentleman Jim. Sometimes he played Patsy Cline but normally Jim Reeves. She knew all those songs so well, and whenever she played one of Jim's songs, it reminded her so of her father, and the loss she'd endured too long.

Jim Reeves had died a year, almost to the day, after her father and just a few weeks after her thirteenth birthday. Her hormones had been bubbling. She hadn't had time to get over her father's death when Jim's life was taken so suddenly and so tragically, so sadly. It had broken her heart all over again. Suppressed grief had been the norm until then. She managed to suppress it again, but accidentally seeing his death certificate, that day, awakened it.

Surely it couldn't rain, she thought, as heavy clouds started descending in the sky and the wind picked up. She could feel a headache coming on. She always got this headache just before the weather broke. A peel of thunder rumbled in the distance.

She could hear the gentle heartbeat, in her mind's ear, of Jim singing, *Precious Memories, How they Linger*. Jim, travelling life's pathway and softly crooning to cooing singers lullabying in the background, as a guitar softly strummed. She had loved her father so much. She'd been a daddy's girl, and he'd been such a lovely man. Tall, dark, slim and handsome. He was kind and calm; direct when he needed to be, but always kind and calm. When he held her hand, his hands were clean, warm and soft. When he lifted her up, she could feel his warm heartbeat. He was fun and funny and always had time to play with his 'special girl'. She looked at him with her mother and, even as a child, wondered what on earth he was doing with her. He could have done so much better. Still, Mother was a workhorse of a woman back then, and that left more time for father and daughter; hearing about each other's day, sharing secrets, funny stories and listening to the Jim Reeves songs they both loved. She couldn't have wished for more love.

But that was a long time ago and she was a woman now, an old woman, and Mother had remarried. A contrivance for the convenience of all concerned. But, whenever she thought of him, she couldn't help but regress to being his special girl again. She smiled sadly, remembering all the lovely times, and that last afternoon they'd had at the pictures and then in the park. She gazed out of the car window on the way back from Maidstone, witnessing the dreadfully slow passing of that unloving, unholy day as the rain started to hit back at her from the other side of the glass.

Then, in her mind's eye, she saw those words on his death certificate that she'd never wanted to see, 'immediate cause of death: cerebral hypoxia by hanging'.

9

Returning to work again after the Christmas break was tougher than previous years. She guessed this was because the end was now in sight, almost within reach. Just twenty-five weeks' time, she'd be retired.

The months since her jaunt to Hull had passed with nothing of any consequence. Martin had moved in shortly after he and Linda tied the knot that September and had sold his own place. He'd quit his part-time job at the care home and was now fulfilling the role of full-time carer for his new bride, making him eligible for the carer's allowance.

At work, Jenny was still on maternity leave and occasionally boring her childless colleagues with pictures of baby Toby and news of his progress. Mel, issued with her temporary contract of employment, due to end less than a week before her visa, had settled in well and continued to bring a refreshing cheerfulness to the office. Her attitude was of unbounded positivity; not in a Pollyanna-ish way, but in her pragmatic and helpful approach to tasks and making things work. With Mel, equilibrium was restored, and all was in balance.

Hazel, still the backbone of the organisation, worked feverishly to keep the good ship Trethendar afloat. Stuart remained as obnoxious as ever. He kept dropping suggestions that Janice should really think about handing over some of her tasks. His nervousness was, she believed, born out of a fear that she may choose not to retire after her next birthday. She had every intention of handing over everything to him when she retired, but when she was ready, not a day before. She wouldn't tell him this, though. It was far too much fun to watch him squirming on the hook. She'd keep him dangling for just as long as it continued to give her pleasure.

It was still too soon to get in touch with Mike about the new boiler, but at least the board had approved the cost. The work was scheduled for the summer. It had been tough having a board meeting that first Wednesday of January, just the second day back in the office after nine days off. Trethendar, like many employers, closed over the period, and staff were required to take three days' annual leave on the Christmas closure days between Christmas and New Year's Day. It had been long enough to properly unwind and relax. The downside was that it took at least a day or two to get the building warm enough to comfortably work in. No one complained. What was the point? Hazel beavered away at her desk in her hat and little girl coat.

Myra had received a letter from Mr Savile, the man handling Ben's estate. It hadn't said much. Just that he was in communication with someone in Florida, that matters were in hand, and that he'd be in touch again, as and when he had something concrete to report. She'd read it absently and done nothing with it, just added it to the pile of papers at home to be filed away. Neither had she done any delving into the pension fund to see what the loss of the two beneficiaries did to the pot or to her own pension plans. She was dying to know the status of things but opted to resist and wait to be told rather than to ask questions. She didn't want to draw attention. She had heard of the police staking out scenes after a fatality, knowing full well that perpetrators invariably return to scene of their crimes. The only connecting factor in this case was the pension. She pushed it from her mind.

As for Irene Hartley, Myra was in no hurry. It had been a good three months since Margie Miller exploded. Perhaps that was a respectable enough period. Perhaps she should soon take the short train journey across to the Isle of Sheppey where Irene lived and reflect on the good old days with the old cow.

Get on with it, she thought. She looked across at her mother and glanced up at Martin. "Come on, Mother."

"I'm still looking," she said as she rifled through her hand of cards, looking for a pair. It was more fun with more people, the downside of having just three playing meant that each of them had rather a lot of cards in their hands at the beginning. To help with this, Myra was playing two hands, one for her and one for her best-beloved elderly tortoiseshell.

"I think you'd know by now if you had a pair."

"I said I'm looking."

"She's looking," chimed in Martin, wetly echoing her tone without irony; not helping.

Distractedly, Mother said, "Honestly, Myra, you can be a nuisance sometimes." Then... eventually... "I don't think I can go. I start looking at the cards from one side, and by the time I get to the other, I can't remember the ones I saw at the beginning. It's the same if I start at the other side, too. No, I don't think I have a pair this time. I probably do, but I don't think so."

"You need to let me choose one of yours then."

Mother held her hand up so Myra couldn't see. Mother found it tricky to hold her cards with her thinly gloved hands. She was clearly feeling it today. She'd rub her fingers between rounds to try and force a bit of circulation back into them.

Myra picked her card and after a quick scan, pulled a card from her hand and put down the pair. She held her hand out to Martin. He was too busy organising his own and admiring the images on the rather beautiful set of cards. "Pick one for Bimbo," she said. Bimbo was theoretically between them; in actuality, he was on the sofa, completely oblivious.

"Come on, Martin," said Mother, "pick one for Bimbo." Her hands felt numb with cold; she wanted to rub them again.

To an outside observer, her relationship with Mother may have looked peculiar at best and dysfunctional, possibly even mutually abusive, at worst. But regardless of what they said to each other or how rotten things looked to anyone else, there was a fondness there. They'd always been able to make each other laugh and rather enjoyed shocking when in company. Myra smirked at her. Her mother looked up and smirked back.

"You really are an awful old woman," said Myra.

"Takes one to know one. Just because you go to church and work for a charity doesn't make you any less of a… witch."

"Now, now," Martin said. He really didn't 'get' them, even after living there for the past few months and having known them both for years. "I don't want my too favourite girls fighting." They both chuckled. He took a card for Bimbo and put it into his hand, which lay face down on the table. Myra checked to see if it meant he had a pair. It didn't. Miss Athleta Burke looked like a Victorian lesbian, and Uncle Ben Lovechild had to be a kiddy-fiddler. Mark Gaze esq. looked like a confirmed bachelor, like Martin. There was a card that bore an uncanny resemblance to him actually – Master Phil Tubbey.

Poor Bimbo. Not only couldn't he make a matching pair, but there she was, staring back up from the little cat's hand, the Old Maid. Myra wouldn't know if she'd moved it to Martin's hand until next time she looked at Bimbo's. Not a flicker or emotion moved across her poker face as she held Bimbo's hand out to Martin, face down.

"And now one for you," she said.

He reached out and took one. She watched his eyes to see if there was any tell-tale sign. He looked up at her and smiled as if to show everything was alright. That was it, she concluded; that was his 'tell'. She'd deduced the Old Maid was now in his greasy, porcine hand.

It was an odd way for two adults and one senior citizen to while away a Friday evening. She loved the game though and always had done, ever since she'd first played it with her parents. Martin had bought it as a Christmas present for Myra's mother, and it had become a favourite pastime ever since.

How Myra and her father had laughed with glee when Mother ended up with the hated Old Maid card. It was a highly addictive and perverse game. She liked the fact that instead of there being one winner and many losers, there were many winners and one loser. The unsurpassable glee of offloading the curse of spinsterhood to someone else, without permitting your face to betray you.

It reminded her of writing references for jokers who left to work for other organisations. You can be sued by the subject of the reference if it's too bad and sued by the prospective employer if it's too good, when they are actually lousy. References had descended into a safe, factual, two-line confirmation that the individual had worked where and when they said they had, followed by a large disclaimer, absolving the writer of all liability. The blandness of the references she wrote meant that the risks to Trethendar had been removed entirely and the new employer wouldn't know what lazy, half-witted incompetents they'd inherited until it was too late.

"Ooh, I know what I meant to tell you," Martin said suddenly, "and this will be right up your alley, Linda."

It irritated Myra, him calling Mother 'Linda', but she put up with this and the other things she'd begun to hate about him because he prepared such good food, albeit a bit too rich and exotic for Mother's dicky colon. Maintaining Mother's digestive tract was a delicate balancing act, an art. Too much of one thing and it clogged her up for days, and all she'd muster, regardless of the straining, was a Malteser-sized, bullet-like dropping. They'd have to break out her home enema kit and start pumping. Too much of another kind, and it was an embarrassment of riches. The moment it went in at the top end, it practically fell out of her bottom at the other, without touching the sides, like Brown Windsor soup down a kiddies' water flume, and it stank.

It was very difficult to know which food led to what. But after years of experimentation, they found the one thing that without fail would help Mother tread the fine line between chronic constipation and diarrhoea (the latter coming on with little to no warning and such an alarming and relentless ferocity), and that was those frozen savoury crispy pancakes. For some reason, they maintained Mother's colonic status quo beautifully. While Martin's ample girth had been adequately maintained since his arrival, poor Mother had seesawed from one unhappy extreme to the other. It didn't seem to bother the old woman. She was clearly fond of him, but Myra had begun to go off him, and the effect of his cooking on her mother's failing bowels just added insult to injury.

The way he had moved in felt more like a muscling in, stamping his presence on their environment. *That was probably unfair*, she'd tell herself, he was unobtrusive, but just the fact that he was there at all was an irritant. She couldn't avoid him now even if she wanted to. He kept referring to Bimbo as a 'she' and a tabby when *he* was tortoiseshell; and Martin and Mother were getting closer. Obviously not as close as a married couple would be, but extremely cosy. She was out so much of the day, and could see he was now spending so much of his time with her mother that she couldn't help feeling... marginalised? Excluded?

What was it that they had joked with each other about the other day? Oh yes, it was the fact that Myra didn't drive. In fact, she had never owned a car but had learnt to drive and had driven a lot initially. But when she was working in London, there was no need for a car. It would just have sat at home with Mother; another rusting, unnecessary expense. They'd both guffawed at the thought of her driving now and were listing the kinds of car she might drive. She didn't know the makes they were laughing about or what made it all so funny. "You'd need a crash helmet if you were ever in a car with her," he'd said.

She began to get annoyed all over again, just thinking about it. Martin was a wedge between her and her mother, the thin end. She wanted him to go. Not die, just go, he was a friend, after all. Anyway, when he did pop off, it needed to be after Mother, not before, if the inheritance tax avoidance was to pay off. He was there to stay, for the time being, now he'd sold his own place and burnt his bridges.

"I saw this thing," he went on, "at the Horsebridge. There's an event for senior citizens at that thing run by a group that's moved into that old church hall off the high street."

"What group?" she asked.

"I forget what they're called but they're into running community events. The something Fellowship, they're called. It's basically multifaith. It's all the main religions coming together to do things for the local community. Anyway, whatever they're called, they're doing this Black and White Party thing for the senior citizens. I wondered if you'd like to go, Linda?"

"When is it?"

"Sunday. They give you lunch and sing songs. It sounds fun," he said.

"Does it?" Mother asked. "Maybe you should go then."

"I don't think she has anything black to wear; or white for that matter," Myra said.

"I'm sure it won't matter. They're not going to throw her out for that, are they?"

"Maybe not for that, but I'm sure as soon as she opens her mouth, they'll be throwing her out for something."

Mother cackled. "I'm not sure it's me, Martin. I mean, it's a lovely thought, but I'm not sure…"

"I thought Janice and I could drop you there. There's line dancing around the same time at the Horsebridge."

Myra looked up. "Is there?" she asked. "Why don't you go, Mother? It will be nice for you to get out and do the… what is it again?"

"Singing along and clapping mainly, I think," he replied, his eyelids feeling heavier.

"Why don't you? And Martin and I can go line dancing."

"…You could still go to the Horsebridge without me having to go to that." There was a silence. "For you to go line dancing is what I mean… Oh alright, I'll go, but I'll wear what I want to wear. I'm not going in just black or white."

Myra noticed Martin pinching the bridge of his nose. "Alright, Martin? Not going hypo, are you?"

"No. I took a pill and it's just kicking in. It's nearly time for me to call it a day, I think."

"I married a druggie."

"I suppose I should wean myself off them; they were helpful when I worked shifts at the home and my sleep patterns were so irregular. Something to help me sleep, something to pep me up – there's *so* many things I have in common with Saint Judy of Garland. Anyway," he said decisively as he scanned the cards in his hand, squealing with fresh excitement, "I've seen one of him somewhere. I'm sure I have." Even his happiness irritated Myra. At some point, one way or another, he really would have to go. "Here he is!" he said, proudly displaying his pair. He offered his hand to Bimbo to pick one.

They continued to play. Bimbo was first out. The pace of the game quickened as the number of cards in each of their hands began to dwindle. The Old Maid, who had been flying around from one hand to another had now stopped with Myra and stubbornly refused to budge. Mother put down her last card in a pair and then

Martin, leaving Myra with the Old Maid. She was the subject of almost hysterical laughing and finger pointing.

"Bad luck, Myra," Mother laughed. "Of course, it doesn't mean anything. It's just a game."

"Although, interestingly," Martin said, "she does end up Old Maid a statistically significant amount of the time."

According to the instructions that came with the archaic game, once the losing player is publicly declared an Old Maid, 'the other players may ride her around the room'. Myra drew the line at that. What might have been acceptable in a Victorian nursery would almost certainly end in a trip to accident and emergency at their age.

"Oh, don't be horrible, Martin."

"I'm sorry. You know I don't mean it, don't you, Janice darling?" She didn't answer. "Well, on that note, it really is time for me to turn in. Is that alright with you, Linda? You don't need me, do you?" he asked.

"No, you're alright. Goodnight."

"Night then. Night, Janice."

"Night, Martin. Don't let the bugs bite."

He left the room.

Mother watched as she moved the table back to the side and put the cards away. She sat on the sofa next to Bimbo. She slowly stroked his velvety ears.

"Everything alright, Myra?"

"Just a bit tired."

"Me too. You're not going off him, are you?" Mother asked.

"Martin? No. What makes you say that?"

"I don't know."

"No, he's fine."

In a hushed tone, she said, "I'm not sure about his cooking though, Myra, if I have to be honest. Are you? I'm alright with just a crispy pancake and some mixed vegetables from the frozen section or even just a hardboiled egg. It's too late at night for all that; it's too rich. All that garlic, butter, brandy and goose fat. I'm not sure if my bottom can take much more of it. I'm scared I won't make it out of bed in time. Will you talk to him?"

"Why don't you?"

"Well, he's your friend."

"He's your husband."

"…He's your stepfather."

Myra laughed. "OK, I'll speak to him."

"I think I'd prefer to be clogged up, if I had a choice. Do you remember the big poo, Myra? When I hadn't been for days? Do you remember?"

"How could I forget?"

"You said it'd have been easier if I was up in stirrups and used a pair of birthing tongs on it. I'm not even sure I know what that was we ate tonight."

"It was duck in cherries," she said under her breath, with an audible smirk.

"A fuckin' what…?"

"Duck… in… cherries," she enunciated with a laugh. "Duck. You heard."

"Ooh it was nasty, though. Too sweet. Sweet *and* savoury. I think it was off; definitely past its sell-by. I bet he got it cheap. Don't you think it was off, Myra? It tasted all old and rotten to me."

"You are what you eat."

"No, you are."

The next day, Martin dropped Mother at the church hall, then parked in town and headed, with Janice, to the Horsebridge. They hadn't been totally sure what they were leaving her to do when they said goodbye. The multifaith, community, fellowship people seemed pleasant enough and well-organised.

They said they'd expected about twenty, so "the turn-out was a little disappointing" but there was, "still time for more late-comers". They weren't late but she didn't let her irritation show. She never really let any authentic emotion show; she smiled and twinkled her eye as she screamed inside.

In the hall, there were twenty swivel chairs in a circle, facing the walls. There was a middle-aged man unloading CDs and tinkering about with a beaten-up CD player but the other four were women; three, about the same age as herself, and one younger, possibly someone's daughter. One of the four picked up a case from the back. One of those cases that opened into tiers of smaller containers. The kind of thing that someone would use for fly fishing, sewing or crafting. There were also about seven confused-looking senior citizens. None of the others were in black and white either, so perhaps that part of the lunch and happy-clappy sing-along had been ditched. At least Mother wouldn't stick out as a colourful party-pooper now.

Although harmless enough, the fellowship people were very quick to ask for the £7.50. She had assumed it was free, for the community. She was told it was to cover the cost of the lunch, which smelt overly cabbagey as it cooked in a room at the back somewhere. The charge was apparently not a charge but, 'a donation for a recommended amount'. They were told she was in safe hands as they said goodbye, and Mother was led to one of the swivel chairs.

"Now I think, as the music is nearly ready, we ought to make a start," said the grinning fellowship woman from the other side of the door as she and Martin walked away.

Just as before, she and Martin had a wonderful time with their thumbs tucked into imaginary belts, heel-turning and toe-tapping the hour away. *I really must sign up for the regular class*, she thought; it gave her real pleasure.

They had a light lunch at the Tudor Tea Rooms. But instead of going for one of their delicious cakes, decided to go for a potter around the shops with a view to stopping off at Tea and Times for coffee and a bun later, before it was time to collect Mother.

Martin suggested she walk to the hall while he brought the car around to pick up Linda. It made sense. It was a short walk back from where they were and it would only take him a minute, so she walked quite slowly, the long way round, rather than nipping down one of the alleyways.

She turned the corner. An ambulance was parked outside the hall. There was no one around and the road was quiet. No siren. No blue lights. Just a distant, muffled, echoing music. Barely recognisable, only just discernible: *De Camptown Races*. It wasn't uncommon to see an ambulance parked on a back road, so she knew there was no reason to be worried. So, why was she? Her pace quickened slightly.

She could only see the front of the ambulance as she approached. She'd expected to see the two crew members having a sandwich or something, but there was no one there. An empty street and that dreadful *De Camptown Races* doo-dahing from somewhere. Nearing the hall, she could see the double doors were open and, getting closer still, as the music grew louder, saw more of the inside. She saw a small pile of dirty dishes piled up on a tray at the back. One of the women saw her approach and rushed across to her, ashen faced. The paramedics were working on someone on the floor.

"Oh my God."

"It happened at the big reveal," she said. "She's going to be OK. Once we'd done all the face-painting, that's when it happened."

"The what...?

The chairs were no longer facing the walls but facing the centre. The old people looked equally shocked and upset but, to her horror... their faces were blacked up with white lips and white around the eyes, all wearing bowler hats with stripes of pink and yellow, like old fashioned, boiled sweets. She could see that more than one of them was crying. Her eyes searched for Mother. It was like a dreadful throwback to a time of mainstreamed sexism, homophobia and racism. Like one of those appalling black and white minstrel shows, but without the production values. She couldn't see her mother. Her eyes turned to the two paramedics, and she ran towards them, instantly recognising her mother's bony ankles and her shoes poking out between them.

"Oh my God."

"We just turned the chairs around," the well-meaning, multifaith do-gooder said, "and we thought it would be a lovely surprise. But they started screaming and shouting at each other and your mother, she screamed too. I don't know what got into them all, but they all just started screaming and crying and she just… your mother slipped from her chair. I'm so sorry."

She pulled the paramedics apart.

"Please let us do our job," the lady paramedic said as she turned.

"It's my mother," she said, recognising her skinny face, blacked up like Al-fucking-Jolson and the ECG pads and wires leading back to the machine.

"Myra," she said weakly. "Myra, thank God."

"We had to shock her. She needs to get to hospital right now." They started to prepare her for the ambulance gurney.

"What were you thinking?" she snarled at the fellowship volunteers. "In what world is this OK? In what world… is what you've done… in any way OK?"

"Excuse me," the paramedic said kindly to her as they lifted the gurney and locked it into place so she could be wheeled out. "You're welcome to ride with us if you want to."

"Thank you."

"Janice?" called Martin as he appeared at the door. "What's happened?"

"It's Mother. She's had a heart attack, I think. Is that what it is?"

"Yes, and we've got to go now, right now."

The gurney sped towards the hall doors, out into the light of day and then bumped and rattled across the pavement, onto the road and the ambulance.

"Myra," Mother rasped weakly through the oxygen mask on her face, as she was rolled into the back.

"Jump in if you're coming," said the paramedic. She did as she was told.

"Shall I come too?" Martin asked.

"No. I'll call you," she said tersely.

"Do you know which hospital?"

"QEQM," said the paramedic.

Martin clapped his hand over his mouth. "Not Margate," he exclaimed.

The paramedic pulled the doors closed; the other was already in the driving seat. "I'm going to have to ask you to sit back and let me work on her if I need to."

"Yes of course."

"Myra..."

"I'm here..."

The ambulance pulled out; its blue lights flashing, and siren sounding in fits and starts.

"Myra..."

"Don't try to talk."

"No, actually, talking is good," said the paramedic.

"Talk, Mother. Keep talking."

"Please make sure that they know..."

"What, Mother? Know what?"

"I hadn't felt right all day. I think it was the duck in cherries and I didn't know what they were doing. I'm not black. I must have dozed off. Then they counted one, two, three and spun us all around at once..."

"I know."

"I've never been so scared in my life. It was horrible. I'm not racialist…"

"I know, Mother. Don't worry about them. They're irrelevant. Can we get this stuff off her face?" she asked.

"That's fine, just please don't disturb the monitor or move the mask please." She handed three or four wipes to her. She began to wipe the black grease paint from her mother's skin.

She couldn't fault the care of the ambulance crew or the staff at the Queen Elizabeth the Queen Mother Hospital in Margate. Arriving at the hospital, people thought Mother had been in a house fire, her face covered in what looked like thick soot. An hour or so later, when she'd begun to stabilise enough to be moved to intensive care, a lovely girl gently wiped the remaining black from her face.

She called Martin around 7pm to say Mother was out of the woods and sleeping now, but that they were keeping her in overnight. She reminded him to give Bimbo his treats, which was just as well, Martin had completely forgotten. He knew Linda was worse than Janice let on. She must be if they'd felt the need to keep her in. The reality was it didn't look good at all.

She'd been asked if she wanted to sign something to say they shouldn't resuscitate if that situation should arise. She knew exactly what this meant; how violent and intrusive a process that could be. For someone with a low likelihood of survival in the long-term, it was far from the kindest thing to do. How much of her mother might they bring back anyway, and for how long? She knew instantly that the answer should be 'no' but made it look like she needed to think about it before signing.

She stayed in the waiting room and asked to be notified if there was any change. As evening turned into night, the hospital quietened, except for the occasional sound of someone walking on those squeaky-clean floors.

She was awoken by a nurse, the same one who cleaned her mother's face, touching her shoulder and softly saying, "Excuse me." Myra looked at her and then at her watch. She instantly knew what she was about to hear. It was seventeen minutes past midnight. The girl sat next to her and said that she was sorry to wake her. She said she was afraid she had to tell her that her mother had just passed away. She said she'd fallen asleep and slipped away peacefully. She said it appeared her heart and circulation were in a very poor state. She was just too weak, and it was absolutely the right decision not to resuscitate. Even if it had bought her a little extra time, there would have been no quality of life.

"Is there someone I can call for you?" asked the nurse.

"No, thank you. I have a cab number. Is it alright if I just go home now?"

"Of course. I'll look after everything here for you."
The nurse held Myra's hand in both of hers. Around the
girl's smooth, dark honeyed neck was the most beautiful
pendant of deep indigo, lapis lazuli. "I'm so sorry," she
said.

"Thank you."

Martin was in bed by the time she got home. She
could hear him sleeping. She decided not to wake him.
She needed to get to bed herself and couldn't face a
conversation with him at that moment. The house, snug
in its thick, coniferous cocoon of leylandii, already
seemed half-empty without Mother. The dent in the
sofa cushion was still there from that morning when
she'd stood to leave, when Martin had said the car was
ready. Myra got into bed. It was so dark it was hard to
know if her eyes were open or closed.

*The next thing. What was the next thing? The next
thing that had to happen*, she thought, was that she and
Martin needed to marry. But it couldn't be so quickly
that it appeared inappropriate. At the same time,
although he didn't look like he was going to pop his
clogs any time particularly soon, it was best to do it
sooner rather than later.

She didn't know if she'd ever be able to forgive him
for suggesting that awful fellowship thing to her mother,
but at the same time knew that he couldn't really be
held responsible. They could probably co-exist in the

house indefinitely if she could retain her own space without invasion from him. She certainly wouldn't be trespassing into his space.

She decided to wear Mother's cobwebby Raynaud's gloves from now on. Always. Even at home. Until she was ready not to. The only time she would take them off would be to wash her hands. Her mind flipped to those dreadful fellowship people, who talked the talk and espoused values while doing such dreadful things. Hate-filled people who preached against judgement, lest they be judged, yet judged with sanctimonious impunity, knowing they could do what the hell they liked if they maintained their weekly acts of absolution. How far removed from the institution of the church were the actual words of Christ? If he had had strong views about people who were gay, for example, surely he'd have mentioned it. Paul did. So those people are Paulian then? Not Christian at all. Jesus didn't say one word in judgement of others, not one. Except against hypocrites. Only words of acceptance, humbleness, kindness, forgiveness. Perverted through time, however, by people of monstrous ego, who sought to control the masses through fear, grew the church. The other religions were the same and it grew worse in the Old Testament-thumping States. How far from those wonderful values were these types, who'd patronised those helpless, old people in the most offensive, racist way and that led to the premature death of Mother. They weren't doing good for others. Their motives were entirely self-serving; penance to appease their own sinful self-loathing and feed their own swelling sense of self-righteousness. How she loathed them. One thing was certain, she'd never do the flower arrangements at church on a Sunday now. They could all go to fucking hell in a handbasket and rot, for all she cared.

She lay there in her darkness, eyes wide open. A sixty-year-old orphan. There was no wind outside. There was no sound inside or out, but she wouldn't be allowed to sleep. Her mind raced furiously. Everything was still and alone and silent, but in her head, for some unknowable, random reason, an earworm from a long-distant time took hold and began to replay and repeat to torment.

Oh, deary me,
Mother caught a flea;
Put it in a teapot to make a cup of tea.
The flea jumped out
And made Mother shout
And in ran Father with his shirt hanging out.

She'd not recalled the rhyme for decades. Where was this coming from? Why now? She heard the little girl handclaps and the skipping rope whip-cracking on summer tarmac. Patent leather buckle shoes, over the obligatory white socks, tapping on the playground as they hopscotched without a care in the world. She squeezed his hand. After feeding the ducks, the merry-go-round, spinning wildly; hexagonal, heavy wood and iron. Must hang on. Spinning too fast now for a little girl to jump off.

She squeezed her eyes shut to block out the memory and a tear rolled out. The beautiful torment of that last day in the sun in the park. A long-forgotten summer, when her father didn't come home, replaying over and over and over...

Oh, deary me...

10

On Monday, she called in to work. She spoke to Hazel and said her mother had died. Hazel was possibly somewhere on the autistic spectrum because when it came to emotional intelligence or social pleasantries, she tended to sound uncomfortable, embarrassed; she'd much rather stick to work-related topics like membership statistics or subscriptions. She wasn't creative either. She was, however, objective, analytical, clear-headed and logical in a tight spot. Although neither understood where the other was coming from, there was a mutual respect, like Spock and McCoy.

"Do you want to speak to Stuart?" Hazel asked, sounding keen to remove herself from the situation.

She paused. "No, it's alright. Please just tell him I'm a bit upset. I do need to talk to Mel though, if she's there?"

"I'll transfer you now. Bye, Janice, and sorry again to hear your sad news. My… er, commiserations."

"Janice?"

"Morning, Mel. Look, I'm sorry I won't be in today, but my mother died at the weekend."

"Oh no. I'm so sorry."

"Thank you."

"How are you doing?"

"Well, you know. It's hard."

She could hear Hazel whispering to Stuart in the background. "...her mother just died ...over the weekend... I don't know..."

Martin touched her shoulder on his way to the kitchen and mouthed to her if she wanted another coffee. She shook her head. "No, thanks."

"Look, if there's anything I can do...?" Mel went on.

"Well, there isn't anything in particular, but I'm probably going to be away for a couple of weeks. There's a lot of things I need to take care of. I don't think there's anything in my diary but, just in case, can I give you access to my calendar?"

"Yes, no problem."

"In case there's anything you'll need to cancel for me. I'm sure there isn't, but I'll give it to you anyway. You'll need to log on as me, then send yourself an invite from me to share calendars."

"OK. I can do that."

"My password is bimbo49; no spaces, all lower case."

"Got it."

"Bimbo is my cat."

"Ah, cute."

"And forty-nine is... just forty-nine; the number of times I've had to change my password, actually. Are you ever first to arrive?"

"Sometimes. I just wait for Hazel to get in to open up."

"I'll give you the security code for the door too. It's 6751. You just put that in when you arrive, and the beeping will stop. Same on the way out if you're ever last to leave. You just need to remember there's just thirty seconds between putting the code in and getting out and closing the door behind you."

"OK. What happens if I get the code wrong?"

"You get three attempts to get it right. You'll be fine. There's a spare set of keys in my top desk drawer."

"OK. 6751."

"If you make a mistake with the code... if you put it in wrong three times or set the alarm off by mistake, it will flash up with the security firm, Appleyard Security Services, and they give me a call on the mobile. They can attend site or reset it remotely if I can't get there in time. The police are only called if they can't get me on the phone for some reason." She was wittering. Too much detail. "But you'll be fine. The mobile is always on if you need me."

"OK. Got it. There's just one thing. I'm going back to New Zealand to see Chris. I'll be leaving the same week you're back by the sound of it."

"Yes, I'd forgotten that."

"It's only for a few weeks. Will that still be alright?"

"Not a problem, I'm sure I'll be back by then anyway. Thanks for this, Mel, and look, please don't hesitate to call if you need me for anything."

"I won't. Thanks, Janice. Look after yourself."

"Bye." She hung up and turned to Martin, who put another coffee on the table next to her.

"I made you one anyway," he said.

Although there was so much to do, there was nothing they could do until Monday. The hospital rang and asked if there was a local funeral director she wanted to use or whether they could call someone for her. She opted for a local one. She dropped in to one on the high street shortly after 10am. They were incredibly kind, and much to her relief, took control of all the arrangements; just asking her the odd question periodically. Did she want this or that? What was the budget? Was there insurance cover for funeral expenses? Did she want an open casket? Did she want to be buried in something of her own, or did she want to select from one of the coverings they did? What will the date be? Burial or cremation? They asked her to think about music and readings for the various points in the service, or alternatively they could pick something suitable. Did she want a religious service or humanist?

She hadn't ever considered a world without that sour-faced little woman. That scrag-end Steptoe; tough as nails and manipulative as anything. She was convinced she'd never die. Well, heaven wouldn't want her and as for hell… they'd be too afraid she'd try and take over. The chemicals, colourings and preservatives in her favourite frozen crispy pancakes that kept her colon ticking over so nicely were surely enough to preserve the shrivelled up old husk well into the next millennium.

With the help of the funeral home, she'd taken care of all the arrangements herself. Martin had offered, but she'd rather do it on her own, she told him. He respected that, which was good of him.

"I never thought I'd ever get married, not to a woman," he told her as he polished off the last mouthful of fish and chip lunch in the Tudor Tea Rooms, "so I'm very grateful to her for that. And to you, of course. Even though it was all too short."

"Can I get you anything else?" the girl asked as she cleared the table. "Dessert menu?"

"Just a white coffee and a slice of the coffee and walnut cake, please," she said.

"Dessert menu for me, please."

The girl took the plates to return shortly with the menu.

"What was I saying?" He perused the dessert selection. "Yes, marriage. When I was growing up and still not being open with myself about... my sexuality, those relatives, the ones you'd see at family gatherings and who'd insist on telling tell me how I'd grown, well, when I was in my teens and early twenties and they were all getting old and wrinkly, they'd come up to me at the family weddings and say, *you'll be next, I expect.*

I'd get my own back when I saw the same relatives at family funerals and think the same about them; *you'll be next*, I'd think." The girl returned with her pad. "Knickerbocker glory, please."

There was no danger of him going hypo that afternoon. He'd become so much more sedentary since he moved in. That, coupled with the income released from the eventual sale of his flat and the lack of things to do at his new home, meant he'd quickly put on at least another stone in weight. He moved only between bed, sofa, fridge and toilet. He'd say he was going to get back to the gym, as he tucked into whatever snack he happened to be enjoying at the time. It made it sound like he'd once been a regular gym bunny but, to her knowledge, he'd never even set foot in one. She smirked. Saying you're planning to do something is not the same as doing it. She'd believe it when she saw it.

"Is it too soon to talk about us?" he asked as they stood to put their coats on. "I'll get this by the way." He went to the till and the waitress totalled up what they'd had. He paid and dropped some change in the cut glass ice cream goblet for tips, by the till.

"What do you mean?" she asked as they left.

"Well – and tell me if it's too soon to be discussing this – the original arrangement was that once your mother passed away, that you and I would marry."

"I'd forgotten about that," she lied.

But it interested her that he should be the one to raise it and this soon. Of course, there was an advantage to him, but she really hadn't given it much thought. The fact that he raised it may be an indication that he thought she'd be the one to go next and that he'd scoop the all the death winnings. She wondered what had given him that idea if he did harbour it. A gust of wind blew a cold smell of fish and seaweed in her face and a gull screeched. They were about the same age, but it was common knowledge that women tended to live longer, and she didn't have any pre-existing conditions like he did. He wasn't planning to shove her down the stairs or something, was he? Or meet with some other untimely accident? No. It wouldn't have crossed Martin's mind for a second. He was a care worker, for God's sake. No violent thought ever crossed his mind. That mind, encased in an increasingly bloated face. He was probably just asking because they'd made a deal, and he was ready to deliver on his part.

"We can talk about it if you like," she said.

"It's not something I suppose should happen straightaway."

"No," she said. "I suppose not."

"Perhaps in a month or so? I could get onto them at Maidstone again and organise all that side of things if you like."

"Alright. Thank you, Martin. You are a good friend. Won't it look a bit strange though? I don't want to raise any eyebrows."

"Well, I've thought about that and... what if it does look odd? What are they going to do? It's not like one of us is a foreign national and it's a scam to get a British passport. They might think we're up to something, but there's no evidence of anything dodgy... because there isn't anything dodgy. We'll just brass-neck it."

"We can do that. I'm sure it will all be fine," she said,

"There's something else I wanted to ask you. There's this Princess cruise I've seen, around the Med." She stopped and looked at him. He hated when she did this. She would just turn and stand there in front of you, looking, no emotion on her face, just listening. It was disarming, being suddenly listened to, with no warning. "Of course, I'll be here for the funeral, but it leaves early the next day. I can get a very good deal. It's only a week."

"For both of us? Like a honeymoon?"

Awkwardly, he replied, "Well, if you wanted to come too, I'm sure we could arrange it if we're quick."

She stared at him for a moment. "No, you're alright going on your own if you want to. I'll be fine."

"Well, if you're sure. You'll probably need a break from me at that point anyway. It's Saturday to Saturday so I'll be back on the twenty-eighth. Perhaps sometime in the first or second week of February, then? For the wedding?"

"That will be fine." They walked past Thompson's and back towards the car. "So where does this cruise take you?" She asked.

He couldn't help but sound excited. "It starts in Rome. The first stop is Palermo, Sicily, then La Goulette in Tunisia, back to Italy for Florence and Pisa, then on to Genoa, then Toulon, France and ending up in Barcelona. I had some money left over from the flat..." he said by way of explanation.

Interesting that he felt the need to explain, she thought. He obviously wants her to know he's not squandering her mother's money on his cruise. She was more than a little annoyed that he'd want to go off on some jolly so soon after Mother's death, leaving her alone. She didn't want him around, but he shouldn't be going. What kind of friend was he anyway?

"And tell you what," he went on, "when I'm back I'll make a start on those leylandii."

"What do you mean?"

"Well, I was going to thin them out a bit. Let some daylight in. It would be nice to be able to use the garden too."

"But I like them," she said plainly. "I like that they press against the windows. It's comforting. I don't care about the garden or more light."

Mother had planted those trees, originally as a hedge, for a bit of privacy. She'd planted far too many, too close together and too close to the house. For years, it had been buried behind a beautiful, thick black, impenetrable forest. The neighbours, whoever they were, never complained about them. If it ever looked like a branch was going to break a pane, she'd open the window, saw it off and stuff it down as far to the ground as it would go.

Anyway, she thought to herself, *there's no point discussing it with him. It will never happen. He's all talk. He'll start a gym membership before he clears one of those trees and besides, I'd really need a professional to come in and fell them, if that's what I wanted to do, and I don't.*

Returning home, she went straight to her bedroom and lay on her back. Laying on her bed in the middle of the day was something she never did. Hermitting herself away. She'd told Martin she had a headache. She didn't. She just didn't want to be in the same room as him, breathe the same air as him and he always had the TV on too loud. She heard a familiar and gentle creaking nearing her room. He stuck his head around the side of the door and meowed.

"Here, Bimbo. Here, best-beloved," she said, tapping the eiderdown. He jumped up.

She rolled off the bed and pushed the door closed and lay back down again. He was looking more and more scrappy with old age, like brown, moth-eaten tinsel. His coat didn't pop back up after a nap the way it used to. He looked like a fur stole that had been folded up and stored in a box from a time when it was acceptable to wear such a thing. He walked up her body, eyes slowly blinking, and lowered his frail, arthritic frame down on hers, so they were nose to nose. He closed his eyes and purred. She put one hand on his lower spine and stroked his ear with the other. She closed her eyes. She didn't sleep. She just lay there with Bimbo, warm and furry on her bosom. His pink paw beans and velvety nose and ears. His comforting rattle and contented sighs. Bimbo was more a part of her family than Martin was. There's a distinct difference between friends and family. You can't choose family. Bimbo, however, was very much a family member; a living, breathing connection to Mother.

The funeral was a miserable affair. The weather, cold and drizzly, and the turnout, poor. Neither was much of a surprise; it had been a typically dreary winter and Mother didn't have any friends to speak of, not that she was aware of anyway. There had been friends once, but they'd slipped out of touch for whatever reason. It was just her, Martin and the humanist minister. It was short and sweet. She hadn't chosen music or readings, nor had she provided the minister with anything to say about her mother; there was little point as it was just the two of them. Sad that a long life should be signed off this way. But Mother was dead and wasn't likely to care much.

She wondered if she'd have a similar send-off one day. Probably. Ben was gone and she was still planning to move. She still hankered after that honey-coloured cottage in Burford in the Cotswolds. She'd start a whole new life there. Perhaps she'd join a class or volunteer or have an allotment or make jam. She could learn bowling and join the local club, or line dancing! Yes, line dancing; she could take that up properly. She could buy a spangled cowgirl outfit; white leather with tassels and rhinestones and a hat. Perhaps she could write her recipe book. She'd already started to note some of her creations down in the notebook the office had given her for her birthday. She pictured herself pottering around her cottage garden, pulling up home-grown carrots and snipping blooms for the table. Making quince jelly, drying lavender in the kitchen window as homemade blackberry wine bubbled through its gallon jar airlock, soon ready for bottling for Christmas. Making apple sauce from the ample fruit from the ancient tree in the garden; pickling vegetables, making chutneys, baking breads... It would be an idyllic life in her little honey-coloured cottage in the Cotswolds.

As soon as the service was over, Martin started to prepare for his cruise. He'd booked Ray to drive him to and from Gatwick so he didn't have to drive himself and think about parking. It was marginally more expensive this way but at least it gave him an hour or so extra snoozing time in the car.

They seemed pleased to see Janice arrive at work after her two weeks' compassionate leave. She worked that Monday but spoke to Stuart and asked to take the rest of the week too, as she didn't feel quite ready. It wasn't convenient as Mel was off too, but he couldn't, and didn't, say no. It was only four days more, anyhow. She had next to nothing to do there, and it was hardly likely the organisation would disappear down the pan that week. She said she'd be on call, in case needed, knowing they wouldn't dream of calling her unless something terrible happened.

The reality was she'd not intended to spend more than a day that week at work anyway. There was only one reason why she felt the need to go in. There was that phone number she needed to retrieve from an archived personnel file. She needed to cross reference it with the contact details as they appeared on the Trethendar pension fund beneficiaries list, to ensure it was correct. It was. She noted the current address as well. Still Sheppey.

She didn't get out of bed until after 9am the day after her aborted return to work. She only arose then because Bimbo kept walking across her and nuzzling to get her up to replenish his water and dry food bowl. As soon as he saw his daily needs had been catered for, he'd go straight back to sleep again. He was losing weight and moving more slowly. She could feel his bony spine when she ran her hand down his back.

After toileting and showering and dressing, she walked into Mother's room. She stood in the centre, wondering what had brought her there. It felt as if Mother was about to pop in at any moment or call out to her, "Myra. Myra." But there was no calling out. No one to call her 'Myra' now. She opened the curtains. No light flooded in. The black-green leylandii pressed against the pane. Outside, as inside, it appeared completely airless, like a stage set. Just her own reflection in the obsidian, collard green glass.

She crossed to the chest of drawers and pulled one of the two top drawers open. Underwear. She closed it. She opened the wardrobe. Inside were her shoes and outfits. Those clothes, so associated with her mother, as if they *were* her. If you looked at the shoes, you could see her narrow, bird-like ankles sticking out of them. If you looked at the collar of a dress, with its residual foundation make-up around the edge, you could also see her necklace, her testicular, turkey neck, her jawline, her hair, those aged eyes, that smirk.

She sat on the side of the bed and looked at the window of the hermetically sealed room. She opened the top drawer of the bedside cabinet. No books. Not with Mother's eyesight. She'd never been much of a reader even when she could see. Her glasses, a pen, a pencil case containing dog-ends of make-up and, at the back of the drawer, her home enema kit in its handy travel case. She un-popped the popper and folded open the case on the bed. The transparent tubes flicked out from their coiled position, knocking to the floor one of the two attachments (the longer of the two) that facilitated an easy rectal insertion. She put it on the bed. She lifted out the two-litre transparent bag with its hook. It was at this point she realised her eyes should fill with tears for the first time since her mother had died and finally let that sea of emotion flood over her. But nothing came. She forced a sob to try and get things moving, but nothing. She couldn't really understand how it was possible she could feel such a sense of emptiness. None of it meant anything. The only emotion she felt was that it should mean something and it didn't. She returned the enema kit, in its case, back to Mother's drawer.

She drifted into Martin's room. She didn't spend long in there. It was neat and tidy enough, in fact it was incredibly neat and tidy, but that smell that she'd feared would follow him had indeed followed him. The old man smell hung in the air. Stale, hard to pinpoint and describe. A subtle, musty, composite. A blend of vintage jackets in need of a clean, stale sweat, dried urine droplets, the breath of an old man who doesn't floss his teeth, rounded off with the faint, but nevertheless quite distinct, smell of greedy man's shit.

The last room she glanced in was her own. Bimbo looked up at her from his corner of her bed and smiled a slow blink. She smiled back. He put his head on his paw with a sigh and went back to sleep.

Downstairs she made herself a cup of tea. She put it on the table where they'd played Scrabble and Happy Families and Old Maid. She moved the phone towards her. She didn't have the number. She collected her bag and rummaged through it as she made her way back to the lounge. She sat back down at the table and put the bag on the floor at her feet. She held the paper with the address and phone number on it. She stood suddenly and went to where the phone books and maps sat, then returned to her seat with a road map of Kent. She looked at the address: Sunnyside Avenue, Minster-on-Sea. Her eyes scoured the map. Eventually she found it. Sunnyside Avenue was off Power Station Road. The short, curved road looked more like a cul-de-sac. It curved, nowhere, then ended.

She traced it back with her fingernail. From Sunnyside Avenue, turning left into Power Station Road and following that to its end. Then turning right onto Halfway Road. Following this all the way up, into Sheerness and the train station. She'd never visited before; it was so close, and she'd lived in Whitstable for so long. Sittingbourne was only the next stop on the train, after Faversham. She knew the announcements, heard over the years, that you changed at Sittingbourne for Kemsley, Swale, Queensborough and Sheerness-on-Sea. She didn't know how long it would take, but it couldn't take more than an hour from Whitstable to Sheerness on the Isle of Sheppey.

You could see Sheppey from Whitstable. The beach across the estuary was a piss streak of bright yellow on the horizon, often mistaken by DFLs for Essex. She'd always assumed this was sandy beach but had heard it was the rape that flourished there. She'd also been told Sheppey had the highest incidence of mental illness per square mile than anywhere else in Western Europe. She didn't know if this was true or not, but it could well be. Apart from the docks, there were three prisons, one of which was maximum security, along the lines of Broadmoor. Sheppey was a small place, with one road in and the same road out.

She followed the road with her fingernail back again from the station, down Halfway Road, left into Power Station Road and turning right into Sunnyside Avenue. Her nail scraped to the point where the road ended unsatisfactorily; unfinished and untidy, abandoned. She tapped the spot.

She picked up the number and moved the phone a little nearer. She picked up the receiver and put it to her ear as she started to dial. She suddenly stopped and put her finger on the hook to stop the call. There was a number you could dial to stop the other end being able to retrieve the number of the last caller by dialling one-four-seven-one. The only time she'd ever used it was when she called Margie Miller. She went back to the useful numbers section of her phone book. She tapped in the number, then started to dial again. She looked up, waiting for the ringtone. Her face reflected darkly in the window, blackened by the most unneighbourly of evergreens.

The phone rang the other end. She waited. She didn't know what she was going to say. Anyway, she was better working on the hoof. By the way the phone was ringing, it was clear the old bitch wasn't anywhere nearby. Perhaps she was in the garden? Not on a day like today. More likely she was at the shops or the doctors or post office or something. She probably volunteered somewhere too or was a trustee of something or a school governor. She couldn't imagine her just sitting in her own piss, looking out of the window at all that shuffling isolation and mental ill-health. There was still no answer. She'd let it ring ten more times. She started to count. Maybe she was taking a shit. It was unusual for someone not to have an answerphone. But perhaps not so unusual if you're retired and alone. She hadn't really needed one herself as Mother was always on hand. The thought struck her that her house now belonged to her stepfather, currently cruising around the Med, with skin salty like pork crackling. He should have been there with her. Ten rings passed, and she didn't hang up. She didn't know why. She would in a moment. Her mind was drifting. Then suddenly, that voice—

"Hello, Irene Hartley," she answered, sounding very business-like. Myra didn't know what to say. She put her hand over the receiver. "Hello?"

"I'm so sorry, I think I've dialled a wrong number."

"What number are you trying to call?"

"I, er…"

"Who is this?"

"No, sorry – wrong number. I wanted the coin-wash launderette."

"Well, you have dialled a wrong number, and very vexing it is too. I'm disabled, and it's difficult enough for me to get to the phone nowadays without it being a false alarm. I wish people would be more careful."

"I'm very sorry."

"Well, really…"

"I'm sorry. Goodbye."

"Goodbye," said Irene as she hung up.

She slowly replaced her receiver. Her shadow smiled back at her from the pane. She'd gleaned invaluable information. The phone number was current. She'd recognise Irene's voice and that prickly tone anywhere. Tough as old boots and fit as a fiddle, she'd not changed a bit. Except, that is, for the fact that she was not quite so invincible, formidable, and untouchable as she'd once been. Not with a disability. A mobility issue? Irene was vulnerable.

Now she'd pay.

11

It was all too horribly familiar. A dreadful, groundhoggy, déjà vu day. The same dumpy, bespectacled registrar with her eyebrows and glasses. The words that had sounded almost spontaneous and sincere at the September ceremony for the first Mr and Mrs Blair, exactly five months before, now sounded so hollow.

The registrar was visibly puzzled when she recognised the two people in front of her. She was sorry for their loss on hearing the first Mrs Blair, just like the first Mrs de Winter, was no more and just as unmentionable. 'I am sorry for your loss' are words rarely heard at a wedding and the registrar knew this, despite hearing them tumbling from her own mouth. Ray the driver was witness to this wedding as he had been at the first. Martin, whom the registrar hadn't really seen as the marrying kind at all, was now onto his second wife in five months. What a rampant womaniser he must be. What on earth was the secret power he had over first the mother and then the daughter? Money? A twelve-inch penis? A tongue like an eel that he could lick his own eyebrows with?

"There now, please be seated while Martin and Janice sign the register." Everyone seemed in a hurry to get the signing over with, and just exactly as before, the registrar continued by saying, "To conclude the ceremony, I will now present you both with your marriage certificate. May I be the first to congratulate you both on your marriage and wish you both a wonderful day today, a very..." she hesitated as if her words would jinx their union as perhaps they had before, "long and happy marriage and all the very best for your future lives together. Congratulations, Mr and Mrs Blair."

Ray took just one photograph this time, of the new Mr and Mrs Blair. There was a bit of debate about whether they should take one at all this time, but as they couldn't decide and were both in a bit of a hurry to get the whole thing done and dusted, they opted to have the picture taken in the same spot as before, on the steps in the apothecary's garden. Then it was back in the car, with Bonnie and Clyde speed, and home to Whitstable to pick up their Saturday where they'd left off, with absolutely no mention that they were now husband and wife. A girl to marry her stepfather within one month of her mother's death, although possibly normal on the Isle of Sheppey, would feel so incestuously wrong if it had been based on anything other than convenience, a financial arrangement. Both decided it was probably best not dwelt upon, though neither said this to the other. They didn't talk about it at all.

Normality soon returned. Martin eventually stopped talking about his cruise, and Janice had returned to work. Mel was back too, from seeing her significant other in New Zealand, although how she could sustain a long-distance relationship for so long seemed unfathomable. They seemed to get by on phone calls and video chats over the internet. She didn't say much about Chris and didn't carry a picture of him – not one that she shared anyway. She was bright, sparky and infectiously cheerful, but at the same time seemed keen to keep her home life private. She hadn't shared much about her hopes for the future either, except a dream to set up an arts project for people who'd suffered debilitating injuries. She'd been inspired by volunteering for a charity at home in New Zealand, which worked with a similar client group.

The latest topic of conversation at Trethendar (possibly arising to distract from the fact that the ship would probably sink in the very near future, and that they should seriously start considering lowering lifeboats), was that 'the mouse' was back. Hazel said she saw it in the kitchenette part of the flat at the top of the building. As this was a facilities issue, it fell within Janice's remit to sort out.

It wasn't a new issue. They'd had mice before. Jenny had been adamant, back then, that only humane traps be used that didn't hurt the mouse. This had been complied with publicly, but other traps (with poison) were also set all over the place; around the fridge, in the toilets, behind the filing cabinets and everywhere else she could think of. It was an old building. She wasn't overly worried by mice; their sleek, little dust-coloured, dust-covered bodies darting about, seen only from the corner of your eye.

She issued a notice that no food was to be left out, unless in sealed, airtight containers, and no food at all was to be left in the building over the weekend. It was hard to know how the rodents got into the desk pedestals, but they obviously did as a family pack of individually wrapped corn snacks in Stuart's had been chewed open by the mice, and their shitty, pellet droppings left on his differentials and last month's issue of *Payroll Manager*.

Everyone in London knows that, wherever you are, you are no more than six feet away from a rat and that if you saw a mouse, it meant at least ten more were close by. But the level of denial still amused Janice no end. The way they all referred to 'the mouse' rather than 'the infestation'; the scavenging multitude currently scurrying between the old building's wooden floorboards, squashing their tiny heads flat to squeeze under doors as well as through and up inside the walls.

"It's all the building work," said Mike the plumber with the air of an expert.

"How do you mean?" she asked as she followed him down the stairs to the basement. He was there for the (late) six-monthly boiler check. He'd had to reschedule as he had another installation job on, but better late than never. He also wanted to remind himself, so he was prepared for when he fitted the new boiler later that summer. They descended into the damp dark.

"A few doors down," he went on, "what are they doing? Starting a demolition?"

"Not completely," she said as she flicked on the light at the bottom of the basement steps, "I think they're just gutting it. The front is protected, so they'll be leaving that, but knocking pretty much all the rest down. They've only just started."

"I was going to say; shame to lose the front of a lovely, old Victorian house. You always get it though, the mice. Whenever there's building work, the rats and mice all make a run for it into buildings round about. You're doing the right thing with the traps and stuff, but to be honest, there'll be so many of them it probably won't make much of a difference till the work's done. They breed so fast. Tip of the iceberg, I'm afraid."

"You are a comfort, Mike," she said, arid with sarcasm.

"I'm just saying, Janice. Anyway, you know I'm right," he said approaching the boiler in the corner, behind the partition of grimy filing cabinets. "You can leave me if you want. I know what I'm up to."

"OK. I'll be upstairs if you need me," she said, turning to leave. He immediately lifted the front of the old boiler and stood it to the side.

"And I bet you this is where they're all getting in…" he muttered to himself.

She stopped and turned. "The mice?"

"One of the places anyway. Remember this?" he said as he tapped the metal lid covering the hole under the boiler. "See there? That tiny hole between the stone floor and the lid itself."

"That's disgusting. What do we do? Can we fill it in?"

"Probably best not to right now, as it might cause me problems when I come to fit the new boiler."

"What problems?"

"I don't know. I could maybe put a bit of filler in there for now. Some mastic or something. I'll see what I can do for you." He stopped. "Did you hear that?"

"I can't hear anything." She wanted to go for a pee. What was it about that basement that always made her want to pee? The dark? The musty smell? Mike? She couldn't hear anything over the noise of boiler's furnace rumbling.

"Listen…"

At first she thought it was her imagination. Neither of them breathed. From the tiny black hole between the metal covering and concrete floor there came a sound. The hole was no bigger than the width of Mike's index finger, but the sound from that pitch-black hole was unmistakable, echoing. The sound of starvation. The sound of panicking in the dark confinement. The sound of the eating of the young, the weak and old. The sound of survival. Beady eyes and yellowed teeth; hairless, squirming tails. It was the sound of scratching rodents squeaking and seething below, in the dark, swarming. Scurrying over every surface, over each other in that horrible pit, like a spillage of a million graphite pencil nibs; an ever-churning legion, moving as one chaos.

"Oh my God," she said. "That's disgusting. Mike, is that what I think it is? That is completely disgusting. Please, do whatever you can."

Where there're mice, there're rats and fleas and disease. Anyone from any European city has an inherent fear and repulsion for rats, a collective inherited memory of infestation and plague.

"I will," he said sounding equally shaken and repulsed. "And you need to get more traps down here, a lot more. This place will be full of them before long if we don't." Before he could finish, he heard her scurrying up the steps out of that ghastly hellhole and into the light, scratching her suddenly itchy arms, forehead and scalp.

She told Martin about the mice that evening over dinner. He'd made a lasagne and didn't really want to hear about it.

"Well, I hope you washed your hands," he said.
"Of course I did."

She missed Mother's mean old presence, the smells she made and the sound of her doing something in the next room, rummaging through her bag or busying herself with something. She didn't miss the things she used to have to help her with, like the enemas and getting in and out of the bath. Martin had moved in to care for her and had done a decent job. But there was an awkwardness now. They were friends and had often chosen to spend time together as friends do, but the element of choice had gone. It was really her home, and Bimbo's, but Martin had burnt bridges to be there and now had nowhere else to go. It crossed his mind to move out. He had no need to be there, and it might save his friendship with Janice. She was cordial towards him but living with her was very different to seeing her for lunch one afternoon a month, or for a coffee or glass of wine. After years of that kind of friendship and that level of contact, they were now thrown together with a new, rather unwelcome, level of intimacy. She was growing colder towards him. Direct, monosyllabic, terse. He didn't like it. He felt uncomfortable, unwelcome, no matter how hard he tried to make it work.

They ate in silence until their plates were clean. He ate faster to get away. He sat there politely until she'd finished. He looked at her plate. He looked at her thin lips moving rapidly as she chewed. There was something of the rodent about her. The narrow gap between her eyebrows and her hairline may lead you to think she had a full head of thick hair, but it was thin and flat and hung at the sides like short, wafer-thin sheets of pale Welsh slate. There was always the feeling she was thinking something else; not letting on, not sharing what she thought. What could pass for a commendable skill of active listening was somehow not. He hadn't noticed it before, but there was something rather withdrawn and scheming about darling Janice. Now that he thought about it, there always had been. She would smile and laugh – he had even seen her cry once many moons ago – but overall, there was little unrehearsed feeling displayed. Her reserve was so pronounced it was almost as if she had not a shred of empathy, but was at the same time, shrewd enough, and a sharp enough mimic, to keep that fact concealed. He wasn't even convinced her current grief was genuine. People grieve in different ways, and maybe it hadn't hit her properly yet, but he'd expected some display of emotion, no matter how small, private or fleeting; some loss of control. As far as he knew, there'd been nothing. Not one tear. And even that one time he had seen her cry, they hadn't been tears of sadness. They'd been tears of frustration and rage when reality had failed to meet her expectations. He wore his heart on his sleeve, always had done, but she... did she even have a heart?

"Thank you, Martin. That was lovely. I hope you won't be offended—"

"Offended?" he said, too quickly, too defensively.

"I was going to say, I hope you won't be offended, but I'm rather tired so I think I'll read in my room before going to bed early."

"Oh."

"...Rather than watch television. You don't mind?" She stood and cleared the table. It wasn't a question. An answer would make no difference.

"Of course not, Janice, darling." It was early, but he didn't think there was much on anyway. He hadn't taken one of his dwindling sleeping pills yet. They took an hour or so to kick in. He seemed to be getting through them faster than normal. He'd only just picked up a repeat prescription, but the new bottle already seemed half empty.

Bimbo followed her out. Martin was left at the table on his own, in that atmosphere of... awkwardness. He was currently reading one of the Norse sagas and couldn't help picturing Janice whenever the Nordic hag, Hel, was mentioned – daughter of Loki and ruler of the underworld. Condemned by her plainness to stagnate in the pit forever. To preside over an eternity of inertia, queen of her own private Helheim, dark and dank. Was it really '...*better to reign in Hell than serve in*

Heaven?' Probably not. *Must ask Janice one day,* he smirked.

"By the way," she called from the kitchen as she piled the dishes into the sink.

"Yes?"

"I'm away this weekend. You'll be alright on your own, won't you?"

"Of course, Janice, darling. Yes, of course."

She climbed the stairs to her room. "Night, then."

"Sleep well."

The week swung by in a paper-shuffling-about sort of way; random attempts at appearing busy, filling in time with nothing special until it was time for her to up sticks and head home fifteen minutes early for the weekend.

The whiff of jammy toast and melted butter filled her nostrils as she came downstairs that Saturday morning. Martin munching at the table in the same position she'd left him in the night before, except this time he was in his robe. Was he never not eating? A little snack here, a little snack there. Buttery lips.

"There's coffee if you want some," he called cheerily to her.

"No, thank you. I'd better be off."

"No time for even a bite? It'll give you strength. They're working you too hard, Janice, darling." She didn't correct him. It suited her perfectly if he thought she was spending the weekend away for work; he wouldn't ask for any of the dreary details. "When are you back?"

"Sunday afternoon. I'm not sure which train I'm getting at this stage. I should be home for supper." She put her overnight bag by the front door in the hall and peered through the door at him. He didn't know she was watching. He was checking his blood sugar at the table.

"Marvellous, darling," he chimed distractedly. "I shall do us a roast if you like, all the trimmings."

She looked away and buttoned her coat. He closed his kit. She took a few steps into the room towards him. "You alright, Martin? You look peaky."

"My blood sugar's a bit up the spout, but nothing jam can't fix."

"You should see the doctor."

"I know. I tried calling the surgery, but they've changed the system again now apparently. You have to go in between 8 and 9 if you want to get seen that day, and they give you a ticket or something. It's bloody hopeless. You can't speak to a person anymore. I called and left a message yesterday. At least I think I did. It didn't say the 'leave your message after tone' thing; there was no... no outgoing message, you know? There was a beep, so anyway, I rambled on until there was another beep. I'm not sure if it worked. I'm going to call again in a minute. I don't know if there's anyone there on a Saturday though; probably not. It's all gone to buggery." He looked up at her. He wished she'd let him do something with her hair, it was so flat and lifeless. "I'll see the doctor on Monday. Sweet of you to care."

"Righto," she said. There was that awkwardness again. "Where's Bimbo? Have you seen him?"

"Yes, he's been in. I gave him his biscuits. He's probably out chasing birds." She was rather sorry she wouldn't see him before she left the house. Seeing Bimbo before leaving for the day was like ticking a box and she felt out of sorts if she left without seeing him. Now Martin was here, Bimbo got fed earlier in the morning so she rarely saw her cat first thing anymore. Bimbo's schedule had changed with his arrival. Something else she resented Martin for. "And when you come back, I'll have a lovely surprise waiting for you."

"What?"

"Do I really need to explain the concept of 'surprise' to you again, darling?"

"Martin, please don't. I don't like surprises. What is it?"

"You'll see. What train are you catching?"

"The 8:50."

"Well, you'd better run then, hadn't you?"

She arrived at Sheerness-on-Sea a little after 10am. There'd been a bus replacement service from Whitstable to Faversham, which came with its own delays. Then she got the train from Faversham to Sittingbourne, changing there for Sheerness. The most bizarre of the stops before hers, was Swale, under a flyover taking you across a narrow band of swampy water to the wretched isle. There was nothing at Swale other than the platform and the steps down to a layby under the flyover. There wasn't a house or a shop or anything. Just a road to nowhere, the flyover and swamp. She looked across the brownfield scrubland at pylons, sick-looking horses and a distant place where literally hundreds of delivery lorries were parked.

Through her train window on that dreary February morning, she saw wasteland industrial parks for businesses that had no business still functioning in this decade. Large numbers of fenced-off capacitor banks, which must have looked very fly and space-aged when they were built, buzzed sadly with a lost greyness. As train rides go, this one rated near the incredibly low end of the God-awful spectrum.

Then there was the long, straight run up to the town. She was puzzled as to why Sheerness needed two platforms, one to arrive at and another to leave by, when there was only the one track in and out, this was the end of the line. The platforms would have looked rather lovely when they were built in their Edwardian heyday. White-painted ornate ironwork now greying and leaching tears of rust. The track was marked with hefty sleepers between iron posts painted white except for a thin red line through the middle, like a cartoon

Victoria sponge. There were ugly and depressed teenagers on the platform; pierced, tattooed, acned. Presumably they were trying to get out for the day, to see the wonderful sights of exotic Sittingbourne. Or more likely just hanging around the station till there was something on TV or their tea was ready, or their medication kicked in. Her overthinking kicked off.

They have so little imagination nowadays, she thought, *no idea how to occupy time. If someone suggested something, to them they'd moan about it being 'so lame'. If it isn't served up to them on a plate, they complain, and if it is, they complain. There's no getting out there and making things happen. There's no mending and making do; no borrowing or sharing; no effort or goodwill, although they have so much more than my generation ever had. A spoilt generation who'd never suffered hardship, never wanted for anything, but at the same time, complained bitterly and sneered and criticised and moaned relentlessly about how difficult things are for them. Too much wishbone and not enough backbone. No rolling up of sleeves and mucking in. No contribution. No accountability. Just whining and an overinflated sense of self-worth and entitlement, but they'll have a rude awakening one day*, she thought, *when they realise that in the real world, they won't get a gold star for just showing up and there's no one there to hold their hand, or give them what they want or need, or comfort them*

*or give them a job, or that money or anything else they
felt entitled to but haven't earned and so don't fucking
deserve. The world owed them nothing, and they were
too spoilt and ignorant to know it. Innocence was not
what filled their dead, grey eyes, it was malevolence;
brooding and bitter.* Her lips tightened to nothing; she
was so angry. She despised them, the wasted youth.

She'd tried to book a room at the local Premier Inn, but
surprisingly they were fully booked for a conference.
She decided to chance her arm and just show up at
Sheerness and see what she could find. She could always
go back home if she came unstuck. There was bound
to be an hotel near the station, there always was. A
surprisingly ornate red brick building with large
surrounding windows, arched in red and white. The
alcove windows jutted out over the street supported by
the same leafy stonework that formed the architrave
moulding over the entrance on the street corner. She'd
waited at the reception desk for nearly five minutes
before the girl arrived, vacantly pushing a vacuum
cleaner. She apologised profusely and said she didn't
know anyone was waiting. She explained that guests
could check in any time after 11.

"Can I check in now?"

The girl looked at her for a moment. "Have you
booked?"

"No."

"…Yes, that will be fine." She started to type. She passed her a card to complete: name, address, car registration if relevant, signature. She explained the price didn't include breakfast although they did serve it from 7 to 11am in the dining room for £7.50, continental or the full English. "It's payment in advance, please. Cash or card?" She passed her the cash. "Lovely. I'll show you to your room, Mrs…" She looked down at the card. "Mrs West."

She put her bag on the bed and unzipped the sides. She travelled light. Between her neatly folded blouse and tomorrow's underwear was just the street map, her mother's home enema kit in its travel case and a small-sized, ziplocked freezer bag containing about thirty of Martin's sleeping pills. She hung her clothes in her cupboard, zipped up the sides of her bag and put it in the wardrobe. She put her handbag strap over her shoulder, retrieved her key from the sideboard (an actual key on a plastic fob rather than a card in a torn paper wallet) and left her room.

She strolled by a large Tesco opposite the station, passed a tired, ghastly-looking shed with 'Funhouse Amusements' on the side in dull shades from the 1950s, and a sinister-looking yellow clown face, with more than a passing resemblance to Donald Trump. There was a burger place and some filthy bins outside shaped like penguins facing the sea with their mouths open, full of rubbish, covered in gulls.

The sea was as leaden grey as the sky, choppy. The brown, gravelly sands churned noisily in the grimy shingle. She wanted to walk along the front, but it didn't look like she could turn left and walk along that way. The sea there lapped against the concreted beach and the path was fenced off. Behind was a city of shipping containers. She walked the other way. On her right was the back of the town's high street shops, and on her left were some wide, concrete steps down to the sea with a narrow strip of wet, diarrhoea-coloured beach. The tide was high. The steps ran the length of the walkway and were possibly nicer in the summer.

She walked for about ten minutes before finding a small bench inside a wooden hut, out of the gusting wind. There was a bunch of dead flowers tied to the bench, and a deflated balloon with the word 'gran' written on it. She'd already had enough of Sheppey. She looked at her watch. It wasn't even quarter to eleven. She sat down feeling instantly relieved to be out of the windchill. The promenade too was concrete and separated from the shoddy-looking buildings by the sea defence wall in yet more concrete. Barren and bleak, the town to horizon was devoid of colour, just gritty concrete and soulless shades of grey.

On the wide steps she saw letters painted upside-down. She stood and walked across to read them. The words ran for some distance, so it was hard to make sense of the whole thing. She turned and stepped down a step with the sea lapping, splashing on the lower steps behind her. *'Buried in the belly of its liberty… Snapped in half… This wartime souvenir…'* A poem or something.

"Morning." It made her jump. She looked up to see a surprisingly cheerful old man in front of her. "You can see it on a clear day."

"See what?"

"The Montgomery." It was clear from her expression that she didn't know what he was talking about. "That's what it means when it says 'wartime souvenir'. You can sometimes see its masts sticking out of the water." She looked at him blankly. "It was heading home at the end of the war but sank in the middle of the estuary there; blown off course into shallow waters. Full of high explosives. They managed to get about half of them out, but after a few days the whole thing broke in two. It's still got 3,000 tonnes of explosives packed in its waterlogged hull to this day. I reckon the actual amount is significantly higher than that. It was too dangerous to try to do anything about it at the time, so they left it there, marked out so no ships go near it."

"It can't still be dangerous, can it?"

"Different experts have differing views. They say that if it does go off it would be the biggest non-nuclear explosion there had ever been. It would destroy all of this." He said gesturing to the delightful seaside town. "Locally, we call it the Doomsday Ship. It would blow out the windows of east London thirty miles away. It would cause a tsunami too. That's what this bit means." He pointed to the letters on the step at her feet.

She read them to herself. '...*But whisper to yourself, that you can see the end of the world from here*'. She looked up, back up at the little man. He had a big smile on his face. She started to chuckle and looked out to sea to see if she could see the end of the world. She stepped back up onto the promenade. The old man chuckled too.

"Shouldn't really laugh though," he said sombrely, "it's a very real and present danger for the people here." In the silence she nodded respectfully. They both guffawed. "Best to go out with a bang though, I suppose," he said as he continued his morning constitutional, giving her a cheery wave as he did so. She wondered if she'd recognise the end of the world if she did see it, looming on her horizon.

It was cold. She walked briskly back to her hotel room. She wasn't in there more than two minutes. No time like the present. She stuffed the street map, enema kit and pills into her bag and was soon outside again, heading towards the street that turned into Halfway Road. She didn't need to get the map out. She'd traced the route with her fingernail.

The road was residential, quiet and unassuming. There wasn't a soul around. It turned out to be further than she'd thought. She was beginning to feel breathless.

Suddenly, there it was, with a flutter of butterflies in her tummy, Power Station Road. Her pace quickened as she turned right, and the wind gusted up. In just a few minutes she'd be just one door away from Irene. She didn't know what was going to happen after that door opened, but that was not going to stop her.

Almost immediately she saw the turning on the right, Sunnyside Avenue. She took a deep breath and turned into it, passing the first few houses and then on to the house where she must live; and there it was. That must be it. She drank it in, but her pace didn't slow.

The house was detached, pebble dashed and ugly; two-up, two-down. Plain. So plain in fact that it stood out from the others. It looked neglected. The wheelie bin at the front was stuffed so full that the lid couldn't close properly. She could see dirty carrier bags full of household waste and loose fizzy drink bottles stuffed in the side. Crisp packets. She began to doubt she had the right house. This didn't look like Irene. Maybe things had slipped since Trethendar. Maybe she'd always been a secret slob at home as well as a total tight-arse. She couldn't see Irene eating crisps and drinking pop though.

There was a small aluminium gate painted dark green. She pushed it open with a squeaky swing and walked the few steps up the pebbled, cast concrete path to the front door. She pushed the doorbell but didn't hear it ring; she waited. The door had two long windows of textured glass. It was dark inside. There was a sliver of daylight at the far end. The kitchen? The house felt empty. She rang the bell again. Still no life. She looked up to see if there was any sign behind the upstairs windows. She glanced over her shoulder. Not a soul in sight. Not a twitching net. She knocked on the door with her gloved knuckle and waited again.

She stepped backwards, off the front step. Then, a noise inside. Was it from Irene's or next door? Sounded like a door closing, then footsteps. It wasn't the neighbours. The muffled steps got louder as someone hurried down the stairs. She took a deep breath. How long had it been since she last saw Irene? A figure took shape and loomed nearer the door. But something was wrong. Reaching for the lock of the door through the wobbly glass was a younger woman's hand. The door swung open.

"Yes?"

She was in her mid-thirties, early-forties. Brusque with insincere courtesy, like an estate agent on her day off. Not Irene.

"Good morning," Myra said to the stranger with warm smile. "I'm so sorry to trouble you. I'm... I'm looking for Irene Hartley?"

"She doesn't live here. She moved."

12

"Perhaps you can help me, then." The woman frowned and looked over Myra's shoulder. It was clearly a bad time. "My name is Janice Lucas and I'm from Reeves Plaistow International. An independent market research agency based in London. Ms Hartley used to help us out from time to time by taking part in lifestyle surveys and as a thank-you for taking part, she'd be entered into free draws for cash prizes up £2,000."

"Oh, I see. Well, she moved about two months ago."

"Could you tell me where she's moved to?"

"I don't mind doing it, if you want?"

She smiled, floored for a flash. "That's incredibly kind of you, but it's a tracking survey. Ms Hartley was a panel member, you see. We ask the same people the same questions to track how their views, opinions and levels of awareness and so on vary over time."

Disappointedly, she replied, "Oh."

"So, it really is Ms Hartley I need to speak to. I'll make a note of your address, though, if you like and ask them to send you an application."

"Alright, I don't mind." She had scratchcard grey under her fingernails.

"So, do you know where she moved to?"

"Yes, she's at Heath Drive. Number twenty."

"Is that far?"

"Ten minutes or so if you're walking. You need to go back the way you came, then when you get to Halfway Road, turn left. When you get to the T-junction, turn right. That's Queenborough Road. Heath Drive is the second or third road on the right, I forget which."

"Number twenty."

"Yes. It might be the third road on the right. If you notice St Peter's Close, you've gone too far. It should be signposted." She reached inside. "Oh, and you couldn't you give her these, could you?" She pulled out a stack of about twenty or so assorted letters, giving them to Myra. "She said she had the mail redirect thing, but they still seem to be coming here. I mean I don't mind, but it's a bit annoying." She took a step inside and closing the front door.

"Thank you so much. Sorry once again to disturb you." Myra walked back towards the gate.

"No bother."

She walked briskly back the way she'd come. Her flush of nerves dissipated. At the end of the road was a grey-looking office or factory or something. She turned left, passing a long rusty, corrugated building covered with lichen. At the end of the road was the T-junction with a worn-away white roundabout painted on the tarmac, overlooked by a friendly-looking pub. She turned right, away from Minster, and passed a tyre replacement centre and Chariots minicabs. It was all so bleak.

The Victorian terrace looked like it had been picked up from London's East End and dumped on this wasteland. The absence of parked cars added to a Dickensian feel and hinted at the average income of the locals. Then some larger houses appeared, perhaps twenty years old, and some larger open spaces that looked like private land, but none of it was any less flat, or desolate.

The houses thinned out and the road, obviously a busy main road by Sheppey standards, was flanked by more empty space, with industrial-looking spikes and blocks on the horizon. There was a graveyard then a large, well-stocked garden centre. She waited on the kerb as a car pulled in, giving her a smile with raised palm of thanks. The natives seemed friendly enough. Maybe she had misjudged the place. The Sheerness Holiday Park had some flashy, modern trailer homes and entertainments for adults as well as the kiddies.

The road turned into a low-lying bridge over a wide expanse of still water. On one side a traveller site with horses, cackling kids playing roughly and piles of tyres and scrap metal. On the other, another Victorian terrace. She must be nearing the town again soon, she thought, realising she'd walked nearly a full circle, clockwise from the Station Hotel.

The first on her right was Belmont Road with signs to a discount warehouse. There was a funeral director, a school, some bungalows, then Western Avenue on the right. She carried on. Neatly trimmed lawns between the pavement and widening road appeared on the leafy avenue. These smartly kept bungalows, with clipped hedges and well-established shrubs and rockeries were a far cry from the nearby Victorian streets. More like suburban Surrey. Turning right into Heath Drive, she walked more slowly, beginning to savour her approach. She checked the house numbers. Irene's must be a bungalow on the right. Sixteen. Eighteen. And there is it was.

The small house was perfectly symmetrical, with a path that divided the handkerchief lawn in two equal parts, taking you from pavement to door. A red, shiny mobility scooter sat under a plastic cover. A gentle concrete slope led to the front door (sheltered by an overly large porch) and white handrail, both looked like recent additions to this home of infirmity. The grass either side of the path was almost ready for its first cut of the year. Two baby monkey-puzzle trees were planted, unimaginatively, either side. There was a drive of sorts, an off-road space for a small car, but no car. Large, double-glazed windows, more plain nets. There was no doorbell, just a slimline, brass-effect knocker. She knocked. She immediately heard a voice inside.

"Coming." It was Irene Hartley. The voice was unmistakable. Myra was conscious of some huffing and puffing and difficulty getting to the door, which eventually opened with a, "Good God!" She instantly recognised the woman on her doorstep from her wheelchair. "Janice. Janice Mead!" Her ginger hair had given way to the grey. Sheppey drained the colour from everything.

"Hello, Irene."

"What on earth…? How lovely to see you! What are you doing here?"

"I'm sorry I couldn't call ahead. It was a bit of a spontaneous thing."

"Won't you come in?" she said as she manoeuvred her chair backwards. "I hope you don't mind a bit of mess."

She stepped inside. "Thank you. I can't stay too long unfortunately."

"Come on through. How ever did you find me?"

"Well, I always meant to visit. I only live in Whitstable after all…"

"Of course you do. I remember. Please sit down." She pointed her towards the sitting room.

"But I was passing, and I had some news so…"

"News? Oh dear, that can't be good. Tea? Coffee? I was just making one. I'm afraid I don't have any milk if you don't mind drinking it black…?"

Myra said, "Coffee please. No sugar." Irene wheeled herself to the kitchen.

"I called at your old house first. I have some post for you."

"Oh, thank you. That's kind. Though it's probably all junk."

Myra stood in silence, gazing through the nets and out into the bleak, deserted road.

Irene wheeled herself back in. "Please sit down. Take off your gloves and coat. Myra sat on the sofa to the side of the window just in case anyone approached the house and managed to see in. She took off her coat. "Well, I'm blowed. Thank you for being postman. I'll go through them later. I just can't believe it. It's so lovely to see you, Janice."

"You too, Irene. It's been a very long time."

"Yes, it certainly has. I almost shudder to think how long." There was a silence for a moment. The kettle came to the boil and clicked off. "Two ticks." And she was gone again. She seemed slightly desperate. A little too happy to see her. Irene had always been brusque and brutally direct. Perhaps retirement had mellowed her. Perhaps she had softened. Perhaps it was her new-found predicament, her disability, her vulnerability, loneliness, which meant she had to develop some charm, a warmth, a little humanity even.

"Can I help you with anything?" she called out.

"No, thank you. I need to be able to manage." She rolled back into the room very slowly with the tray balanced on her knees with two half-empty cups, the bottoms sitting in pools of coffee and/or tea. She wondered for a moment, absently, why Janice was sitting all the way over there, at that end of the sofa when what was clearly her own armchair was at the other end, pointing at the television in the corner with a perfect view of anyone coming up the path. "So how on earth are you?"

"I'm very well, thank you."

"And Trethendar? Still going from strength to strength?"

"Well, things have been quieter recently. We've had a few difficult years."

"You must be coming up to retirement yourself pretty soon, I should expect?"

"Yes, I am. July in fact. Just under five months now. Not that I'm counting."

"Make sure you have plenty to do is my advice. I've seen too many good people keel over prematurely, within months of retirement, for the want of some proper stimulation and activity."

"Do you manage to keep yourself busy?"

"Oh heavens, yes. I'm on the board of several local charities. I'm governor of the school just down the road here. There's *Sheerness in Flower*. What else? I bowl now, would you believe it? And I even have a column on upcoming events in the local rag. My feet barely touch the ground, in fact." Her face clouded with a slight bitterness. "This wretched situation is a new development. It takes a bit of getting used to, but it will take a lot more to keep this old bird down."

"You're not in pain, are you?"

"Nothing to speak of. I can't complain. Anyway, what about you? I want to hear all your news."

"Well, there's nothing really." She shuffled awkwardly to the edge of her seat and picked her bag up. She put her cup on the occasional table to the left of the sofa arm. "I couldn't be a pain and use your loo, could I?"

"Of course. You passed it on your way in. Turn right and it's the door on the left." She stood sheepishly to leave the room. "Please excuse the state though. I've got someone in doing some improvements, access improvements..."

Myra looked to the left as she exited the room. At the bottom of the corridor was a door to the kitchen. Dulled morning daylight kept just enough of the dark out. There was perhaps a door there leading to a back garden. The door down the same end, on the right, must be the bedroom. She turned as instructed and stepped into the bathroom.

"...He's making some home adaptations for me. Handrails and so on. Ridiculous really, but it's a free government thing so I may as well take advantage.

And he's local too. Luckily I'm up with the lark and he has a key, so we don't get into each other's way too much."

The bathroom smelt of soap scum. An unpleasant avocado suite with limescaled showerhead hooked into a grimy attachment over the bath. Alternate tiles had a tacky floral motif stickered on, the grouting was missing in places and there was mildew on the mould-proof filler around the edge of the bath. In clear plastic wrapping to the side, the handrails waited to be fitted, a box of tools and a tub of grouting. The shower curtain was opaque and stiff with soap and scale. Towels, still damp from this morning's ablutions, hung on a cold radiator. Though the bath, curtain and walls were bone dry. It was a larger window for a bathroom than you'd normally see. There was a roller blind that could be pulled down over the nets. High over the pedestal handbasin, possibly too high for Irene to use now, was a mirrored cabinet and directly over the sink, a plastic cup and toothbrush holder. There was a range of bathroom accessories on the sink and more in the wicker and raffia corner stand behind the door.

She took the cup from its holder and looked at the grime inside. The flowery pattern matched the wall tiles. Still holding the toothbrush cup, she stepped out silently and hurried down the corridor to the kitchen. The kettle was still steaming. She poured some water from the kettle into the cup. She emptied it, so there was hardly any water left inside the cup, but just enough. It would do. Silently she hurried back towards the bathroom.

"Find it alright?" Irene called out to her.

"Yes, I was just trying to find my hanky," she replied from outside the bathroom. "Found it," she said, sounding like she had as she closed the bathroom door behind her, pulling the little bolt across, locking it.

Putting the cup on the edge of the sink, she rummaged in her bag for Martin's pills. She sat on the toilet seat, held the little cup between her knees and tipped a few of the pills in. She swished it around for a moment. *To hell with it*, she thought. She emptied about three quarters of the freezer bag of pills into the hot water. She continued to swill it around. The crisp, sugar shells started to dissolve. She swished it. It took too long. She stood and put the cup on top of the bathroom cabinet, nicely out of Irene's reach. She turned and flushed the toilet. She turned on the taps for a minute, then turned them off, paused and unbolted the door and stepped out and back into the sitting room with Irene as she adjusted her gloves.

"I couldn't help noticing..." Irene nodded towards her hands.

"Oh these. It's a bit of a nuisance."

"I hope you don't mind me asking?"

"Not at all. My hands feel cold all the time and it can be tricky to grip things. It's an annoyance more than anything else. A circulation thing. The gloves help." She sat back down again.

Irene looked frail. Birdlike, bonily perched in her wheelchair at an uncomfortable angle with scrawny, bare elbows on the thin metal arms and durable, wipeable, NHS padding. That watch she always wore with the oval face, and her liver-spotted hands and buzzard's forearms. There were bandages around her ankles under dark stockings, and her crinkly, old, scrotum neck craned forward as her head bobbed slightly with age. The whites of her eyes now the colour of antique ivory on a pub piano. Her teeth, yellowed, and the odd white whisker protruding from a random part of her face that her fading eyesight no longer had the ability, thankfully, to see.

"You said you had some news?"

"Yes, it's rather sad news, I'm afraid. You remember Ben?"

"Of course."

"Well, he passed away last year. July."

"Oh, I'm sorry to hear that. He couldn't have been that old."

"No. He was no age really."

"I remember that awful time," she put her hand to her forehead, "when we really thought Trethendar was going down the pan. Well, we were, we really were. Membership was down. No large legacies for God knows how long. There were just too many people employed there, many with precious little to do. We had very difficult decisions to make, but we had to think, first and foremost, of the members and the long-term viability of the charity. I remember the cuts and poor old Ben…" She laughed dryly as it all came flooding back to her. "I mean a lovely, lovely man, but what a dreadful waste of space he was." Myra looked up at her. "Really, if it hadn't been for Vera and I, Trethendar wouldn't have lasted more than two more years. Possibly three, at a push. I suppose, if I'm honest, I contributed to the financial problems as much as anyone. I blew things a bit with the marketing and the rebranding exercise. Both over budget and not as successful as I'd have liked. A gamble, an extravagance, you might say, but we had to invest. You have to speculate to accumulate." She smiled. "It was naughty of us, but Vera and I plotted for weeks and then, when he went on one of his long holidays in the summer like he always did, we struck. You won't have been aware…"

"I remember it."

"You do?"

"Yes, I had to do his compromise agreement."

"That's right, of course you did. Weren't you his secretary or something before you took over on the personnel side of things?"

Myra nodded. "It's called human resources. HR."

"Yes, of course it is. That must have made it quite difficult for you, I suppose, with hindsight. But you were such a pro, Janice, a real trooper." She thought for a moment. "Still, a lovely man, but when you're on such a downward trajectory, an organisation needs a leader at the helm, some ruthlessness, not a chap like him."

She smiled, "Do you have a garden?"

"Yes," she said, relieved for the change in subject, but without knowing why. "Let me show you around." She wheeled herself back and to the left so she could have a clear run at the door. She could go fast in her chair. Myra followed, down through the kitchen to the back door. They peered through at the gloomy garden, flat and rectangular. It had a lawn with borders around the edge, beds meant for flowers, but empty except for the odd weed sprouting. There was a child's swing squeaking in the breeze. "The previous owner had it for his granddaughter. You don't have to rush off, do you? Will you stay for lunch?"

Lunch was a hardboiled egg salad with some pieces of tinned tuna thrown in. Irene talked about her volunteering work and Myra, for the most part, just listened. She hadn't forgotten what had brought her there but wondered if there might be anything Irene could say that would change the decision. The old woman clearly wanted to talk, but there wasn't anything she said that changed Myra's mind. She loathed Irene Hartley now just as much as she had then, when she'd made her compromise Ben out of his job, and the charity he built and loved. Where had any of that horribleness got this woman? Absolutely nowhere. She had worked her whole life. Laboured, schemed and plotted and strategized, but for what? For this?

Trethendar would never be what it had once been. All work was, at the end of the day, fundamentally pointless. It all seemed so important and worthy at the time, but the charity's work had not moved the needle one iota. If Janice Mead had disappeared back then too, would anyone have been in the slightest bit bothered? Some of the members had of course benefited from the organisation, but the effort invested was totally disproportionate to the outcomes delivered. Trethendar seemed to exist predominantly to keep some of the world's most unemployable, employed. Sometimes it's better to just let nature take its course and let the fruit whither on the vine rather than try and keep it alive indefinitely, unnaturally. Couldn't Irene, at that time, just have been nice about it, though? No. She had enjoyed the plotting and ousting Ben; pleasured herself with the drama. But he was never the same; broken and hurt. Irene had been responsible for his declining health and, ultimately, his death but she hadn't dirtied her hands with any of it. She'd made Janice Mead, *personnel*, do it. A part of Irene got a kick out of ruining this lovely man's life. She enjoyed it. She'd laughed about it then, she was still laughing about it now, but there are consequences. *There is a price*, Myra thought, *and now, after all these years, and in this sorry little backwater of a dead-end fucking place, it's time to land a hard and long-overdue punch, for Ben.*

"Another cup of coffee, Janice? Or perhaps a little dry sherry?"

"Another coffee would be lovely but let me get it. I'll wash up while I'm there if you like. But I really must go after that." She collected the plates and went to the kitchen. She washed her own plate and fork, dried them and put them away. She left the soapy water in the sink but left Irene's dirty plate and fork to the side. She boiled the kettle and put a teaspoon of decaf into each cup.

"Do you take sugar, Irene?"

"Just one please."

Silently and unseen, she walked to the bathroom and retrieved the toothbrush cup from the top of the cabinet, peering into it as she walked back to the kitchen. The tablets had dissolved. She wondered if the coffee would be enough to cover any taste from the pills, there had been so many... She swirled the drugged water around in the cup then emptied the contents into Irene's cup and gave it a good stir, adding two more sugars. She rinsed out the bathroom cup, dried it and returned it to its original position.

"Sorry I took so long," she said, coming back in.

Irene had been resting her eyes. "You're here now, but I mustn't keep you. Not that this hasn't been lovely. I hope you visit again soon."

"I'd love to." She passed the cup to Irene.

She took a sip. It was hot. Sweet. "Ooh, it's a strong one."

"Is it?" she said with a smile.

"I hope it doesn't keep me up."

The conversation slowed and the pauses lengthened until it all but dried up. There came a point when anyone with an ounce of social awareness would realise they were outstaying their welcome. Irene put the lights on as it started to darken outside, looking drowsier as time dragged on. She didn't know what time it was, but it was twilight; it must have been around 5pm. She didn't want to appear rude and look at her watch, but she couldn't understand why Janice was still there. It was getting late. Was she going to be put in the position where she'd have to make her excuses and ask Janice to leave?

Her sleepy eyes nipped, and her head started to loll. Myra stood, taking her bag to the bathroom. She pulled the roller blind down. She thought about turning the light on, but the orange glow of a streetlamp a few doors down gave her enough light to work.

She had given the old woman more than enough chances and every opportunity to redeem herself, but she'd said nothing. Nothing said had made her think twice about what she had gone there to do. The evil old bitch deserved everything she had coming to her.

She took the showerhead off the wall bracket and hung up the blue enema bag, screwing the clear, rubbery connecting tube into place. To the loose end with the little tap, she fixed the longer, more flexible of the two attachments that came with the kit. Back in the lounge, Irene's chin was on her chest, out for the count. Myra switched off the light and rusty orange streetlamp light filled the room. Walking around the edge of the space, she drew the curtains.

Back in the bathroom, she ran the taps, tipping some of Irene's bluey-green bath salts into the water. She took the shower head and flipped the mixer-tap lever so the water sprayed out, using the jet to stir the bath and dissolve the herbal crystals more time-efficiently. It was difficult to know how deep the water should be. Deep enough, but not so deep that it could splash over the sides. She filled it about three quarters full, body temperature. She turned off the taps and looked around. Everything was ready. She'd been careful not to touch anything, even with gloved hands, that she didn't absolutely have to. The tap dripped once, twice, then silence.

Irene was in the same position as before. Breathing very deeply now, almost unnaturally deeply; snoring softly like Bimbo sometimes did. She took the handles of the wheelchair and pulled the old woman gently into the bathroom, next to the bath, without waking her.

She hurried out again and went to the bedroom, drawing the curtains. Flicking on the light, glancing around, breathing quickly, shallowly. She took Irene's dressing gown from the bed, removing the cord as she headed back to the bathroom.

When she re-entered, to her horror, Irene was awake, sitting there looking around sleepily.

"Janice…" she said weakly.

"It's alright," she said. "I've called an ambulance. You had a nasty turn. They said I had to get you ready." She started to unbutton the old woman's blouse as her head lolled, her heavy eyelids closing.

Moving faster now, she pulled her forward and yanked the blouse off. She undid the bra clasp and pulled it off, over her shoulders and down her arms. She pushed her back and took the dressing gown cord, using it to tie her wrists to the chair. She threw the dressing gown into the corner of the room so it wouldn't get wet and pushed the door shut, bolting it. She went back to Irene and reached behind her waist and then to the side, looking for the clasp and zip to her skirt. She found it, pulled it off and threw that too into the corner of the room with the rest of her clothes, as far from the bath as possible. She had to work quickly. It was important she didn't mark the woman; she looked over-ripe, and she'd easily bruise. She removed the deadweight's underwear with a struggle. She paused, breathless, standing over the elderly woman's tiny, naked frame, unconscious, tied to her wheelchair.

She took the toothbrush cup from the sink and, double-checking that the tube tap was in the off position, used it to fill the enema bag with bathwater. Filling it right up. She held Irene's chin, but her mouth wouldn't open, so she squeezed the corners of her jaw like she did when opening Bimbo's mouth to give him a worming pill. Her jaw opened enough to put the tube's end in, and she stuffed it down her throat. Irene's eye's opened as she gagged, sudden dawning panic and confusion. Myra, with one hand holding the woman's chin up with the tube in place down her throat, turned the tap, filling the scrawny, bitch full of bathwater.

Her feet kicked about, and her wrists pulled against the robe cord holding her to the chair as the bag emptied into the woman, much quicker than Myra could have hoped. She turned the enema tube tap to off then refilled the bag. The turning of the tap and the filling of the bathwater bag made Irene struggle more. In between, there was almost a stillness, almost a calm as she took on the bathwater, her stomach slowly distending. She hardly made a noise. Just gurgling, gentle gagging and dutiful swallowing. An occasional belch, that stank rank and sulphurous, of coffee, egg and tuna. She couldn't talk with the tube down her throat, although there was some moaning and whimpering. But Myra worked so quickly and within the blink of an eye this phase was over, and she had filled the old woman with five enema bags-full of bathwater, stopping only then because she started to retch more frequently and more ferociously.

It would have been easier to suffocate her first then put her in the bath, but she knew they'd have found no bathwater in her stomach and conclude that she must have died prior to entering the bath. But now the moment was upon her, it dawned that she hadn't brought anything in to suffocate her with. She could fetch a pillow from the bedroom, but that was too obvious, and the wet... She mustn't create evidence. She could put her hand over her mouth, but she could get bitten and bleed: evidence.

The next bit would be trickier. She scolded herself for the error with a cold objectivity. It would have been easier to put her into the bath lifeless, but now, thinking on her feet, she would have to do it in the bath. Decanting the old woman over the side when she was still alive would be tricky, possibly splashy. She pulled the tube from her mouth and unpicked the dressing gown cord knotted round the wrists as quick as she could. *How do you put an old woman in a bath? Top half first or bottom half? Probably top half.* She put her hands under her armpits and around her back.

"Janice... Janice? What are...?" she mumbled incoherently.

She leant forward as far as she could, her back bent and her face over Irene's shoulder. "I'm afraid," Myra said, as one of her hands found the other behind Irene's back, "you are now surplus to requirements." One hand gripped the wrist of the other, pulling the old woman to the edge of the chair. "And you've put me now in the very difficult... unenviable position..." With the angle she was at, she was in danger of putting her back out, but there was no other way. With a sharp wrench, she yanked belching Irene out and swung her round so her bottom was sitting on the rim of the bath. She then lowered Irene's floppy top half into the bath as slowly as she could, her lower legs dangling over the side from the knee, trying not to let any part of her hit anything too hard and, if possible, with no splashing. It was inevitable though. Her grip loosened and the old woman's loose back skin slipped through her fingers, like boiled chicken slipping off the bone, and into the bath. Myra stood, realising she was now sweating profusely from the exertion.

She picked up the bony knees next, her lower legs hanging side-saddle over the edge of the bath, and let her hands slip down to her ankles. Then she bustled around to the foot of the bath and without pausing, pulled her feet up with one great slippery tug, so that Irene's head and face plunged under the water and her greyed, red hair swam in the warm water like mucous at the public baths. She reasserted her grip on the skinny ankles, as they'd started to kick about in the air above the bath.

Irene's underwater eyes opened wide in blind panic. She writhed feebly, as far as her infirmity would allow. She coughed below the surface, her chest heaved and convulsed as she retched from the pit of the stomach, pumping vomit from her mouth, spat into the turquoise, scented water. Small pieces of hard-boiled egg white and masticated salad greens filled the bath around her face with red specs of chewed tomato skin and sandy-coloured coffee, brown like the churned estuary sea.

It didn't matter. In fact, it was all window dressing for the scenario being created. Irene's hands reached for the sides of the bath as large bubbles of air from her mouth broke the water's surface. Her frail, bony fingers trying, uselessly, to get a grip on the sudsy bath sides. The water between her legs turned a deeper lime green as she pissed in panic. Her guttural, animal croaking and choking, muffled by her breath bubbling submarine. Irene tried to get some leverage to pull her bodyweight up and out of the warm, soapy water, but she was too heavy for her thin arms and the angle of her wrists was wrong. It was all wrong, she weakened and, eyes wide, gulped.

Myra tightly held the ankles, occasionally giving a tug if it looked like she might get a grip and lift her head up. She didn't want her to get her nose or mouth above the water level. She couldn't risk her taking even one breath and using it to cry out. The property was detached, but even so. How much longer? It was taking an eternity. Even as she held her there and watched her drown, she imagined that less time may be passing than she was perhaps perceiving. Perhaps it was all less than a minute rather than the four or five it felt. The struggling stopped and after a few spasmodic jerks, no more bubbles came from Irene's mouth. Myra's grip on her ankles loosened a little.

"I'm afraid, Irene," she said, "I'm going to have to let you go."

She gently placed the old woman's feet in the bath and attempted to arrange her knees to make it look like she'd slipped under. But her knees kept falling open, exposing the old woman's quim, like a mouldy orange. She didn't want that. She decided to leave one foot poking out, the ankle resting on the bath edge. It looked a little casual, but to Myra it appeared in keeping with the tragic scenario she was trying to create and still preserve some post-mortem modesty.

She stood in the silence. Hard to know how long; long enough to ensure there were no moments when Irene suddenly gasped for life and leapt from the water to attack her. But no such shriek-inducing, twisting-in-the-tale happens in reality. She looked at her watch and decided she'd wait there for exactly five more minutes before doing anything else. Myra knew there was no hope of survival of the brain if it was deprived of oxygen for three minutes, so opted for five, for the avoidance of doubt. She sat on the toilet and stared at the dead face under the water, the wavy, grey, seaweed hair, now frozen in time in a pool of vomit, piss and luxury bath salts.

She looked at her watch. *Time's up*.

She took down the enema bag and hung the showerhead back on its wall bracket, put the bag and tubes into the sink and flicked off the worst of the water, then tightly wound the tubes up and wrapped the blue enema bag, the driest part, around them and put the whole thing back in its carrycase, and back in her bag. She took off her gloves and immediately replaced them with her spare, dry pair.

She dried the cup used to fill the bag and replaced it in its holder over the sink. She hung the dressing gown on the back of the door, threading its cord back through the loops.

She took the clothes to the bedroom and folded them neatly but casually and placed them by the side of the bed. She turned over the duvet at the side and switched on the bedside lamp. Cosy.

In the kitchen, she ran the tap then took off her gloves to wash up the coffee cup she'd used. She put her gloves back on to dry the cup and put it away. She left nothing that might imply the old woman had been anything but alone, careful not to touch anything with an ungloved hand.

She left it all looking like Irene had had her supper as normal and then left the plate and so on by the sink to wash up in the morning. She'd been too tired to do it that night. She was new to the house, and the disability adjustments had not yet been completed. It would all look like a terrible accident, and because she was old and had had a good innings, no one would look more closely. She'd be discovered on Monday morning by the man coming to finish the work to make the bathroom safe. When there was no reply, he'd let himself in as she'd lent him the spare and she wasn't used to the mobility scooter yet. He'd think she was probably out the back and wouldn't think twice. As for the sleeping pills, surely there'd be no suspicion of anything other than what it clearly was, a tragic, but perhaps preventable, accident. She'd probably thrown up most of them anyway and he'd inevitably pull the plug and drain the bath when he saw her. Though understandable in the circumstances, he might be criticised for that. They rarely ask questions when an old person dies. It's hardly unexpected and her quality of life was not what it was. It was probably a blessing. Irene had no family either, that anyone knew of. She must have been lonely. It was a release, possibly even a kindness.

She made one final check of the bungalow, room by room. She stood in the lounge for a moment to ensure there was no one outside to see her leave. Then, quickly and unseen, she left.

13

It was about 6:50pm when Myra arrived back in her hotel room with the dreadful chicken burger, chips and can of cola she'd picked up on the way. She considered leaving there and then and getting the next train home, but that may have drawn attention. She sat on the edge of the lumpy bed and bit into her chicken burger, chewing slowly in the dark room. She hadn't considered it would have taken as long as it did. She wanted to get back to normality as soon as possible, but instead circumstance required her to remain frozen in the moment. She resolved to stay, watch television and have an early night. She wouldn't stay for breakfast. She'd check out at the earliest opportunity in the morning and return home.

It took her ages to drop off and she didn't sleep well. Normally, Bimbo would jump up after she'd rolled onto her side to sleep. He'd lie next to her, his pink nose almost touching hers. His paw resting on her hand and if she rested her hand on his, he'd pull it out and put it back on top again. He needed his paw to be on top. He needed to be the one giving the comfort. He'd close his eyes and purr with a contended smile. Sometimes he'd reach out his arm and put his velvet paw on her cheek. He'd leave it there as long as he deemed necessary, before removing it and resting it again on the back of her hand. He was a comforter. Also a sage, confidante, comrade, Zen master and comic genius. He was old now too and a dear friend. In that moment, she needed him more than ever. His gentle touch and benign, trusted, trusting face. Her best-beloved.

It was one of those nights where she felt she'd not really slept at all, but probably had more than she thought. She awoke at 6:37am feeling refreshed.

After her normal bathroom routine, she was packing her things, then checking and double-checking herself in the almost full-length mirror on the back of the wardrobe door. A final quick scan of the room for anything left behind. Confident, she exited the room and went down to reception. She was asked if she wanted breakfast but said she didn't really eat breakfast; she'd rather just check out. She'd paid in full and there were no extra charges, so it was just a case of handing the key back and saying goodbye.

The station was a stone's throw away. She didn't know when the next train would be. She crossed the road. All she did know was that there would probably only be one every hour as it was a Sunday. She might be in for a wait if she'd just missed one. But having waited only fifteen minutes, the train left at 8am, arriving at Sittingbourne at 8:17. Unfortunately, she then had to wait until 8:55 as the essential rail works were still going on. She'd have to get the bus replacement service from Sittingbourne back to Whitstable, arriving ten minutes after its scheduled arrival time of 9:35.

As she walked towards home from the station, her pace quickened at the prospect of seeing Bimbo. It had only been a little over twenty-four hours since she last saw him, but still. She missed him. She was going to be a lot earlier than she'd told Martin she'd be, but hopefully that would mean he wouldn't have time for whatever this surprise was he was planning. Maybe it was tickets to some dreadful, local amateur thing. Martin did seem rather hardwired into the local community and its goings-on. She hoped the surprise wasn't anything too radical like reconfiguring the furniture in the sitting room or reorganising the kitchen drawer.

She didn't have to arrive home before the nature of Martin's surprise became all too apparent to her. She turned right into Nelson Road and looked up to see her home at the end, looking back at her from the T-junction, the other side of Whitman Road and her jaw dropped open. Her leylandii. What had that fucking bastard done to her leylandii?

Its surrounding protection from the harsh light and prying eyes had been hacked away, exposing the house; the trees, brutalised by an amateur. He'd sawn and chopped at the branches, but not all the way up. Only as far as he could reach using a short ladder. He had clearly cut some branches from the upstairs windows too, but the job was unfinished, and the five trees now stood like poodle tails. Ugly trunks, rudely exposed up to the windows with thicker foliage above the window level. Branches lay piled at the front, hacked off and untidily heaped like a pterodactyl nest. The shutters covering the upstairs windows, and always hidden from view by the trees, were now exposed. The house that wouldn't have attracted a second glance was now an attention-grabbing eyesore; the house of a weirdo, a hoarder, a crazy cat lady, or some other subcategory of nutter.

She was incensed by the mess; as exposed as her house. She didn't want anyone to see her like that, knowing her business, staring, gawking in through her windows. She didn't even know who her neighbours were. A good fence makes for good neighbours and the house, with its impenetrable dark green wall, had always screamed loudly and clearly, to all who laid eyes on it and had wondered, to mind their own business and keep the fuck away.

She turned her key in the lock and took a deep breath.

He was obviously up and about because the curtains were open, as was the kitchen window, but the house was quiet, and she knew in an instant it was empty. Perhaps he'd popped out for a paper or a tool to finish his handiwork. She went straight upstairs and put her bag on the bed and began unpacking. She started to put the enema kit away but then decided to throw it out instead. She wouldn't be needing it anymore. She hung up her clothes and put her toiletries back in the bathroom. The only thing left to put away was the sleeping pills.

His door was shut. He always kept his door shut. She hadn't used all the pills; best to return the leftovers. She stood there at the top of the stairs, of that empty house, with them clenched in her hand. The house was too still. She could tell when he was in or had been there recently. She could even tell if Bimbo had moved from one place to another and stirred the emptiness, but he hadn't. It was the kind of stillness you'd get after returning home after a week away, before collecting him from the cattery.

"Bimbo?" she called in the voice he was so familiar with and responsive to. "Bimbo?"

Silence. Stillness.

She went down to the sitting room and checked the spots where he normally sat. She looked in the kitchen. His bowl was half-full. He'd obviously been around. In the garden, perhaps. From the kitchen window she saw a similar sight of barbaric desolation as at the front. It was as if he'd just hacked and butchered away at anything he could reach. Clearly beyond his capabilities. If he really wanted to do it, he should have called professionals in, but no, he had to try and do it all himself. A complete and utter mess. Martin had no sense of the scale of a task, of what things involved and the level of knowledge, skill and experience required to complete it effectively and efficiently. Instead, he'd stride in there, armed only with good intentions, the kind of 'good intentions' used for paving roads to ruin, and create ground-zero disaster zones for someone else to clear up and fix for him. He'd have a little-boy-lost look on his face and try and charm his way out of sorting it himself; and feet-draggingly, shuffle off, looking for something else to stick his unwelcome fucking oar into.

"Bimbo?"

She hoped he was OK. Perhaps he'd taken him to the vet. The vet's closed on a Sunday, but there's that emergency vet you can call, out of hours. Martin wouldn't know about that. If something had happened, he'd have called her first and asked her to come back and deal with it. It didn't make sense. Where were they? She continued to look till she'd looked everywhere.

She went back upstairs to get her mobile phone, to call Martin, wherever he was. She sat on the side of her bed, putting the leftover pills on the bedside table. She dialled his number. A pause, then she heard it ring. It rang inside the house. She stepped out of her room onto the landing. The ringing was coming from Martin's room. The one place she hadn't checked. She stopped the call and knocked on his door.

"Martin? Martin, are you there?" Silence. She turned the handle and pushed. It wasn't locked, but it wouldn't open either. Like someone the other side was trying to hold the door closed. "Martin?" She shoved harder. The door opened just wide enough for her to realise the thing stopping the door was on the floor. She put her shoulder to it, this time with all her body weight and the door opened just wide enough for her to see Martin flat out on the floor inside. She continued to force the door until it was wide enough for her to squeeze through if she breathed in and put one limb through at a time, going in sideways, stepping over his shoulders. She had to pull her skirt up over her knees so she could get her legs wide enough apart to get one through, then the other.

He was lying on his stomach, arms to the sides. A bloated, purply-grey cheek pressed against the carpet, pushing his jowly mouth ajar. She stared at the face. It didn't look like Martin. It didn't feel like a person. His eye, half-open, was dry and matt. His body was still; flatter but no thinner, he spread over the floor, stone-dead.

She'd have to call an ambulance. Would they call the police? An undertaker? Was this suspicious? Would they ask what relation he was to her? She'd have to say 'husband'. He'd been married to her late mother. They'd know how long he'd been dead. They'd ask why she hadn't discovered him sooner. She'd have to say she'd been away. She'd have to say Sheppey, because if she lied, she knew there was a possibility she'd get caught in that lie. She'd been to check in on an old disabled friend. A former work colleague. How would a person who couldn't walk get into a bath? That's why the towels had been wet, but the bath and shower curtains had been dry. There was a possibility, possibly a high probability, that her lies would be found out, probably a certainty. Better the question never arose in their minds, than permit circumstances that could germinate suspicion and a question that might elicit a lie. Better that than have to field more questions with more lies and the inevitable unravelling as all trust crumbled away, irreparably, permanently. Or you tell the truth. How much truth you tell is a choice, of course. You can lessen the full force of judgement by giving the facts but create an alternative scenario that explains them; a context that maybe even generates some sympathy for you. A half-truth isn't the truth. Not telling the truth fully or fast enough, will be perceived as concealment and trust crumbles again. She'd need their trust. The answers must be complete and right first time. If you change the story, they'll conclude you were either lying then or you are lying now. You'll always be caught in a lie. Better by far to maintain a position that is completely beyond all suspicion. Her actual innocence in this one thing could unravel everything. Everything. *Focus.*

So, if they asked why she was in Sheppey, what would she say? She had no reason to be there. Would they check the station CCTV? They could ask where she stayed. They might call the hotel and find her name was not in the register. How could she explain that? She hadn't done anything to Martin, but her alibi, the truth, placed her somewhere she couldn't be, and *it was all his fault.* Irene would be found soon, too. She would be connected to that if they dug hard enough. Martin had ruined everything as per. *Focus, Myra.*

She had to stay calm. She had to stop. She had to stay calm. She had to do one thing at a time. Just one. She had to do the right thing first and right first time. Then decide what the next right thing was, do that and so on till it was all done. She needed to put his sleeping pills back in their bottle. The longer she was home without calling for help, the greater the suspicion that might fall on her. *Do it now.*

She squeezed through the door and back to her room to collect the tablets. She squeezed back into his room, through the narrow gap in the door and put them back in the bottle in his bedside table drawer.

Shit! She'd taken off her gloves when she unpacked her things. She had to work harder to focus and ensure she made no more mistakes.

She went for a wee on the way to her room to fetch her gloves. She peed when pressured. Pee first, gloves next. It was OK that her prints were on his door handle, in fact they had to be there for her to have found his body. It would look odd if they fingerprinted the place and they weren't there. She was overthinking, but better to overthink than miss an essential detail. She decided to fix the prints on his door handle once back outside his room. She forced her way back in and rubbed her gloved hands all over the handle of his bedside drawer and pulled it open so she could wipe the pill bottle too. Just before leaving, she scanned the room. Just under the edge of the bed she saw an unopened jar of raspberry jam on its side. She knew she had to leave it exactly where it was. She looked back down at Martin and stepped over his shoulders as she squeezed out for the final time, one stretched-out leg and then the other, closing the door behind her.

She had to call the ambulance now. She had to call right now. She couldn't arouse suspicion. She had to make it look like she'd called within minutes of discovering his body. Outside his room, she took her gloves off and put them in her pocket. She knocked on the door.

"Martin?" she called, hurriedly enacting the tragic, discovery scenario. She gripped the handle and pushed the door open. It opened about six inches before being obstructed by Martin's corpse. She tried to get in and realised she'd be able to say, and if needs be, to demonstrate, that she was just a little too wide in the hip to squeeze through the gap into the room and a little too weak to push the door any wider. She ran downstairs and dialled 999.

The ambulance arrived quickly. She'd told them she thought her husband was dead. That she hadn't been able to get to him, but she could just see his face and it was all grey and he didn't appear to be breathing, and she couldn't get the door open.

As it pulled up outside, a horrible dread surged that the paramedics would be the same ones who attended to her blacked-up mother about six weeks before; thankfully they weren't. One of them sat with her downstairs while the other went up to see to Martin.

"Had he been unwell?" asked the one sitting next to her on the settee.

"He's diabetic. We hadn't been together long. He kept that side of things to himself."

"Do you know if everything was under control?"

"He was complaining yesterday about his blood sugars being up the spout. He was calling and leaving messages with his doctor to try get an appointment for early next week. I don't know enough about it. Do you think that's what it was?"

"Possibly."

A minute or two later the other one came down and asked the one sitting with her for assistance. She asked if they needed her to come up too, but they said it wasn't necessary. She heard movement upstairs and muffled voices.

She heard one of them counting. "One, two, three…" *They must be lifting him*, she thought. Then it went quiet. She waited.

She heard the floorboards creak and the door to Martin's room being closed and soon she heard them quietly coming down the stairs. The one who went upstairs first popped out to his ambulance and the other came back to sit with her again and explain.

"We've put Martin on his bed. I'm very sorry but it looks like we were too late. There is a formality in that we need get a doctor to confirm that Martin has died. It's looking like his blood glucose levels fell very low, too low. We found a jam jar under his bed. I suspect he started developing symptoms and… thought he'd have some jam. People can feel shaky, get headaches, blurred vision and so on. Sometimes there's no reason for it, it just happens."

"Poor Martin."

"It could be triggered by missing a meal or some physical exertion—"

"Well, he was…" she interrupted. "He's been doing work in the garden. The leylandii had got rather out of control and was blocking out all the light. But he's not a fit man and a bit… you know. He's a large man. I told him we should get a professional in to do it, but he wouldn't listen. He wouldn't listen."

"Well, that may well have been it. He probably went upstairs to take a break, lie down and have some jam. It looks like he closed the door behind him and collapsed. He lost consciousness, probably instantly. He wouldn't have known anything about it."

She wondered if it looked unusual that no tears were coming. She looked at the young paramedic in front of her. She decided to go for stunned silence and hoped that would explain her apparent lack of grief.

"Can I get you a cup of tea or something?" he asked. She shook her head, then looked to her knees and put her hand over her eyes, supporting her elbow with the other. She kept shaking her head slowly. "I can't... I just can't believe it."

"My guess is that it happened yesterday," he said slowly. Something in the pit of her stomach rose suddenly to her throat and hovered there. "When did you find him?" This was it, the questions.

"Just now," she said quickly looking up and him, looking her straight in the eye. "Well, just before I rang 999. The last I saw him was yesterday morning. If only I'd stayed at home. If only I... maybe I could have helped him..."

"I'm so sorry," he said. She assumed her previous position, covering her eyes with her hand. They sat in silence for a moment. "There is one other thing."

"Yes?" she looked up at him again.

"Do you own a cat?"

"Yes. Bimbo. Why?"

He knew his partner was hiding in the ambulance, probably still pissing himself laughing, leaving him, the new boy, to deliver the news. The poor woman had already had one dreadful shock. He couldn't not tell her the other thing, and the longer he continued to not tell her, the worse it would look.

"It looks like Martin fell... on the cat."

"I didn't see him." She stood up. "Is he alright?"

"I'm afraid he fell right on him. Maybe he didn't see him and tripped. He was lying right on top of him. You wouldn't have been able to see from the door but when we lifted him up, we found the cat... underneath."

Her lip started to quiver, her eyes filled with thick, hot tears that fell from her eyes and down her cheeks. The other paramedic returned and stood in the doorway.

"Someone will be here shortly," he said.

"Is there anyone I can ring for you?" asked the other.

"The vet...?" she asked. He gently shook his head. She couldn't be seen to cry more for her cat than her husband, but she couldn't help herself. They weren't to know who she was crying for. "I need to see him. I need to see... my husband."

She slowly opened the door to Martin's room. There was no obstruction this time. He was lying on his back on the bed, the jam jar on the bedside table next to him. She looked down and to the right, behind the door, saw the lifeless Bimbo, looking more like a stole than ever. His back legs lay flat against each other as they often did when he was napping but his front paws were straight out and crossed at the shoulders, clearly broken and both pointing the wrong way. His neck was outstretched, his chin pressed flat into the floor, and his pink tongue tip poked out, his eyes still half open. She pushed the door closed and a guttural sob, audible to both paramedics below, burst from deep within her chest. She knelt next to him and stoked his flat, cold fur.

"Bimbo. Kitten-cat…" she whispered. His body stiff. It looked like they'd moved him to the side when they'd lifted Martin off. She was broken. 'Overwhelm' was a long-forgotten concept. She couldn't recall how best to respond. She wept over her friend's clumsily spatchcocked frame.

When the doctor arrived, he was met by her tear-stained face, red-raw and swollen with grief. He was shocked when he saw Martin. They'd been 'brothers' in the same masonic lodge. She hadn't known Martin was a Mason but didn't let that fact betray her. The doctor didn't know Martin was married. He hadn't thought he was the marrying type. He had known him for perhaps eleven or twelve years. He was deeply sorry for her loss. Someone from the lodge would be in touch to see if there was any way they could assist her. This unexpected kindness was disarming. He called the undertaker on her behalf and completed the paperwork required when one is pronounced dead. Cause of death – suffocation brought on by hypoglycaemic coma.

Soon the paramedics and doctor and undertaker and Martin were all gone. The house had never felt so empty and still. Nor had it ever felt so exposed. She called work and left a message on Stuart's phone to say she'd had some bad news and needed to take Monday as special leave. She said she'd call that afternoon if it didn't look like she'd be in on Tuesday either.

When darkness fell, she turned the kitchen light on so it shone through the window into the dark garden, to illuminate her work. She found the new saw Martin had bought for his final activities lying to the side of a balding patch of grass. She'd never owned any gardening equipment before but needed a spade.

She dug a small grave with a serving spoon, near the back, where the earth was softer and there were fewer tree roots. She laid Bimbo in the ground, inside a freshly laundered white pillowcase and gently pulled the earth back over him, patting it down. She marked the spot with a broken corner of pinkish paving stone; part of the garden path, leading nowhere except into gloom.

If Pollyanna were here, she'd suggest looking for something to be glad about. Pollyanna needed a kick. It did mean the house was hers now and that all that was Mother's and Martin's was also hers, but it was hard to feel glad about anything when she'd just buried Bimbo. Perhaps Martin had tripped over Bimbo as the paramedic suggested. Perhaps Bimbo had decided to take out her husband of inconvenience and take one for the team in the process.

Irene, and the others, were distant memories now. All she needed to do was sit and wait for the five months to pass until her birthday, when she could retire, sell up and move to her honey-coloured cottage in the Cotswolds, beginning the next chapter of her life.

Just before climbing into bed, she did enjoy one satisfying thought. When the undertaker re-entered Martin's room with his colleague, he'd apologised for interrupting a private moment. To them, it must have looked like she was whispering her final words of adoration to her dear, recently deceased husband, when in fact she'd been hissing in his ear, "I really fucking hate you, you fat, fucking, greedy *cunt*."

All her secrets were safe after all.

Mel passed Stuart coming downstairs as she was going up with the post. "Just popping out for a sandwich," he said. "Still no sign of Janice?"

"She emailed; sorry, I thought I'd said. She's not feeling well, but reckons she'll be back tomorrow."

"Ill? She's never ill."

"I'm sure she's fine. I can give her a ring if there's anything specific...?"

"No, I was just curious. Oh, and if Philip O'Brien calls, can you take a message and tell him I'll call him right back."

"Of course, no worries."

Hazel was out most of the day at external meetings, so it was rather nice to be left alone and have the office to herself for a bit. Back at her desk, Mel opened the post. There was never very much and most of it was junk or bills. Occasionally there'd be a cheque donation. It wasn't a bad place to work, but it was a bit quiet. She answered the phone, holding it under her chin as she slid a letter knife through the corner of a handwritten envelope.

"Good afternoon, Trethendar. Mel speaking. How can I help you?" She scanned the handwritten letter to determine who it was for, probably Hazel.

"Hi, it's Philip for Stuart if he's there, please?"

"I'm afraid you've just missed him. He won't be long though. Can I take a message?" She took her stapler to fasten the two pages of notepaper to the envelope. It was for Hazel. A member requesting some money from the Trust. She clipped it with her stapler, but it just bit the corner of the papers rather than stapling them.

"No, it's not urgent. I'll call back later."

"OK, I'll tell him you called. Bye."

She hung up and rummaged through her draws for staples. Plenty of paper clips but no staples. She knew Janice would have some so rolled her chair across and pulled open the top drawer of Janice's pedestal. She had a quick scan. She didn't want to see anything she didn't want to see. No spare staples there either. A paperclip would do but she'd just have a quick look in the large bottom drawer, where the files hung, before giving up. Perhaps that's where Janice kept her stash of stationery. Pulling it open, there were just some files. Should probably be locked, to maintain confidentiality.

There were some that were obviously to do with facilities like the one marked 'new boiler' and ones for invoices and so on, but there was one marked 'pensions' too, which should probably be locked away somewhere.

She'd have to use a paperclip.

She pushed the drawer closed and began to roll across to her own desk, but the drawer hadn't closed properly. She didn't want Stuart to find her looking in Janice's desk, so quickly moved back again and gave it another shove. It still wouldn't quite close. She opened it and leant over to see what was jamming it. It's so annoying when something slips down the back of the inside of the unit. It's hard to reach in and over the back of the drawer. The wider you open it, the further you need to reach for whatever's there. She could see it was an envelope in the way. It was folded over at one end. She reached in, with her cheek pressed against the side so she could just touch the corner and pinch it between the tips of her index and middle fingers. She pulled it out.

The end of the long, unsealed envelope was folded over, at the edge of the contents. She didn't know why she looked inside, but she did. She opened it, taking out the passport. There was a business card bookmarking the photo page. It was a card for Frank Savile, whoever he was. Passport pictures were always pretty funny. She opened the passport up with a slight smile on her face wondering how old Janice would be in the picture and what she'd be wearing. The smile turned to disbelief when she saw the picture. It was Janice but not as she'd ever seen her. A sister, perhaps? Why would she have her sister's passport? It looked just like her, but the flat, grey hair with the old-fashioned side parting was gone, replaced with tight, blonde curls. She was wearing make-up too and Janice never wore make-up. The clothes looked bright, nothing like anything she'd ever wear. But the date of birth – she was pretty sure that that was Janice's. It was personal and she shouldn't be looking at it. She put it back in the envelope, opened the top drawer and laid it on some papers, towards the back. She closed the drawer and rolled back across to her own desk.

She tried to put it from her mind. It didn't make any sense. It looked like Janice, and the date of birth was the same, but at the same time it couldn't be; and the name was wrong. It wasn't Janice Mead – it was Myra Westrell.

14

She was never late for work normally, but that Tuesday, she had no interest in arriving on time. Walking on automatic pilot, without the normal multitude of thoughts flaring up and fizzling out at varying rates and varying levels of volume and intensity, jostling for attention; she just didn't care. Nothing much obscured her mind. A peculiar calm as she walked, eyelids drooping, physically drained, like the source victim of the zombie apocalypse.

She stopped at the crossing. Someone else could push the button to stop the flow of white van men. She waited, staring into Smithfield Market's Grand Avenue the other side of the road. A couple in business dress snogged in an alcove by a pub. A bit early in the day. Probably having an affair. She'd normally glance up at the clock at this point, but she couldn't be arsed.

The traffic stopped and she crossed. Walking diagonally across Market Avenue, so she'd come out near the Cowcross Street crossing, side-stepping pallets, plastic wrapping, nylon cable ties. Normally she'd try and avoid any suspect-looking puddles, but today she just walked as the crow flies and whatever stood in her way, got stepped in. People often commented on how tiny her feet were. The bloody footprint trail she left looked childlike.

She crossed over Charterhouse Street, then Cowcross Street and, in a short while, the Trethendar Welfare Annuity Trust loomed a short distance away. Scaffolding fronted the nearby hospital buildings as the demolition work continued apace around the loathsome Victorian pile on the corner where the road split. With its grimy, dust-covered windows and ghastly heavy blue double doors it looked more derelict than the nearby buildings being gutted.

She made her way through the ground floor, its space wasted with filing cabinets. Heavy, metal and dark, tank green or battleship grey; they seemed to attract dust and absorb any vagrant light that drifted, confused, into the room. Each step up the staircase to the first-floor office seemed heavier and slower than the last. A deep sigh before the final one and she stepped inside.

"Morning, Janice," said Stuart. Hazel chimed in next, followed by the energising breeziness of Mel.

"Morning, all."

"How are you feeling?" asked Mel.

"Fine, thank you. Better anyway. Not too bad." She sat down and turned her PC on, pushing her bag under the desk. "Did I miss much?"

"Not really," said Mel. Hazel exhaled and shook her head almost imperceptibly (Mel perceived it) before getting back to her rapid typing.

"That's good," said Janice absently as she simultaneously opened her desk diary and the top drawer to her pedestal. Glancing in, she froze. Sitting on top was the envelope containing her Myra Westrell passport. It hadn't been there before. She knew she'd misplaced it, that it would turn up, but it had not been in her desk when she last looked.

"Oh," said Mel sensing a situation, "I ran out of staples, so I had a quick look in your desk to see if you had any." Janice, devoid of energy before, was now coiled like a spring, a snake. She slowly looked across at Mel's sweet face, within spitting distance. "I... the drawer wouldn't close so I fixed it for you. Something had slipped down the back," she said with that antipodean upward inflexion that turned, rather irritatingly, every statement into a question?

"That's alright, Mel."

Mel felt uncomfortable; fixed by Janice's beady, needle-eyes; a butterfly pinned to a collector's board. Janice knew the moment's void would soon be filled with a sudden flash of, 'the next right thing to do'. Until then, she'd simply wait. If she mentioned the passport as being hers and made light of it, it would open doors to questions about the name, the photo's step-change look. If she didn't make light of it and got angry, Mel might think she had something serious to hide. If she referred to it at all, Hazel and Stuart would hear and have their interests piqued. Maybe Mel had already told them. Maybe she'd not peaked inside the envelope.

Peripherally, she could see Hazel typing and Stuart deeply engrossed in whatever spreadsheet he was intently scrutinising. If they knew... if they'd seen the photo, they'd be waiting for her response with an inner smirk, but they weren't. They couldn't know. Mel was discreet. If it was unspoken and unseen, it didn't happen. She'd not refer to it at all.

"Did you find them? The staples?" Mel shook her head. Janice lifted the papers out, with the passport envelope on top, and placed it in the centre of her desk. "I normally keep all those sorts of things in here," she said as she reached to the back of the drawer, "there should be some. Here." She passed the box to Mel. "You can always help yourself, you know, but you should have a much better rummage next time. I may have a clean desk policy, but my drawers are exempt."

Mel smiled. Janice was still looking at her, smiling now, Mel didn't feel any less uncomfortable. She realised Janice was waiting for her to refill the stapler right then and there. She tipped a half strip of staples into her hand, pushed back the spring and loaded them. She put it on her desk and passed the box back to Janice. Janice returned the box and papers to her pedestal desk drawer, but not the envelope; Mel noticed the envelope containing the passport and business card that had been on top, was gone. In the moment it had taken to load the stapler, and without any discernible movement or sound from Janice, the envelope had gone, as if it had never been there at all.

Janice turned and continued to log into her PC. The incident would be forgotten in an instant and if it wasn't, it could always be flatly denied with a dash of relaxed, bemused guilelessness. But as she started her day's work, she knew there was the possibility that, either wilfully or accidentally, Mel had opened the envelope and seen the passport. It was now securely secreted inside the bag at her feet. She'd have to be careful. She'd have to remain focussed if she wasn't to make any more careless errors.

She took an early lunch. She'd get a more expensive sandwich than the regular egg mayonnaise and cress, and large, skinny, hazelnut latte. She'd treat herself. She found a sunny bench by the back cloisters in the garden adjoining the ancient church of St John. A suntrap, out of the breeze. It smelt more like early spring than late February. She tucked into her crayfish with rocket and dill mayonnaise. She'd have the coffee as dessert and pick-me-up.

She would have three urns of ashes soon. She'd need to get Martin done quickly and hoped there'd be no need for an inquest or anything. The doctor and ambulance crew seemed satisfied Martin had not suffered a violent or unnatural death, unlike poor Bimbo, so it seemed unlikely a coroner would need to be appointed, but she didn't know. No one had made any mention of it and Martin was now on a slab at the funeral directors, cold, under starters orders and ready for the off. There'd been no particularly difficult questions, so no potentially flawed answers. She had demonstrated the appropriate level of grief, not that they knew her tears were for her cat rather than the gay, diabetic who'd killed him. She meditatively chomped her sandwich in the peaceful and sunny solitude. Everything was as it should be. All she had to do was sit and wait. What was today? February 21st. So, eight days till the end of February. 'Thirty days has September, April, June and November all the rest...'. So, ninety-one days in quarter two, plus thirty-one days in March, the eight left until the end of February and then the last six until her birthday on June 6th. One hundred and thirty-six days until her birthday, her retirement.

Her honey-coloured cottage in the Cotswolds. There'd be no Mother, obviously, or Ben or Martin or Bimbo, but she'd have her pension; all of it. She'd also have the inheritances from Martin and Mother. She'd be quite comfortable, thank you very much. It didn't bother her that she'd not have anyone to share it with. She wasn't much of a sharer, happy in her own company.

She'd meet new people in the Cotswolds. Perhaps there'd be a local line dancing class or a Scrabble club. She'd get another cat, in time; not that Bimbo was replaceable, but another cat would be a comfort in her snug cottage with its thick, honey-biscuit stone walls. By the hearth, with an open fire and a mug of warming country vegetable soup. A piece of fudge while the wind blew up a storm outside and the rain beat against the windows. Maybe a big ginger boy between the fire and her toasting toes.

She folded her sandwich packaging down into a flat triangle, opened her bag and took out her diary. She flicked the business card with her fingers; sounding like the playing card Daddy once pegged to her bike, thrumming the spokes as she sped. Ben had suggested she call his man, Savile, if she needed anything. Now was that time. She needed financial advice and help with her mother's and Martin's inheritances. She dialled the number, a mobile. Unusual there should be no landline on a business card. No address either. Did Ben say he was a legal adviser as well as finance? The card didn't give much away. It rang too long for it to be diverting to a business.

"Hello, you've reached Frank Savile. I'm sorry I'm not able to answer your call just now—"

She stopped the call and put the phone, diary and business card back in her bag. Almost immediately, her phone buzzed and vibrated like an angry wasp. She reached for it glancing at the display. Number withheld. She answered anyway.

"Hello?"

"Good afternoon. I just missed a call from this number. Can I help you?"

"Mr Savile?"

"Yes," he said, a smile shined in his voice. "Who's this?"

She spoke quietly. "You don't know me, but I'm a friend of Ben Westrell."

He paused for a moment. "Then you must be Janice, is it? Am I right?"

"Yes."

"Ben said you'd be calling. Poor chap. Funnily enough, I was going to call you this week if I didn't hear from you. I've been tying up his estate."

"I was calling to see if we could arrange to meet?"

"Yes, we absolutely must. I'm afraid I'm away on business, outside the UK, for much of March, but I'm back before Easter." She rummaged for her diary and a pen. "How about... Do you have a pen?"

"Yes, I'm ready, Mr Savile."

"Oh, call me Frank. And may I call you...? Now, Ben referred to you as Janice but, I also have you down as Myra...?"

"Call me Myra."

"Lovely. Then how about Thursday 5th April? 12:30?"

"That will be fine," she chirruped like a schoolgirl.

"Thursday the 5th it is then."

"I don't have an address…"

"We can meet in a hotel or something. Let's arrange all that nearer the time. I'm so sorry, but I should fly right now. That's all in the diary."

"Alright."

"I'll catch up with you soon."

"Yes, alright. Thank you, Mr Savile."

Chuckling, he replied, "Frank."

"Yes of course, thank you, Frank."

"Bye for now. Ben told me so much about you."

"All good, I hope," she said, laughing back, but he'd already gone. "Oh."

The hotel was next door to the Pope's Head, on the corner of Wimpole and Queen Anne Street. An independent boutique, deceptively small from the outside but extending so far back it was unexpectedly spacious. The Georgian frontage belied a spotless, slick and unapologetically modern interior. Clearly a place local professionals disappeared to, to conduct business away from the open-eyed and apparent transparency of the surrounding glass-fronted business blocks. There were many turns and corners with low, dark wood tables, faux leather chairs, dim lighting and crimson, quilted tissue coasters. A place where discretion was king. When asked who she was there to meet, she was ushered to a secluded booth nearer the bar, far from the entrance and reception.

"Myra, how lovely to meet you," Frank said as he rose to take her hand. "You found it alright?" It was odd hearing that name, on the lips of someone other than her mother.

"Oh yes, it's very central... easy to find. Lovely to meet you too."

He was a half-inch or so taller than her, in his sixties perhaps. It was difficult to tell when portliness plumped out the wrinkles. His eyes were blue but had lost the sparkle they must have once had, the whites turning sepia from drink and tobacco. His face had a pinkness from the thread veins, and a fondness for a glass or three. His grey hair thinned on top, and his suit, although pristine, was silvery, a bit too shiny, belonging to a different decade.

She realised she too probably looked like she'd just stepped out from a time that had passed. Her slight frame meant she now had a slightly scraggy neck. She was all too aware how flat and lifeless her hair was with its safe bob cut, old-fashioned parting, and slide to keep it out of her grey-blue pinhead eyes. Martin had always eyed her hair pityingly. She hoped she could trust Ben's friend and be frank with Frank.

"Thank you for the statements and the other papers you sent across."

"No problem."

"I find it cuts through the crap. Our time together can be spent much more fruitfully if I have all the documents and background in advance."

They ordered coffees and a jug of iced water for the table. There was small talk about Ben and how it was surprisingly warm for the time of year and "do you have anything nice planned for the Easter weekend?", "not really", "no, nor do I", and then they got down to it.

"So, just so I have the context, let me summarise things as I see them. ...Janice *Myra* Mead...?"

"It's actually Myra *Janice* Mead."

"Thank you. Myra Janice Mead married good old Ben in June of last year. Ben died later that month. I've been dealing with his estate since then. Your mother, Linda Mead, marries Martin Blair in September; she passes away in January. The following month, you marry Martin Blair; two or three weeks later, he too passes away." He paused. His eyes rolled up from the paper and came to rest on hers. "I'm very sorry for the loss of your friend, mother and... husbands."

"Look I'm not going to lie. I know how awful all this looks. It has been awful. Martin was a dear friend, and my poor Mother wasn't at all well and hadn't been for a long time. We, the three of us that is, decided… agreed… that, to avoid inheritance tax, she and Martin would marry, and then, assuming Mother died first, everything would go to Martin, and then he and I would marry and whoever outlived the other would get everything. It seemed sensible at the time, but none of us obviously had any idea… I mean to say, we never imagined… this would all happen so quickly. You know, in such close proximity. I never thought for a moment I'd be the last one standing either. I imagined Mother would outlive us all. Tough as old boots, she was. My very own 'bag-for-life', I miss her. She had poor circulation, a heart problem, and Martin—"

"You don't have to explain."

"But I feel I must because I know how it looks."

"Any inquests?"

"Not as far as I know."

"Well then. I know Ben was very fond of you. He told me to look out for you and that's exactly what I'm going to do. Your private arrangements are personal to you and really none of my concern." He reached across and sandwiched her hand between his two. He didn't mention the gloves.

"I have Raynaud's disease," she said, a little taken aback. "They're always cold. I have very little feeling. The gloves, they're for protection."

"Cold hands…" he said reassuringly. She sighed. "I'll handle everything for you."

"That's a relief. It really is. I need to ask you, though, and I don't mean to sound rude… can you give me some idea how much it will all cost?"

"Ben paid outright for my services to him, so you needn't worry about that element. For the pensions advice you're seeking plus the work on the estates of your mother and late husband – Martin, that is – and the conveyancing… I assume you're going to sell…?"

"Yes, I was thinking about it."

"It's Whitstable, isn't it? Great place. Well, for the whole lot, how about we call it a flat fee of £2,000."

"Well, that sounds reasonable."

"Thank you." He laughed as he released her hand with a pat. "It is… very."

He suggested talking about opening an offshore account. She didn't know much about them. He said he'd tell her the benefits, ins and outs, then leave it for her to decide. They spoke a little of the paperwork relating to the estates. There was nothing much he could tell her about her pension. He explained the pros and cons of the available options, asked if there were any outstanding debts. It was clear Ben had nothing to speak of in the way of liquid assets, though what little cash there was, was waiting patiently in one account. Martin's estate too seemed straight forward enough, despite there being no will made post-marriage. Again, reassuringly, Frank said he'd handle all this. He said he'd already contacted the lawyer who'd drawn up Martin's will and, as they'd also been named as executor, it should be straightforward. She breathed a sigh of relief. She'd heard all she needed to hear.

"Now, offshore accounts," he said. She wasn't sure what this was about or why he seemed so keen, unless, she surmised, this was how he made his money; commission from selling her some product she didn't really need or want. "What do you know about them?"

"Well, very little. Nothing really. It wasn't something that featured on my list of things to consider."

"OK, well it should be, and I'll tell you why. There are about seventy offshore centres in the world as defined by the IMF. There are varying investor protection benefits, but Bahrain is where I'd recommend you open one. Their fixed exchange rate works well for expats because it removes the need to transact in multiple currencies."

"I'm not sure it's really necessary for me."

Savile paused. He was puzzled. It was a no-brainer. He went into granular detail for about ten minutes, ending with a cheery, "Does that make sense?"

What was he talking about? She'd been with Lloyds for over forty years with no need to complain or change. Like many banks, their 'customer services' was more about deflecting away from what the customer wanted and towards what they wanted and separating them from more of their hard-earned. Every transaction ended with a sales attempt, the banking equivalent of 'do you want chips with that?'. She didn't particularly like or trust her bank, but better the devil you know. She'd never thought in terms of saving plans or investments. But maybe he had a point. If she was going to retire and live off her savings and any meagre earnings from investments made, she'd need to ensure she was getting the biggest bang for her buck. She was entering a new phase, and it required new ways of doing things. She'd heard about big international businesses and celebrities becoming embroiled in tax-avoidance schemes. The country lost millions to tax-avoidance, but to the businesses and probably the individual celebs' points of view, it was tax-efficiency rather than avoidance. It wasn't illegal, after all, even though there might be an ethical question; it was just setting up a new bank account.

She had a few questions on the practicalities, the cons, and what was required. He answered everything, and she listened intently. When he'd finished, she sat in silence, still digesting. Had they really been talking for an hour?

"Well, it seems to make sense. It's not complicated to do?"

"A piece of cake. Just opening an account. I can do everything for you. I'll need you to sign some papers, make some copies of your ID and bank statements, proof of address and whatnot."

"Oh, yes of course." She rummaged in her bag for her Myra Westrell passport.

"I can then have the funds transferred from the accounts of the deceased directly into your new account. I can recommend some investments for you too if you like, and I earn a small commission on these. I'll obviously tell you exactly how much as and when we do that. But you don't have to, of course, it's totally up to you."

She looked him in the eye and held out the passport. He returned her gaze, unflinching, one snake to another. He took the passport.

"If you wait here for a few minutes," he said, "I'll just go and scan this. I'll aim to finish all the work on it for you tonight... on my laptop when I get back to the hotel. I'm not going too fast for you, am I?"

"Not at all. It sounds fine. I understand completely. It sounds sensible."

"I'll be back soon then," he said as he left with the papers and her passport.

She leant back in her chair. She didn't know how far she could trust Mr Savile. All she knew about him was his mobile number and the fact he'd been recommended by Ben. Here she was trusting him with almost everything she had. Ben had trusted him, so must have rated him. She'd obviously retain all control over any outgoing monies. He was clever, and she was sure there were things she wasn't being told. She didn't know the questions to ask. But why should any of that bother her if it didn't leave her any worse off? She wondered who his other clients were. She wondered if he had a home at all. She pictured him moving from one hotel to another, ducking and diving and rolling with the punches, gathering no moss. Frank Savile was just like her. He couldn't be trusted.

He returned with the copies and handed her original documents back. "So, do you have any other properties apart from the house in Whitstable?"

"No, that's it."

"You must be so excited."

"I've been looking forward to retiring for a long time."

"When are you planning on selling up and moving to Florida?"

Flummoxed. "Florida? I'm not moving to Florida. My dream was to move to the country, possibly the Cotswolds, one day."

"So, it'll be a holiday rental?"

Had she missed something? Had they been speaking at cross-purposes this whole time? It would make sense if they had. He'd confused her with another client, surely.

"People do holiday in Whitstable and there are lots of weekend lettings, but I was thinking of selling the house."

"But the other house? Ben's house?"

She'd known Ben's parents had had a house somewhere, but he'd never mentioned anything about still having it. He never mentioned it at all.

"Excuse me?"

"Didn't you get my letter? I've been liaising with the people in Florida. I was going to call you about it just before you called me."

Her assistance with his exit had been more than fully repaid by him marrying her. In that moment, she could almost feel Ben's great big cowboy grin beaming down at her, basking in her surprise.

"Now that you mention it, I think there was a letter. It was months ago. It didn't really register what it was about. I don't even think I ever read it. I've had so much on my plate recently. My God, there's a house?"

"A lovely house by all accounts. Two bedrooms, single story with a pool."

"A pool?"

He nodded. "Near the ocean, the Gulf of Mexico side, I believe. A place called Nokomis, just south of Tampa. He didn't tell you?"

"He never said a word." She felt choked, emotionally. This threw everything into the air. No wonder Frank had been going on about expats and offshore accounts and foreign investments and currencies. It all made sense now.

Frank went on, "Ben really loved that house. It's where his parents moved when they retired. He spent a lot of summers there."

"I assumed he'd cut all ties with America."

"All but that one. He couldn't bear to be parted from it, not Casa Cariño."

"Casa Cariño?"

"You speak Spanish?"

"No. I can order food and get by, but I couldn't hold a conversation."

"Well, casa means house or home, obviously. And Cariño… doesn't really translate directly. It's a bit like a pet name. Cariño, like 'darling', but less formal." Her gloved hand slowly moved towards her mouth, her eyes glazed with tears as he slowly spoke. "It's more casual than that, more intimate," he went on. "Te amo, Cariño." I suppose in American English the nearest translation for Cariño would be something like, *honey*. My Honey's House—"

15

Everything was unfolding for her in the most marvellous and miraculous of ways. She opened the offshore account on Frank's advice and the monies from the estates of her mother and Martin were paid in directly. The little left in Ben's final account was transferred across and, as his widow, a proportion of his pension was now being paid directly into the account of Myra Westrell.

She didn't feel that she was in any position to put her Whitstable home on the market yet, with its lifetime of memories and such close ties to Mother, but it was nice to have the option. It wasn't cluttered by any means, but the amount of clearing required loomed overwhelmingly at times. She adopted the 'Swiss cheese' approach and gnawed holes in the overall task; small inroads made by frequently nibbling away in manageable chunks. She did a couple of uninterrupted hours each weekend, starting with the rooms at the top, working her way down, starting with Martin's room. Items were placed in one of four piles, one in each corner; bin, sell, donate or keep. Progress was slow but steady, manageable, noticeable.

She maintained a semblance of her hard-working work ethic at work. Her colleagues didn't ask after her movements, so an extended lunch here and there went largely unnoticed.

She'd been mooching around and ended up sitting in the garden at St John's when her phone buzzed furiously in her bag and rattled her peace. She juggled her sandwich, pulling it out. A text. Mel was feeling sick again, so was heading home. A dodgy sushi. Should be fine tomorrow. Stuart is aware.

"That's fine, Mel," she muttered under her breath as she texted the words into her phone. "Thanks for letting me know." Send. She put it away, taking another bite of her 'Slimmer's Options' egg and cress.

This was the third time Mel had left work early, or not come in, because she was unwell. She might have to hold an informal meeting of concern with her. She may have to tell her Trethendar is worried about this level of short-term, intermittent absence and ask if there's anything the organisation can reasonably do to support her; or if there's something else the organisation should be aware of... and then it dawned on her. Increasingly zitty and bigger titted, Mel had been back to New Zealand for Easter. She'd be coming up to the end of her first trimester around now. Mel's contract was due to expire on 20th July anyway and her visa expired shortly thereafter, so there was no prospect of it being extended or going perm. She took another bite. It was a good thing she was going, considering she may have seen the passport.

She hadn't decided whether she'd move to Florida, nor whether to pursue or shelve her long-held Cotswolds dream. That original dream felt like someone else's now and the novelty had perhaps worn off. On some unconscious level, she knew what to do. She had plenty of time, there was no rush, and whatever it was she ended up doing, she'd still need to sort the contents of the house first, so clearly the next right thing to do was to make tracks on that.

She'd clear out, retire, then probably put the Whitstable house on the market to gauge interest. She'd need to at least visit Ben's Florida house. She could turn it into a holiday. She could even stay a few months if she wanted to, over the summer of the following year, after her retirement and into the autumn. She could then decide if she wanted to take the plunge, up sticks and move there for good or return to Whitstable. She had so many options and so few ties but, best of all, she had time. The lack of ties and surplus time gave her the options. At last, no obligations, only options.

In the spring, she'd call the local tree fellers to tidy up the hatchet job Martin left of the leylandii, and for the first time in ten or twelve years, sunlight would fall on the compressed earth at the back, where the alopecia lawn had all but balded away. Sunlight would fall on the spot where, fifteen weeks earlier, she'd buried

Bimbo. Sunlight fell on her face, she squinted. She finished her sandwich and headed back to the office.

Time swung round and with just five weeks until retirement and her house-tidying all but done, she'd sold most of the furniture to a local house clearance man. None of it was worth much, but it generated some extra cash. She had her bed, the sofa, the TV and the contents of the kitchen and bathroom left, but where she could downscale, she had done. Why have seven pans when she only ever used the one? Why have eight sets of bed linen when she only needed two?

The rooms grew bleaker, but she liked the echoic space, as if it was about to be redecorated. She could hear every sound and no dust accumulated. It was ready to sell, whenever she was. Newspaper packed the more precious things. There was so little left now that she intended to keep. She had one or two boxes of items to donate, three at a push, and the rest would either be taken with her, get binned or be left.

The unread, unused local papers she'd saved for packing went in the tub for the recycling men to collect Monday morning. She turned to lift another stack when her eye caught a story on the front page, not the headliner, one of the lesser stories about an elderly charity worker who'd died in a freak accident at her home, full story on page five. She took the paper to read in the lounge. It was from back in February.

The angle of the article was the hole left by this local champion of the decrepit, and how it was all too tragic, especially when it could have been so easily avoided. It highlighted the need for greater national and local investment in social care and especially the plight of the elderly and the infirm; a cause, ironically, that had, according to the article, been close to Irene's cold, long dead, heart. Her picture was by no means recent, and the article probably exaggerated the scale of the good works; chair of *Sheerness in Flower,* a micro-charity which raised money to teach first aid to local young people. So not only did the flower competition help the community by making the place look lovely and create a sense of community and shared purpose, but it also had the added benefit of helping people learn how to save lives, thereby increasing their self-esteem. The list went on. There was, apparently, no end to the beatific Irene's charitable works. She was a pillar of the community and would be missed not just by all those who benefited from her good works, but by her colleagues at the local rag, where she wrote a weekly column on community events and local stories with a feel-good fucking factor. There was to be a memorial service for this treasured member of the community. It was enough to make Myra want to heave. She'd been a complete and utter bitch most of her miserable life. Good riddance.

She looked up. The three urns on top of the TV –
Mother, Martin and Ben – looked down at her. She
roughly folded the yellowed newspaper in a scrunch
and stuffed it in the tub with the rest for Monday's
collection.

She could manage carrying the box of items down
the high street; the games, Scrabble, Happy Families,
old jigsaws. She'd become a familiar figure, offloading
junk at one of the local charity shops. She left the
Scrabble until last. It was harder to part with, but she
couldn't play it on her own. She'd only ever played it
with her mother. She didn't want to play it again, so no
point in keeping it. Any emotional tie was easily severed.

At the gardening shop, they had a deal on where you
could buy three plants for £5, so she bought a small
rosemary plant and two lavenders. When she got home,
she went straight to the garden and dug a bucket sized
hole near Bimbo with the serving spoon. She emptied
the three urns into the hole and planted the rosemary on
top with a lavender either side. Rosemary for
remembrance.

She scurried back into town with the three urns,
earth still under her fingernails, to try and catch the
funeral directors before they closed, in case they wanted
the empties back. She was too late. She didn't want to
carry them home again, so she stuck them in the bin by
the bus stop.

The following week, Jenny used one of her 'keeping in touch days' to pop into the office with Toby.

"Oh, isn't he gorgeous," Mel cooed. "How old is he now?"

"Eleven and a half months," glowed Jenny. She had a face flannel on her shoulder and smelt of milky baby sick.

"Is he sleeping OK?"

"I'd love to say yes, but... no. You don't let us sleep much, do you?" she baby-talked, rubbing noses with him.

Hazel exhaled huffily from her desk. Jenny had only been there twenty minutes, but it was a distraction for Hazel who beavered away, bearing the weight of the world on her shoulders, as well as all those chips. Perhaps that was why, Janice mused, she was stunted, buckling under the weight of an overactive social conscience. It was as if Hazel still believed the unstable and doomed organisation was financially viable, as if it could tip back after tipping so far beyond the tipping point. Hazel couldn't not know it was beyond saving. In denial, maybe. She wasn't dim. Stuart knew. He'd consider himself captain, nobly going down with the crew. Melissa was bright, and Jenny... dear, water-retaining Jenny was just too stupid to see the writing on the charity's wall. She'd never leave voluntarily. She'd never earn elsewhere what she made at Trethendar; staying as long as she had, had completely deskilled her.

She was unemployable now, and her role had withered away, in a withering wind, to nothing. A redundant woman walking, with no hope of suitable alternative employment. What took Jenny a week to complete, took Mel an hour. Mel had made many improvements and created efficient new ways of working, so that Janice, Hazel and Stuart could probably take care of the remaining admin themselves. Hazel would put up a fight against redundancy on Jenny's behalf on ideological grounds. But redundancy was the obvious and unavoidable next move.

Myra struggled to maintain her smile. It was probably more of a sickly smirk by now, but Jenny was blind to it.

"Would you like to hold him?"

"I'm so terrible with children," Janice cooed unconvincingly. "I'd hate to drop him." *Or hold it by the foot and dash its brains out against the wall.*

Jenny, both the figurative and literal elephant in the room, had cherubic, pre-Raphaelite hands and chalky-sponge feet, inflated like proved bread dough before it's knocked out. Harmless enough, just irritating. That nauseating smell of sour milk and leaky lactations.

You know your HR days are coming to an end, she mused, *when someone bounds up to you to tell you they're pregnant and you say, "How wonderful, congratulations," but you're really thinking, "Oh for fuck's sake, you have to be kidding me; do you realise* *how much fucking work and inconvenience you've just created for me, you silly brainless womb?"* There's no skill whatsoever in getting knocked up, so why all the privilege? Why the overblown sense of merit and entitlement? Why the interminable need to rub the faces of the childless in their unthought-through birthing? Why the misplaced arrogance? Nobody cares about you or your shitty baby. They really don't.* It was hard to maintain a smile when this was how she felt, in the face of so much pride and joy.

"Can I?" Mel asked.

"Here." She handed the priceless bundle to Mel, who glowed. Although she was a bit spotty, Mel was still beautiful. She really did glow. Fragrant, gentle and kind. She sniffed his head, and her eyes closed as she gave him a little squeeze. She hadn't told anyone yet.

"So, Janice, I meant to ask. Can I have a quick chat about my return date?"

"Of course, let's sit down."

Janice explained that a 'KIT' day was paid at her normal daily rate, even though she was only going to be in for an hour or so. Jenny didn't want to use all her accrued annual leave as part of a phased return, though she did want to take the Monday as holiday as she was due to return on Tuesday 26th June. She was thinking of making a flexible working request too. She wanted it all.

Janice was normally irritated when people wanted to bank up their annual leave rather than take it throughout the course of the year, but in this case, she wasn't. The fact that Jenny would be paid in lieu of accrued but untaken holiday (plus the public holidays and Christmas closure days that fell in the period when she was on maternity leave), would make the redundancy pill easier for her to swallow when that time came. Stuart had said as much to her a few weeks earlier. "We'll need to talk about Jenny when she's back," had been his exact words to Janice. It could only mean one thing. She'd follow the statutory consultation procedures, but Jenny's redundancy would buy the organisation a few more months. *Why not just be done with it all now*, she thought, *and do everyone a favour while there was still enough cash in the pot to give everyone a decent pay off*. He was obviously waiting for Janice to retire so he wouldn't have to pay her a redundancy too.

She said, "That should work out well. Mel sadly leaves on July 20th." They'd agreed to let her take her last two weeks as unpaid leave.

"My last working day is actually Friday 6th," she called across. "I fly back on the 8th."

"So, you'll have two weeks, minus the Monday, for a handover." She paused. That was also the weekend the boiler was being replaced. Her parting gift. "I'll also be leaving on 6th July."

"Of course," said Jenny. She'd completely forgotten Janice's retirement. "Golly, that's come around quick, hasn't it?"

"It has." It hadn't. The time had slowed horribly the nearer her retirement date got.

"I bet you won't know what to do with yourself without Trethendar, Janice, will you?"

"No, I won't," she lied. Jenny knew nothing about her. Her brain had been blended into a fine, pink paste by eleven and a half months' motherhood. "It's true, it's been a very large part of my life but I'm sure, after I leave, I shall learn to laugh again one day. I can't say it will be easy though."

There was an uneasy silence. They still didn't understand her arid humour. They'd each concluded long ago that Janice couldn't make jokes. Her quips were always followed by silence, making quipping all the more entertaining for her.

Stuart will probably be wanting some advice before she retires, especially if he and the board decide to delete Jenny's job. She knew she wouldn't be missed any more than Jenny, but also knew they'd be planning some sort of send-off. A glass of wine and assorted nibbles in the flat upstairs was the norm, but as it was a retirement and she'd been there so long, perhaps they'd push the boat out a bit further. There was nothing she could usefully do at Trethendar now. All she had to do was coast across the finishing line into her long-anticipated, blissful retirement.

On Sunday, she called one of the local estate agents for a valuation on the house. Demand for properties in the town was still high, especially down by the harbour, but she had no idea what her house might fetch. She was just dipping her toe in, to test the market. On some level, she knew she was going to sell and leave. But she was certainly in no hurry. Not half as much of a hurry as the agent, it appeared, as he arrived on her doorstep within forty-five minutes of her call.

She let him have the run of the house with his laser measuring device and clipboard. She didn't mind if he took some pictures but explained she hadn't quite made up her mind yet. She had nowhere else to go. He reassured her that he'd hold off on everything till she instructed him that she'd decided to sell. He called for her while he finished writing up his notes and she met him in the lounge.

"OK, so thank you for letting me see your lovely home, Mrs Mead. It's a big plus for a buyer that the property is vacant. The garden is a little on the small side and the interior needs some modernising but, for the right buyer, looking for a fixer-upper, and considering the current state of the market, I think it would probably sell for around the £525,000 mark. I'd advise you put it on at £526,900 and be prepared to drop slightly to allow for some landscaping, updates, redecorations and so on."

"That's wonderful to know. I'm surprised, I must say."

"Whitstable has seen a slight slowing in the market, but we haven't been hit half as hard as many other places. It's always a desirable location. You're near the station, and there's room for off-road parking, which is a big plus. It'd be great for London commuters. A young professional family perhaps, wanting a bit of a project."

There was a silence. He gave her the spiel about commission rates and that they're a one-stop shop for all her selling and buying needs. The usual patter, delivered in smarmy lacklustre. Another silence. She looked around the empty room, then back at him. He was only young. His suit was too big, and he looked a bit hungover. She smiled at him.

"Wait here," she said as she disappeared into the kitchen only to reappear almost instantly with a spare front and back door key on a ring. She handed it to him. "I still haven't quite made up my mind, but I can always get the keys back if I decide to stay."

"Of course."

"I just need to sleep on it. You've given me a lot to think about."

"That's fine. Thanks for your time."

"I'll give you a ring."

"Here's my card."

"Thank you, Alex. I'll give you a ring on Monday. If I do decide to sell, you can start showing it as soon as you like. I'm out from early till quite late most weekdays, but you can always let yourself in. Just give me a ring on the mobile half an hour or so beforehand, just in case I am in. I'm obviously here at the weekends but I can make sure I'm out of your way."

"Great. I hope you do decide to sell. I already know of quite a few people who I'm sure would be interested. You won't have any problem finding a buyer."

Her first task the following Monday was to put together a spreadsheet of all her passwords. She did all her online banking and retail at work, and her PC remembered her passwords when she couldn't. So, she changed them all and made a record. She had a USB memory stick at work too, so she spent the second half of the morning transferring all her files on to that, not that she'd probably ever need any of the work stuff again. She printed off the spreadsheet with her work and personal passwords and started to delete everything she didn't need. All the personal stuff was removed from her machine and any work stuff that was more than eighteen months old was also deleted. She deleted all her personal files and all emails. When she was done, her work PC looked as empty as her house. She removed the memory stick and popped it in her bag.

At lunchtime, she stepped out to call Alex and say she'd decided to go ahead. He sounded pleased and said he'd work very hard for her.

While she was out, Philip O'Brien of BDI called. Things were moving fast.

"She's at lunch right now. Can anyone else help?" Mel asked. Stuart looked at her quizzically. Hazel was at lunch too, so there was no one else. She started to mouth the word 'auditors' to him. "Just a moment, please." She put her hand over the mouthpiece. "It's Philip O'Brien about the pension scheme."

"I'll take it," Stuart said. Mel transferred the call. "Phil, how are you?" Mel returned to typing her handover notes for Jenny's return the following week. "Hang on, I'll just check my calendar." He switched screens from inbox to calendar. "Don't you normally do this in July?" There was a silence as Mr O'Brien explained that Janice had called asking if it was possible to bring the meeting forward. As he was in London to meet another client, he wanted to suggest Tuesday. It was short notice, but Stuart was hoping to take a bit of annual leave at the beginning of the next month, so it would be good to review it early. He checked Janice's diary. She had the whole day marked as annual leave. "Tomorrow's perfect," he said. "Any time that's good for you… Great. See you then. Bye." He hung up and put the meeting in his calendar. "Mel, are you around tomorrow at two?"

"I should be."

"Can you sit in on this with me, please?"

"Sure."

"It's about the pension. You know where Janice keeps all the paperwork, don't you?"

"Yes," she replied cautiously. She didn't want to piss Janice off, and it sounded like Stuart was up to something. She still wanted to get a good reference off them.

"Janice has a lot on her plate, with her leaving and wrapping things up, so it makes sense I pick this up for her. I'll have a chat with her about it if you like."

"OK, no worries," she said, going back to her notes.

On the Wednesday, Janice arrived back at work early to print off anything that needed to be filed and sift through the personnel files to ensure there weren't items being retained that didn't need to be. A grubby job, and although it didn't really need to be done, she'd told Stuart she'd do it. She had precious little else left to do. No one would be in at that time. Stuart was a nine-to-fiver and Hazel tended to stay late before heading home. So she'd have the copier to herself. She'd had a lazy Tuesday off and only left the house for a couple of hours in the afternoon to go food shopping while Alex showed a potential buyer round.

Arriving that morning, shortly after 8:10am, she was surprised to see that the door, although shut and secure, was unlocked. Hazel must've forgotten to lock up the night before. Unusual but not unheard of, especially if she'd headed home in a hurry. Opening the heavy door she expected to hear the beep of the alarm system sounding, alerting her to the fact that the code needed to be entered, but it didn't sound. Someone was in the building. She paused for a moment to listen. Nothing.

She quietly walked across to the doorway leading to the bottom of the stairs and heard a voice coming from the office above.

A voice, muffled and distant, asked, "What did she say?" Silence.

She craned her neck silently around the door and looked up the stairs with her mouth open, breathing silently as she listened to Mel, on the phone. The person on the other end was obviously doing most of the talking. Slowly, silently, Myra moved up the stairs.

"Have you seen my mum? ...Can you stop by in the week? ...Thanks. ...I miss you too. In fact, we both do. Not long now... Oh, not much. Same old same old. I sat in on a meeting yesterday with the finance guy. Boring. Pensions. I don't really know why I was there. He only wanted me there to pick out the odd file. ...Nothing... No. There was something a bit odd though. I'm probably just overthinking things." She laughed. "Yeah. ...No, it was just a weird coincidence, I'll tell you when I see you. Talking of that, I hope you're not planning anything spectacular." She could hear Mel listening again. Smiling. "Christ, you must love me or something, Chris! ...I know you do. ...I know. I love you too. Look, I'd better go. I just wanted to say hi. You won't forget to stop by Mum's? ...Love you too. ...Bye."

She heard her blow him a kiss and say 'bye' again. She didn't hear Mel hang up so she must have been calling from her mobile. She turned the corner and walked up to the office. As she entered, Mel was removing the earplugs leading to her hard drive.

"You're early, Mel."

"Morning. Yes, I just needed to speak to Chris. There isn't a charge if it's through the net." Mel sounded as bright and breezy as ever.

"I know. It's no problem," she said. "No problem at all."

Mel left to run up to the flat to make a cup of tea and the thoughts flooded Myra's mind. It was clear Stuart had deliberately left Myra out of the loop. She'd called Philip O'Brien to reschedule so she could wrap things up with him before she went, so that no eyes noticed. Stuart knew the pension scheme came under her remit, not his. Although BDI also did the accounts, he'd deliberately rearranged that meeting for a time when he knew she'd be out. She knew a sewer rat when she smelt one and he was one for sure. She hung up her coat and switched on her PC, then went to the toilets. Her mind raced; her pounding heart pulsed in her ears as she peed. But it was natural, she supposed, that now both the scheme and Trethendar were coming to the end of their natural lives, Stuart would need to take more interest in the pension, but the rat could have asked her first. Mel was in that meeting. O'Brien would have given an update on the scheme beneficiaries and their circumstances. He'd have told them that once Janice Mead retired, she'd be the only remaining former employee receiving a pension through it. How come? Because the other beneficiaries had all died in the past twelve months. It would all unravel. The only other person receiving a pension from the scheme was the widow of former chief exec., Ben *Westrell*. Mel would have heard. If Mel *had* seen the passport... if she *had*, and she heard the name 'Westrell', she would twig. Myra had overheard her say something to do with the pensions being 'weird'. Had it already unravelled? What else could that possibly mean?

She knew. Mel knew, and she was about to tell.

16

Jenny returned from maternity leave the following Tuesday. Mel handed her a file with everything she'd need to get back up to speed, plus a few pages of handover notes. They went for a coffee together that afternoon to bond and ended up talking at least as much about baby Toby as work.

Friday week and both Mel and Janice were leaving Trethendar's employment. Mel returning to her old life in New Zealand and Janice starting a new one as a 'lady of leisure'. As Janice and Mel wound down, Hazel and Jenny got more wound up.

The same day they were leaving, the new boiler installation was starting. Stuart didn't know why they were bothering. It would only be ripped out again in six to twelve months when the charity crashed. He was already job-hunting. The board thought a new boiler was a good thing to do and might add value to the property. Any developer would most likely do what they did a few doors down, demolish the core, saving only the protected frontage, and rebuild behind it, modern and fit for purpose. Farringdon was an increasingly desirable location with its trendy agencies, architects, designers and boutique businesses. Demolishing Trethendar's last asset would probably drive the rodents from the basement and back to where they'd come from, a few doors down.

As the previous week had progressed, she'd relaxed. Stuart didn't ask to see her confidentially as she feared he might. Nor did Mel make any passing comment about the name 'Westrell' or the three dead beneficiaries. The focus was on the handover of work and ensuring continuity of service delivery.

Initially, she'd been annoyed Stuart had usurped her role as administrator of the pension scheme and had met with Mr O'Brien in her absence. How noble she'd appeared when he eventually deigned to mention it. He'd obviously done it on purpose, but she couldn't permit herself to appear phased. She'd said of course it was the right thing to do. It made perfect sense that he should take it over now. She was only sorry she hadn't had the opportunity to give him the background before their meeting. She thought that might have made it easier for him, but she was glad it was all sorted now and was sure he'd call on her if he had any further questions. His thanks sounded heartfelt and for a moment Stuart had looked almost fond of her.

She'd asked Mel for a brief summary of the meeting. She said she hadn't paid too much attention to what they were saying, but as she started talking about it, referring to her notes, recalled more. She said O'Brien felt last year's solvency estimate had perhaps been a little too prudent in the light of the intervening actuarial report. There was an ongoing risk of a deficit and the only way to bring this down and rescue the scheme would be to either increase the level of investment return (which was beyond their control) or make a larger employer contribution. They really needed to do both. Stuart said that the only way they could make a larger contribution was if there was a cut elsewhere or the organisation sold some assets.

Well, Jenny could go for starters and the only asset left was the building. It would also mean not replacing Janice, leaving just two employees, Stuart and Hazel. She tried not to care about not being replaced, despite it indicating that her contribution was seen as having no value.

Mel didn't mention the three dead beneficiaries, or that Janice was the only one remaining. In fact, nothing she'd recounted could be considered particularly "weird", which could only mean she wasn't telling Janice everything. But there was no shifty eye contact or any other discernible deviation from her standard delightful self. She didn't appear suspicious. She wondered whether an innocent could be so accomplished in concealment. If it was subterfuge, what was her plan? Impossible to tell. She'd just need to see if Mel did something, and then respond accordingly, with a commensurate level of severity for the circumstances, with the most appropriate and reasonably practicable action.

The other thing Mel said was that she was pregnant. She'd thought she had to formally notify her employer. "What wonderful news." Janice confirmed that in normal circumstances formal notification would be the case, but that as she was leaving shortly, it wasn't necessary. Mel asked if the employer needed to undertake a risk assessment. Janice gave the same response but said they could do one if she wanted one. Mel said she didn't really think it was necessary, she 'just thought...'.

Nothing else was said of the pension.

With Mel's handover to Jenny completed, it was becoming increasingly clear to both that at least one of them was now surplus to requirements. Mel didn't get frustrated with Jenny's snail's pace. Not even when she began to get the impression that all the new, more effective and efficient, systems she'd put in place would be quickly dropped, and they'd return to the old manual systems; not because they were better, but because Jenny lacked the intelligence and competence to understand and maintain the new ones.

Stuart and Hazel met with Janice to give her an opportunity to fill them in on any outstanding matters, through her exit interview. The boiler was due to be delivered on the Thursday before her last day, but she had things in hand. Mike would be in on the Friday for the fit. Not ideal, but just how things had panned out. She said if there were any issues, and she didn't anticipate there would be, she'd make sure everyone, including Mike, had her personal mobile number. She said she didn't mind getting work calls after she'd retired. Stuart thanked her, saying they'd only call her if they couldn't avoid it.

"I know you don't like a fuss made, Janice," Stuart said "but we need to give you a bit of a send-off. It won't come as a surprise that we've had a small collection for you and Trethendar is going to match it from petty cash."

"That's very kind, generous…" she said. She looked across to Hazel, who was making the notes on the exit interview form Janice had designed.

"Is there anything you'd like? We want you to have something you can keep and look back on and remind you of your time with us and your service to the charity."

She thought for a moment. "I really have no idea. I'm sorry, I just can't think."

"Well, if you do think of something, please let us know."

"I will."

"Otherwise, it may just be John Lewis vouchers, I'm afraid."

"A voucher would be fine."

"OK," he said. She smiled at him. He smiled back. "This must be rather strange after so long in the one place?"

"It is a bit. I've seen a lot of change, most of it good. There's been an awful lot on for me too in the past twelve months, one way and another. I'm looking forward to a break and settling into the next chapter, whatever that may be. I was looking forward to retiring, but wasn't sure, when the time came, if I'd really be ready to go. But I am, I think."

He sighed. It sounded like relief. "I've already had to commit your final pay to payroll," he said.

There'd be a party held in her honour. Perhaps a restaurant or something similarly simple after work. She'd book herself into a hotel that night, so she wouldn't have to rush off. Whitstable could be tricky to get back to if you left it too late. Not that she ever did nowadays. In the past, wherever she was in London, if she left later than 8:45pm, it was into the last and last-but-one train territory, and a Big Mac on Victoria Station's concourse.

Her house was a shell now, no longer a home. She'd pack herself a suitcase. That way she could stay out as late as she wanted and not appear ungrateful or rude by leaving prematurely. There was that cheap hotel that always seemed to have vacancies, near the Angel, just five or ten minutes' walk away. She'd book a bed there.

"Of course, I shall need to take your procurement card back," he said.

For fuck's sake. "I can't imagine I'll be using it again. I'll snip it in half if you like and leave it in the top drawer of my desk. In fact, everything will be in there. My keys, the phones, everything…" Stuart looked questioningly. "…my phone and Mel's."

"And the spare keys?" he fished.

"Spare keys?"

"Don't we have a spare set?"

"I thought I'd leave them for Mike. Just for this weekend, with the new boiler. Just in case he needs to come back in for anything. I'll leave everything else in that drawer for you. I'll change the security alarm codes too before I go, and leave instructions for that, and everything else. The new code will be 6161. You should probably change the codes more often than I've been doing."

He smiled at her. Hazel had been writing feverishly.

"It's going to be very strange without you, Janice," she said, looking up at last. "I hope you'll keep in touch with us all."

"Of course I will." She wouldn't. "I'll look forward to hearing all the gossip."

On Thursday, the new boiler arrived, bigger than she expected. Slightly overboard for the building's size. She called Mike as planned, so he could drop by and make sure he had everything for the installation the following day. He said he'd make an early start. She didn't know how he'd manage to get it down into the basement on his own. She didn't ask.

She'd said, "Here are the keys in case you need to be here in the morning before the rest of us."

"Thanks."

"The code for the alarm is—"

"-I have that, I think," Mike interrupted. "It's a sideways funnel." He entered the code into the air with his finger. "7651."

"No, I just changed it. It's 6161." She sounded terse.

"6161. I'd better write that down. I'm going to forget." He took out a pencil, sharpened with a Stanley knife, and wrote the code on the back of the boiler delivery note. "If everything goes to plan, the new boiler will be in, and it will be all finished by about 3:30pm."

"That would be wonderful."

"The one downside is there'll be no hot water for a couple of hours in the afternoon, and the cold will be on and off during the day. I'll give fifteen minutes or so's notice. I'll bleed the rads too and make sure everything else is sorted before wrapping up."

Friday morning, she arrived early and went straight to the hotel. She was too early to check in but arranged to leave her case there and check in later. Packing for London had been a strange experience. Halfway through, she'd switched from overnight bag to suitcase. She'd leave her overnight bag at the house. There was little left there now, nothing she'd ever miss or need to go back for. The house was under offer and although the exchange of contracts would be some weeks away, she'd begun to feel less and less at home, at home. She thought she might be happier being away. She didn't know how long for or where, just elsewhere and for as long as she wanted. If it went through sooner rather than later, she'd just rent somewhere short-term and cheap. Or she could just get on a plane to Florida and never look back.

Attempting small talk, she asked, "All packed, Mel?"

"Pretty much. I didn't want to leave it to the last minute."

Sticking his head round the door, Mike said, "Just to let you know, the water will be off again in about fifteen minutes. It'll be off for an hour this time so if you want to fill the kettle, now's your chance." He disappeared again. Hazel nipped out for a tactical, pre-emptive wee.

"What time's your flight?"

"3pm, so I'll have the morning."

"Not going out tonight?" She tried not to sound inquisitorial.

"I did all that last weekend. And besides, I don't want to miss your send-off." Her eyes began to mist. "I'm going to really miss everyone here. You've all been bloody great, especially you, Janice. I've loved it here."

Janice knew she should be touched, but she didn't really care. "Well, it's been lovely having you. You've been a ray of sunshine, a new broom."

"That's so sweet," she paused. "Can I ask you something, Janice, if you don't mind?" "Of course."

"You remember the lovely cakes you made for your birthday last year?"

"The honeybee buns."

"I know you don't normally share recipes, and I know it's really cheeky of me to ask, but I wondered if you'd make an exception? I've experimented, but they don't come out like yours. I can't get the frosting right."

"I..." she hesitated. "I'm sorry, Mel, but I just don't share. I never ask anyone for theirs either."

"It's just... I'm planning a party when I get home."

"Won't Chris be organising something?"

"Yes, but I wanted to do something special when I tell everyone about the baby. The cakes would be perfect and... it would be like having you there too."

She hesitated. "I know it seems silly but it's just the way I am. I can't."

"No?" she pleaded with a smile.

"No."

"...I'll just have to keep experimenting till I get them right in that case."

Mel lingered. "Was there something else?" Janice asked.

"It was just to ask if you'd managed to do that reference?"

"Yes, I did." She pulled out an envelope from her drawer, empty now except for her own work keys, dust and a few feral paperclips. She'd secretly had another set cut, a keepsake; keys to a moment from her past, never to be revisited. A leaving gift to herself, a souvenir like a carriage clock. Stuart might change the security code again in a few weeks, probably the locks too. Soon her symbolic set would be as useless and redundant as Jenny.

"Thank you so much for this by the way," said Mel, putting the reference in her bag.

"That reminds me—" but Janice stopped. She stood, pulling her bag over her shoulder and grabbing her mug. "No, let's get a tea, while we still can." Mel followed her to the stairs up to the kitchen.

"What were you going to say?"

"...I was just going to say we'll need your work phone and keys back, before you go."

"I can give you the phone now, if you want," she said as she passed it up. She hadn't meant right there and then. She took it. She had no pockets. A bit irritating. She dropped it in her bag.

"But I'm afraid I have a confession to make about the keys."

"What is it?"

"I'm so sorry, I've looked everywhere. I was sure they'd turn up when I was packing. I think I may have packed them or thrown them out by mistake."

Really? she thought. Mel had them a couple of weeks earlier. She'd had them almost a year and now she loses them, just before she knew she'd be asked to hand them back? "Oh, don't worry about it," Janice said reassuringly. She put a tea bag into each mug. There were two bottles of champagne in the fridge and a carton of semi-skimmed.

"I'll pay for some new ones."

"Not necessary, really."

It was feasible Mel had lost them, Janice thought, but what was puzzling was that if Mel was lying and did want to keep the keys longer for some reason, she'd have used them before now. She was flying to New Zealand the following morning. Would she really hang around work on a Friday night till everyone left, only to sneak back in, and do whatever it was? Perhaps the ditzy girl really had just lost them. It can happen – to accidentally bin something when you're moving.

They stood, waiting for the kettle to boil. The proverbial 'watched pot' did not disappoint.

Ever since she'd been excluded from the meeting with Philip O'Brien, there'd been no hint Mel was suspicious. Just bright 'n' breezy kiwi Mel with her perfect skin, perky breasts and preoccupation with 'babbys'. There was not one duplicitous bone in Mel's body. There wasn't the room with all that wholesome, sunshine-and-muesli enthusiasm, and seeing 'only the best' in people; all multiplied now that she was a yummy mummy in waiting.

Just before lunch, Mike told her, "We may have a problem." She instantly switched off mentally, but followed him down to the basement anyway, where he tried to explain. The place was a mess. It didn't look like he was anywhere near close to starting, let alone finishing. "You see this here," he said, tapping the base of a flue pipe or something still attached to the old boiler.

"Yes?"

"That's asbestos."

"Seriously?" she asked.

"I'm afraid so. I'm not allowed to touch it without the appropriate personal protective equipment."

"Have you got that?"

"Not here. Technically, I'm not meant to touch it at all, but I won't tell if you won't. It'll be fine if I have my PPE."

"Well," she sighed. There always seemed to be some-fucking-thing. Nothing was ever simple. "What does it mean?"

"It means it's not happening today, I'm afraid." Instantly sensing her rising displeasure, he continued,

"But I'll tell you what I can do. I'll shoot home right now, get the gear I need and come straight back. I won't get it all finished before half four, but I promise I'll have the old one out."

"And what about the new one?"

"Well, I'll come in tomorrow. I've got the keys and the code. It'll be fine. I was going to come in anyway. To be honest, it'll be easier to do it when the building's empty. I'll call you when it's done."

"It's Friday, it's my last day, Mike. I won't have my phone."

"Have you got a personal one?"

"I suppose so. It's not really on, though. I don't like surprises like this."

"I know, I'm sorry. What can I say?"

"So, you'll go now, get your PPE and take it all out today before you leave?"

"Correct. I'll take the old boiler away with me too and clear up. The only thing I'll need to do tomorrow is install the new one, and that's a doddle."

"What about all this?" she said, indicating the cracked concrete flooring and the hole to nowhere, infested with vermin.

"I'll make it all good tomorrow. I promise you, Janice, you'll not be disappointed."

"Well, if that's the best we can do…"

"I'll do a good job for you. I'll show you what I've done before I leave today."

"Alright." She was already halfway up the stairs out of the basement, muttering.

Mike kept his word and by 4:30pm, the old boiler was out, and he'd tidied the area in preparation for the Saturday morning. She held the front door open for him as he shuffled the old boiler through the front door. She didn't know what he was going to do with it. She didn't care. *Why does everything always have to end up happening at once?*

As she headed back up to the office, Stuart called for her, "Are you coming, Janice?"

"Yes"

She peered round the door into the office, it was empty, so continued up to the flat. Inside she was met with a friendly cheer and a round of applause from Stuart, Hazel, Jenny and Mel.

"Here she is," Stuart said. "We were beginning to wonder if you'd left without saying goodbye."

"No, I was just downstairs with Mike. All a bit of a drama, I'm afraid. He needs to come in tomorrow and finish installing the new boiler so there's only cold water, I'm afraid, till Monday."

Hazel laughed. "Let it go, Janice."

"Yes, your work here is done," Stuart chimed in, coining a phrase.

But it was true. Her work there really was done. She wouldn't return to her desk again. She wouldn't renew her annual season ticket again. She wouldn't see these twats again and she wouldn't be there when the once-great Trethendar breathed its death rattle. This really was it, her leaving do. Four people –the dregs of a once great charity, in a near-derelict building. Her worldly possessions in a suitcase in a three-star hotel that always had vacancies. Two bottles of champagne and three bowls of nibbles bought at lunchtime from Tesco. This was it. No dinner out, so no reason to have booked that hotel. This was the send-off she'd been counting down to. A pathetic end to a pointless career.

Stuart poured her a glass and attempted a touching speech about her years of service. "How many years has it been?" And the great contribution she'd made. He paid tribute to the cakes she'd bring in when someone left. Spoke of the changes the organisation had seen, the 'lean' times and how she'd always provided such a steady and reliable personnel – "Sorry, HR" service. He still didn't understand the difference between the two and they laughed. A safe pair of hands, he praised her professionalism, her thoroughness, her perseverance and her forensic eye for detail; no box left unticked when Janice was on the case. She'd been a joy to work with, would be greatly missed, "So please join me in wishing her a very long and happy— you don't have a glass, Mel," he said.

"No, I'm... off alcohol at the moment." Her face broke into a beam as the pennies began silently dropping.

"You're not, are you...?" Jenny shrieked.

"I am," laughed Mel, "Totally up the duff!"

Stuart and Hazel ran to give her a big hug and a peck.

"Oh my God, I knew it—"

"Congratulations!"

"But I didn't want to say anything."

"How long is it now?"

"Thirteen weeks."

"No! You kept that quiet."

"But, look, hey, this is Janice's moment," Mel said. "We haven't finished toasting her yet. I've got some juice right here."

"Of course, you're right," Stuart said as he raised his glass again, thrown off his stride. "Janice, look... many... thank you and for all your hard work, have a long and very happy retirement. May I present you with this small gift from all of us. To Janice!"

"Janice!" They toasted and gulped as she accepted the A4 manila gusset Stuart was presenting her with. Inside was a copy of the *Cotswold Preview*, an oversized card and John Lewis vouchers – £50. He also gave her a bunch of blooms, yellow-themed.

"I suppose you want me to say something now," she said. "I don't really have anything prepared so I just want to say... Congratulations, first, to lovely Mel. I know you'll make a wonderful mother and I'm sure Chris will be a great father." Mel's eyes flitted shiftily.

"Thank you to Stuart for those kind words. I've loved being at Trethendar. I've had a difficult year with my mother passing, as you know, but you've all been wonderful, and I wish nothing but the best for each of you individually and for the charity. It's a great organisation, it really is, and long may it continue to be so. Thank you for these beautiful flowers and my lovely gift and I hope that when you see the new boiler, you'll think of me." They laughed.

They chatted and ate the nibbles and drank the drink, and soon it was time to call it a night. There'd also been a collection and card for Mel. The whole affair lasted till just round 6pm. Hazel was the first to leave. Then Jenny. 'Do' over, Stuart left the glasses in the sink for Monday. They collected their things from their desks on the way down.

She took a last look at the office, her desk, her chair… then turned out the light for the last time. She knew she was probably keeping them waiting. She'd mentally and emotionally cut all ties to Trethendar as soon as retirement became visible on the distant horizon. She felt cold towards the charity. She thought about leaving behind the keys she'd had cut rather than bin them; her sentimental gift to herself unwanted now, but an extra set might look odd.

They'd already turned the lights off on the stairs. Mel stood in the street, Stuart waiting at the door, he smiled at Janice.

"I gave you the code, didn't I?" she said anxiously to Stuart as she passed him and joined Mel outside. Life in Farringdon started to pick up at about this time on a Friday and the restaurants and pubs were already filling and spilling onto the streets, pints in hand, a warm evening.

"I've got it." He entered the code and the beeping alerted them to the fact that they had one minute to vacate the premises. He locked the door. "Look, I'd ask you if you wanted to go for another drink…"

"I have to shoot too unfortunately," said Mel.

"Same here," said Janice. "I need to get home and—"

"Feed the cat? What's his name again? Bimbo, isn't it?" Mel suddenly felt a rush of embarrassment. That flush you get when you cross a line you didn't know was there.

"That's right. I should get home."

Stuart put his arms out. This meant she had to hug him. Then it was Mel's turn, then the hugging was over.

"It's the end of an era," he said. "Sorry again I can't stay. Have a safe journey home both of you, won't you?" He headed off, leaving the two of them.

"Bye, Stuart. And Janice, thanks heaps. I've learnt so much from you."

Her laugh naturally forced, "Really? I find that hard to believe." She was ready for Mel to let go of her elbows now.

"It's true. I'll miss you, I really will. Thank you." She gave her a squeeze. "Bye then."

"Bye, Mel. All the best."

She stood for a moment of the corner of the Y-shaped split in the road till Mel turned the corner towards the Barbican, out of sight. Instead of walking her normal route, through Smithfield to Cannon Street, she turned and slowly walked towards the hotel.

That was it.

Being free felt strange. Cut loose. She had almost no possessions, no job, no family; but she did have a considerable nest egg to survive off quite happily, thank you very much, until the end of her days. She had a regular income from her generous pensions, which would start paying out in a couple of weeks and she had Casa Cariño in Florida and the memory of dear Ben, hugging her heart. Truly free, for the first time, from all ties that drag you down. Far from feeling fearful, rudderless, she was alive, in the now, exhilarated by the unknown next moment. She was indestructible. She had no idea whether she'd return to Whitstable on Saturday or not. There was no reason to. She had nothing to go back for. Nothing else mattered now.

Cosy in her no-frills room, she made a point of not setting an alarm. She gave herself permission to wake up whenever the hell she woke up. She didn't even fish out her phone, that's how arsed she couldn't be. She'd picked up a sandwich on the way, plus a bumper bag of chocolate buttons and bottle of water. She'd checked in and hunkered down for a night of crap TV, ankles crossed, on her hotel bed, nibbling contentedly like a rat in a cupboard.

She awoke at her normal time. She'd hoped to wake up late for once and miss breakfast. She'd always been up with the lark. She lay in bed for a moment as the 6am sun streamed. Shouldn't she feel some anxiety about not having anything to do, anyone to speak to, anywhere to go? She grinned, then got up for her shower.

She consciously moved at an unfamiliar, unnaturally leisurely pace. She drank all the complimentary tea, coffee and hot chocolate sachets provided as she mooched about. Peering outside, munching the last complimentary shortbread, the street below was quiet. This part of London was mainly businesses. There was literally not a soul in sight. She'd never seen it so deserted. When she couldn't stomach another moment's loitering, she popped downstairs, about 8am, and asked if it was possible to stay an extra night or two.

"Stay as long as you like. We're practically empty. Just let us know when you're going, and we'll sort the bill for you."

Breakfast wasn't over till 10am, so she could always pop back down if she felt peckish. How would she spend the first day of the rest of her life? A gallery?

Back in her room, her stomach churned suddenly at the sound of her mobile phone buzzing in her bag. There was no one who'd be calling her, let alone at that time. A sales call... on a Saturday? A wrong number? It had to be. Irritation building, she'd give whoever it was a piece of her mind. She rummaged in her bag. *Where was the damn thing? Incessant ringing. Where the fuck...?* She emptied the contents onto the bed. Maybe Mike? A bit early for him. *There.* She grabbed it and... noted she still had Mel's work phone. Another irritant. She could always pop it through the letterbox on the way to wherever it was she ended up going. She pushed the green button.

"Hello?"

"Hello, is that Janice Mead?" It wasn't Mike.

"Speaking."

"I'm sorry to bother you so early on a Saturday." Her stomach churned.

"This is Appleyard Security Services. I wasn't sure if we were going to be able to get hold of anyone. The primary number we have for you, listed as the work mobile, went straight to voicemail and the second number, the 01227 number... that one just rang out."

"Yes, I left Trethendar yesterday, retired, so I don't have my work phone anymore and my home number..." She paused for a second to think. "I couldn't get to it in time. What's this about?"

"It's sure to be nothing, but the security alarm at your offices has just been activated."

She stopped breathing. Her head emptied. Her heart was in her throat.

17

"Hello?"

"Yes, I heard you," she said. She looked at her watch. She turned the TV on and turned the volume up, so she'd need to raise her voice to talk over it. Creating a 'home' context. "Sorry, let me just turn the television down." She turned it down, just enough that it would still be audible.

"It's probably nothing, so don't worry. Its normally a window left open, or a pigeon or something. Do you want us to attend site or notify the police for you?" She hesitated. Were those the only options? "Are you at home now?" he asked.

"Yes," she said.

"It's Whitstable, isn't it?"

"That's right."

"I recognise the dialling code, great place. As you won't be able to get there, I can go to the next contact we have for Trethendar. Or do you want us to attend? Or call the police?"

"No. Look don't worry just yet. I'll phone the office right now and see who it is. We have someone doing some plumbing there this morning, so it's probably him.

I'll call you back if there's a problem or we need you to reset it."

She ended the call, noting the caller number. She looked up Mike's. He'd texted her on her personal mobile once. She scrolled through the caller history to find it. There it was. She saved him to her contacts. She pushed 'dial' as she pulled on her Raynaud's gloves.

"Mike?"

"Yes? Janice? What time is it?"

No security alarm going off at his end. Something else was happening; something she didn't understand. She tried to sound casual. "Look, I'm sorry to bother you, Mike. I just couldn't remember what time you said you'd be in today, for the boiler."

"I'm just about to leave so probably about... just before half nine or something. If that's still OK?"

She looked at her watch. 8:17am. "Yes, no problem. I'm sorry, I just wasn't sure. Sorry to bother you."

"No problem. I'll give you a buzz when I'm all done."

"Yes. On this number. Bye."

So, it wasn't Mike. Stuart? No. He lived too far away to be there that early and besides, he wouldn't have set it off accidentally. A break-in then? Most likely a false alarm. It was not Jenny. Hazel? No, didn't Hazel say she was doing something this weekend; and it couldn't be Mel because she'd lost her keys and was flying home today.

She put her purse and Mel's old phone into her bag and turned the volume back up on the TV. She sat on the end of the bed and dialled her direct line desk number. She looked up with the phone to her ear. She could hear it ringing. She waited till her out of office message kicked in. She waited.

That Friday night of her last working day, Mel called New Zealand, just before 7am their time. A shorter call than normal as they were both exhausted and would be seeing each other in the flesh very soon anyway. Just before saying their goodbyes, Chris had asked, "So what was so weird that time? You never did tell me."

"Er... not sure. When?" she asked.

"You said there was something weird after that pensions meeting the other week but never said what."

"Oh that. Nothing. I was going to tell you when I saw you. Just me being me."

"Tell me. Unless you have to shoot or something?"

"No, I'm in no hurry. It'll sound dumb now, but... You remember me telling you I found a passport in my boss's desk, and it looked like her, and at the same time, didn't? All done up, looking like Rose from the *Golden Girls* or something, and with a different name...?"

"I remember."

"Well, that's the first thing, so hold that thought. I know it doesn't sound like much, but believe me, if you knew her, you'd know that was weird. And before you say anything, I know it's none of my business but... and it was an accident..."

"Yeah, you were accidentally rifling through her desk."

"I needed some staples and the drawer got stuck because it'd slipped down the back, so I fished it out. She was probably glad I'd found it for her. Anyway..."

Chris, only half-listening, focussed on making breakfast. She explained that she knew Janice was now drawing her pension, but what was weird, and this was the second thing, was that she was almost certain the name of the only other beneficiary, was the same as the name in the passport. "With Janice's face and the same date of birth but not Janice's face, if you know what I mean."

"Seriously?"

"But that's not all," she said. She said it sounded like three of the other beneficiaries, in fact the only other beneficiaries, had all died in the last twelve months. "Now, call me Jessica Fletcher, but isn't that a bit... thing? She retired today" There was a silence. Chris sat on the couch, munching a mouthful of sandwich, trying to listen to Mel and watch the TV, on very quietly.

"So...? What are you saying?"

"It's weird, isn't it?"

"What is it? Fraud, you think?"

"Maybe. I don't know."

"Well, look it's too late now. You've left. You've probably got the wrong end of the stick. You'll never know, and you don't really want to get involved. Tomorrow you'll be on your way home, that's all I care about."

The subject changed, but Chris was obviously too dozy or distracted to talk or think and the call ended shortly after that. Mel finished packing her world in the enormous backpack, except for what she'd need for the following morning, and turned in for the night. Everything else, she'd given away to her London friends or the local charity shop.

It would take her a good ninety minutes to get to Heathrow from Wood Green normally, but she had nothing to hang around for now. She may as well get up at her normal get-up-for-work time and head off. She'd get there ridiculously early, potter around the airport shops. She'd hung on to her work key and planned to check-in online from the office when she swung by on her way to the airport. She could log into Janice's old PC and see if she could print that recipe off while she was at it. It may be one of the last things saved to her machine, if it was there at all. Her most recent creations would probably be in the notebook they'd given her last year. Janice didn't go far without that notebook, and it looked like she'd almost filled it; beaten up, ratty-looking thing.

She then planned to put the keys in an envelope through the door with a note she'd written to Stuart saying 'what a ditz, found the keys, sorry, here they are'. They wouldn't know she'd been in. She'd get to Heathrow with heaps of time. It wasn't devious. Initially, she *really* had thought she'd lost the keys but there'd been plenty of time before now when she could have returned them. She could have used an internet café for her boarding pass. This was just easier and what's the big deal anyway? The added plus was the cake recipe and she'd always gone the extra mile for them, it was only a recipe and no one would know. Even if they did find out, she already had her reference and she'd be the other side of the planet.

Changing lines at King's Cross for Farringdon, she started to regret not just calling a cab. Lugging her backpack up and down escalators, across concourses and through tunnels. The underground wasn't designed with travellers in mind. She could have just checked-in at the airport too. She could have asked if she could check-in online at work on the Friday. The name in that passport looked familiar. But this way, she'd be able to put her mind at rest about the pension thing and get the recipe. Sounded a bit pathetic now. Must be her baby brain. Was it worth this hassle?

She arrived at Farringdon, deserted, and made the short walk to Trethendar. She left her backpack by the door and pulled out the unsealed envelope with her pre-written note and keys inside. She unlocked the building, opened up and the security alarm beeped, giving her one minute to enter the code. Yanking the backpack inside, and stuffing the envelope and note into her pocket, she went to the panel and entered the code.

The digital display said **** was incorrect, that she had two more attempts. She'd done this before, more than once. Why wasn't it working? She felt sick. She had a minute to get it right. Had she entered it incorrectly? She didn't think so. She must have done. She entered it again, this time slowly, making sure she got it right, sideways funnel shape, pushing each number deliberately and whispering under her breath, "6751".

Incorrect.

"Shit." She hadn't entered the wrong code. "Shit, shit, shit."

The bastard alarm was going to go off. She had one more attempt. The pitch of the warning beep changed. She'd never heard this before; must mean she had only thirty seconds left, or fifteen; how long had it been? She'd have to guess. It's going to be something obvious. It could be the same number but in reverse or the same but with a 2 at the end instead of a 1 or something else, anything, it could be absolutely fucking anything.

"Shit. No." Slowly and deliberately she entered 1576.

The beeping stopped.

Had she done it? Had she? She must have done. Still trembling, she breathed a sigh of relief and smiled to herself. Then the alarm went off. Deafening.

"Oh, please no. No, no, no, no!" she yelled putting her hands over her ears. Piercingly shrill. She started towards the stairs. Then shifted back to the door. She didn't know what to do. She turned the knob to relock the door and, leaving her backpack downstairs, ran up to the office, reaching for the mobile in her pocket as she went. At least it might be slightly quieter up there.

She'd call Janice. She'd understand. She'd just come clean. She'd just say she'd found the keys, was going to pop them through the door but seeing as she was there, thought she'd save time by checking-in. She'd not mention the recipe or anything else. That would be a plausible reason for being there, she thought. Jesus, that noise.

She went straight to the cabinet where the personnel files were kept and grabbed Janice's out, opening it on Janice's desk. She started at the back of the file, rifling through it, scanning then flicking the pages. Eventually, she found a home phone number on a yellowing application form next to her original references. She didn't think Janice had moved since then. It was the only number there. She winced at the relentlessly screeching alarm. She put her mobile on the desk and dialled the number from the desk phone, it would be easier to be heard.

The alarm in the stairwell sounded angrier. What would happen if it just kept going? Janice's phone just rang out, no answer. She didn't want to hang up. She pictured Janice rushing down the stairs in a brown, padded bathrobe, but it just rang. She started looking for another number. If there was, she could call that from her mobile and whichever was answered first...

Scanning and turning the pages, the alarm hurting her ears, she hoped the police wouldn't come. Her flight. Her eyes began to fill. Her understanding was that the alarm was picked up somewhere and someone there then called one of the keyholders before calling the police. She didn't work there. She'd broken in. She should just leave, leave with it still sounding but it could go on all weekend, people would complain. She'd be in New Zealand though. They'd never know it was her. Her keys would be in an envelope with her note on the mat. They'd know she'd been there. They'd understand. She'd just explain.

She found a mobile phone number. Her continued personnel-file-rifling paid off. It was written, in Stuart's handwriting, on a Post-it stuck to a sickness absence self-certification form. Janice had given Mel her personal mobile number once before and this could well be it. She dialled the number from her mobile.

A phone stuck to each ear muffled the alarm. The home number was still ringing and the other number, Janice's mobile, was... was engaged. She hung up

Janice's desk phone and stopped the call on the mobile. She redialled Janice's mobile again. Still engaged. She stopped the call. She redialled again. Engaged. She did this over and over. She'd keep calling till Janice picked up or the police arrived, whichever came first. She glanced through the last few pages of the file in case there was another number. There wasn't. She redialled again. Engaged. Stop, redial, engaged. Stop, redial – suddenly, the phone on Janice's desk started ringing. For a split second, Mel had to think whether she should pick it up or not. What the fuck? She stopped the call from her mobile. Maybe Janice just missed the call and done the 1471 last number recall thing. Maybe the number on the old post-it note wasn't even hers. She picked up the phone. Sticking a finger in her ear to hear.

"Hello?"

"Mel? Is that you?"

Yes, Janice. Thank God. I'm so sorry. I set the alarm off by mistake."

"I know, they just called me," she said with a comforting laugh in her voice. "Did you just try me at home?"

"Yes," Mel said with audible relief. She could just hear a TV in the background of Janice's end, comforted knowing she was now in safe hands.

"I'm sorry I couldn't get to it in time. Look, you need to enter the code to disable the system."

Straining to hear, she asked, "What do I need to do?"

Very clearly, Janice replied, "Enter 6161. It'll reset."

"6161? Nothing else? That's all?"

"Yes. Go and do that now. I'll wait here."

She waited on the other end while Mel ran downstairs to the alarm panel. A moment later the alarm stopped. She heard Mel nearing the top of the stairs again, taking two at a time, entering the office, sitting down at Janice's desk again, picking up the phone, breathless.

"I did it. Thank you. I'm so, so sorry."

She laughed. "Don't worry. We've all done it. No harm done."

"Do I need to call someone?"

"No, I'll sort all that." She paused. "You found your keys then?"

"Yes. They were… in the last place I looked."

"As lost things often are. What are you doing there, anyway? Shouldn't you be flying home?"

"I was just going to check-in online if that's OK?"

It had to be a lie. All lies. Mel suspected. She knew. The deceitful girl, always seeming all that sweetness yet here she was, breaking in, she had no business, hunting, rooting about. Without changing the reassuring smile in her voice or the kindness in her tone, Janice said, "Yes of course. You carry on. Don't be surprised, though, if you hear Mike. He's back in this morning, in an hour or so, to finish off."

"OK."

"Look I'd better just—" Silence.

"Sorry, Janice, you cut out there for a second."

"Can you hear me now?"

"Yes."

"I was just saying I've just stepped out of the house as I have to nip to the shops. I'll call the security company straight back and tell them everything's under control."

"OK, Janice. Thank you. I'm so sorry."

"No problem. Stay if you like and do what you need to do. Safe flight." She cut the call off. She looked up Appleyard's number and without breaking her brisk pace down the empty, early morning London street, pulled Mel's work phone from her bag, and dialled.

"Appleyard Security Services?"

"Hi," she said, in a slightly higher voice, doing a passable New Zealand accent for the first time in her life. "My name's Melissa and... I'm such a ditz, I only went and set of the alarm off, didn't I."

"Where are you calling from?"

"Trethendar's. I think you just called my boss, Janice, a while ago."

"That's correct."

"She just called me and gave me the code, so the alarm's all off now and its sorted. Panic over."

"I'll close the call. Thanks for letting us know."

"No worries. Thanks heaps, and sorry for the bother. Bye."

If she continued at the same pace, she'd be outside the building in under five minutes.

Mel was sitting at Janice's PC, off the hook, waiting for it to fire up. What an effing relief. The username appeared on screen: jmead. She keyed in bimbo49, no capitals, no spaces. She hoped this hadn't changed as well. It would've been bimbo50 if it didn't work the first time, but it did.

There were a few .doc icons left on Janice's desktop. She went to Files. Empty. She went back to the desktop. Janice had cleared everything except the few left on the desktop. Then – 'hbb.doc'. Bingo. She double-clicked and there it was: 'honeybee buns'. Ctrl+P. She ran to turn on the printer/copier; crappy, always jamming, took ages to warm up.

Back at Janice's desk, she double-clicked the internet icon and shut down the recipe while the printer prepared to print it off. A quick search for her airline. She had plenty of time now and the plumber was on his way, but she didn't feel like spending any longer there than she needed to. She flew downstairs to fetch the e-ticket from her backpack.

Back in the office, the printer was making the 'I'm ready to print now' sound. She went to 'check-in online' and entered the e-ticket reference code. All the flight details came up with her name and everything. She selected her seat from the fifteen or so remaining and sent her boarding pass to the printer too. She flicked back a step on the check-in page and had the boarding pass emailed to herself as well, so she could pick it up on her phone, in case. She sat back, waiting for the printer to finish warming up. She went to close Janice's personnel file then stopped. She still had time. She could sneak a peek, no one would know.

She peeled the post-it back to see more of the sickness absence self-certification form, completed by Janice, authorised by Stuart. Thursday 28 and Friday 29 July. Her eyes narrowed, frowning a squint as she searched her memory. Sliding open the bottom drawer of the filing cabinet, for the pensions files, she pulled the one out, opening it at her desk, leafing through until she found it. Mrs Miller, the wife of former employee Peter Miller, died 28 July. A chill creeped her flesh. She looked for the other dates. Mr Westrell died on Thursday 7 July. She grabbed Janice's file; there was nothing there to say she was off sick or on annual leave or anything on that date, but the name; was that the name in that passport? The pages were so tightly bound in the file that once open, they'd roll open, slowly, independently and irritatingly covering the page behind.

If there'd been a pattern... if Janice had been out of the office on the day both died... That name, though, 'Westrell'. The passport picture had grabbed her attention more. Was the name Westrell? The more she thought about it, the more she thought that Chris was right; it wasn't any of her business. She'd never know why Janice had that passport stuffed down the back of her desk. It could have been someone who'd had Janice's desk before Janice for all she knew. Janice was so 'by-the-book'. But seeing as how she was there, for completeness, she might as well check out the last one. Irene Hartley died on 18 February of this year, a Saturday. There was no pattern, it was random. No way of knowing and so unlikely, just coincidence.

She returned to thinking about what she'd gone there to do and shoved the conspiracy theories from her mind. It wasn't her responsibility. If there was something odd it wouldn't get passed Stuart. She'd shoot as soon as her printing was done.She took the envelope from her pocket, with the note for Stuart about the keys, and gazed at it. Was it still necessary? The cat was kind of out of the bag.

The archaic printer eventually sparked into life, making her jump, printing off the recipe and boarding pass, ball-achingly laboured and loud. She left the envelope on Janice's open personnel file and wandered to stand over the printer.

Downstairs, suddenly a sound. Unlocking of the front door.

She'd locked it when she'd come in, she knew she had. She looked to the open office doorway, listening to downstairs. The front door opened and clicked shut. Then nothing. Nothing. No footsteps, no sound nothing.

"Mike? Is that you, Mike?"

18

Too shit-scared to call again. He'd have heard her if it was him. Whoever it was, heard, but didn't answer. Silently, she walked to the door to listen. Nothing. Not breathing, she craned her head, peering round the side of the door and down part of the stairwell. She stepped out silently, starting down, then stopping to listen. Frozen, halfway, looking to sense any movement on the ground floor, the front door. Fearful and at the same time embarrassed by her misplaced (most likely) fear, she waited. There was no one there. All she could hear was the painfully slow, strained efforts of the printer. It had sounded so like the front door. She continued down the stairs, but did so fast and noisily this time, with heavy clomping footsteps, to give any intruder due warning and sufficient scarper time.

The ground floor archive, opposite the front door, a hallway room with its filthy windows, rank carpet, unstacked stackable chairs and membership filing cabinets could have been a smart reception area once, now it was a dusty, dumping ground. No one was there. Her backpack, where she'd left it, untouched. She tugged at the front door. Still locked from the inside. Familiar noises in busy buildings can sound unfamiliar when the building is empty; the noise must have been outside, or next door.

Relief turned suddenly to fear as a sickening realisation dawned. The reason she couldn't see anyone in front might be because they were now standing behind her. She wanted to run, but more than that, wanted to look. She could quickly look and probably still unlock the door and get out. Heart pounding, she turned; no one was there.

Fuck's sake, Mel, she said to herself. *Get a frigging grip*. She ran back up the stairs, two at a time, muttering, "All this cortisol will be doing the baby no good whatsoever. Get a grip, woman. Get your stuff and get the fuck out."

In the basement, against the wall in the dark, staring at the door at the top of the stairs, Myra stood, listening to Mel go back up to the office. The light from the archive room splintered through the cracks round the door and fell onto the new boiler standing, in its cellophane wrap, neatly out of the way. Before going up, she switched on the light and drifted further into the basement, passing the five filing cabinets, trailing her gloved finger along the sides as she went.

"Look at the muck," she'd said quietly at the end, u-turning round, continuing past the partition they backed against, to see the scattered evidence the other side of Mike's unfinished work.

The top layer of his open toolbox was full of screws and bolts, packs of tacks, tape and odds and sods. She lifted the shelf layer out to find underneath the bulkier stuff. A set of three electrical screwdrivers, wrenches, two more screwdrivers, Phillips head and normal, wire, glue, mastic. She picked up the hammer. Not a large one, but bigger than one used for knocking copper tacks into ply, the only hammer in the box. She tucked it down the back of her navy skirt, hammer head hidden by her jacket.

Rearranging herself, she noticed the spot where the old boiler stood before uninstallation. Mike said he was going to make the floor good again before he left for the day, but it looked to her like the lazy sod just upped sticks when he felt like it. He hadn't fixed the floor at all. A botched job, left unfinished, a mess. He was always late too. She hadn't completely believed him when he said he was on his way. She turned and walked back the way she'd come, then swiftly, silently up the stairs from the basement, light left on, door closed.

The racket the printer was still making masked the sound of her climbing the stairs. The printer stopped, struggling to continue, like a paper jam. Mel muttered in frustration. Myra heard the paper tray being pulled out.

Instinct replaced thought, no emotion. Pure, distilled attention.

Nearing the pokey landing, Myra knew Mel would be eight or nine feet from the door if it was out of paper. If it was a jam, though, she'd be right by the door. She drifted ghostlike up the last few steps and peered around the doorframe's edge. Mel stood from a squat and turned distractedly, holding a wrapped ream and gasped, dropping the paper as one hand went to her chest and the other to her throat.

"Jesus!" Mel startled, trying to make sense of the figure in the doorway. "Janice, you scared the crap out of me." She stared at Mel, expressionless, looking through her. "How did you get here?"

Myra glanced at the printer, paper tray out, slowly taking in the whole room. Mel's personal phone on the desk, and some files. She recognised the lever arch as the pensions, the other was a personnel file. *Her* personnel file.

"What are you doing here?"

"I... I was just printing off my boarding pass. It was out of paper, but there's still some in there. It must have jammed. I was going to put some more in. It doesn't like it if it doesn't have a certain amount in the tray. You made me jump."

"What are you doing here?"

She was trying to understand. "I'm not stealing, Janice." She took up the ream, tore it open and loaded some into the paper tray, jostling it back in. "If that's what you think?"

She moved towards Mel's desk. "Shall I put these away for you?" Noting the contents of the pages it was opened at, Myra picked up the pension file, flipped it shut and filed it back where it belonged. The machine sparked back into life and Mel's print job continued.

"I'm nearly done."

Turning her open personnel file on the desk, noting what Mel had seen and expressionless, she joined the dots. She closed and filed it away. She turned back and stared at Mel as the printing finished. Mel smiled at her, uncomfortably. Myra didn't smile back. The final page out, a wave of relief, turning off the printer, Mel folded her printing in half. She didn't want Janice to see she had her recipe. She didn't check if any of it had printed off properly, what with the age of the printer, running out of paper...

"I'm not doing anything wrong, I promise."

"Why was the pension folder out? You don't work here anymore."

"I got it out by accident."

"By accident?"

"When the alarm went off. I didn't know what I was doing. I was trying to find your number."

"Why is my PC on?"

"I was logging in online."

"Why not use yours?"

"Yours was nearer."

"You used my password."

"I was just there right after I rang you. It was easier. I thought you were home." None of it made sense and she knew it, even as the honest words defensively tumbled out.

Myra leaned over her old desk and logged out, switching off the PC. She slowly walked back, positioning herself in front of the exit. "If you tell me what you're looking for, maybe I can help you find it."

"I wasn't looking for anything, Janice, honestly. I was just already at your desk."

"Tell me your experience of databases."

"Databases?"

"What does equal opportunities mean to you?" Something was wrong. Sounding like it was intended to clarify, but maintaining a cold, vacant stare, Myra asked, "Can you tell me about a time when you made a positive contribution to the work of the team?"

Mel didn't know what to say. "I... don't understand."

"I'll repeat the question. What you need to understand is that you not only have to deliver what you've promised but you always need to get what's due to you, so... and I've done everything..." The monotone suddenly fell as her lip quivered, intense emotion contorted both her face and seething voice as she spat the last hissing words and a tear pooled in her eye. "... *everything* to ensure I get what I was promised. I did everything you're meant to do, for years, and I will not walk away now without what's owed me."

"Well... I have to... if I'm going to catch my flight."

"As an HR professional you have to consider, or rather, ask yourself..." Her eyes deadening again, the rage now slipping away, transmuted to an insincere, smiling kindness, patronising almost, quiet, barely inaudible. "...what you must ask is, were your actions within the band of reasonable responses? Are they defensible? In exceptional circumstances, and remember I can't tell you what to do, as ultimately the decision lies primarily with the line manager. It's my job to advise and maintain a record of the meeting on file. With a robust process of regular one-to-ones, annual appraisals and careful performance management... if required, as appropriate and if reasonably practicable, identify any new learning and development needs. Measurable, specific, timebound... Although not express terms, you'll find that this is all part of the implied terms and conditions. There's custom and practise too, and a mutuality of obligation; we can't lose sight of... we do so at our peril..."

"Janice, what's wrong?"

Myra looked her directly in the eye for the first time. "You'll recall me saying earlier that you will have an opportunity to ask questions at the end of the interview?"

Mel hesitated, then calmly walking towards Janice. "I really must go. My flight. You're sure you'll be alright?"

"There are no trick questions so if you don't understand something or something isn't clear and you want me to repeat it, then that's absolutely fine. You can make notes too if you wish. I'm afraid... it gives me great pleasure... I can confirm... in this case, that the principles of natural justice continue to apply."

"Janice?" she said, expecting her to step aside so she could leave.

"We never really had the numbers to justify something like that or found ourselves in the enviable position to claim to be an employer of choice. We don't offer benefits other than the statutory leave entitlement and we only offer that because we have to—"

"Janice?" Mel said, stepping closer, trying to get to the door.

"And there's the bank holidays of course and the three Christmas closure days—"

"Can I just squeeze—"

"And of course, not forgetting—"

"Please...?"

Suddenly she shunted Mel's shoulder back hard, with the heel of her hand. "Our very generous, final salary pension scheme."

"What are you doing?"

"My fucking pension." She shoved her shoulder again, harder this time. "Closed to new fucking members." She pulled her hand right back and belted her across the face. "But you know all about that, don't you?"

Mel tried to push by. "I need out."

"Policies and procedures must be adhered to because the only thing worse than not having a policy, is having one and failing to follow it. Such a failure may lead to the disciplinary procedure being invoked. It's a standard three stage process, in line with the ACAS code of practice. The first stage is informal."

"What?"

"Don't pretend you don't know."

"I don't."

"Well, I'm afraid I have a ticked box on your signed induction form that says different—"

"I don't understand."

"I never leave a box unticked."

She tried to move her out of the way of the door. "I'm leaving now. Right now. You're not yourself." She tried to push past, but Janice had locked herself in position in the door frame. Her silver cross (normally concealed beneath her blouse) caught the light as it swung with a jerk round her neck. Mel tried the other side, but Janice lurched across, arms still locked in the door frame, not letting her out. Mel grabbed her arm and tried loosening the grip and yanking it out of the way, but she couldn't. The woman's upper arm was locked in place like a steel cable.

"If your performance or behaviour does not improve to the requisite standard and within the designated and agreed review period, then we will be left with no option but to invoke the second stage. The first formal stage…"

"I just want to go…"

Mel put her hand over Janice's grip on the door frame, pulling her fingers back, but she was locked there fast. She pulled back for a second, then made a dive under the arm, to squeeze between the door frame and Janice's body, but her arm grabbed Mel's shoulder and her other swung round, tugging her by the hair, yanking down hard, causing her to spine to arch and her jaw to fall open with a scream. They staggered a few steps out, onto the landing. She kneed Mel in the buttock, again and again.

"I don't want to fight!" Mel cried.

She thrashed round with her other arm as Janice, still pulling her by the hair, repeatedly kicked out at the backs of Mel's legs. Kicking, they struggled, gasping. Mel's hand flicked round and grabbed the stair banister, the stairs leading up to the flat, reaching out at nothing. The excruciating, eye-watering hair-pulling pain. She hung on and kicked back, her scalp burning. Mel got her in the kneecap but her grip on Mel's hair twisted, intensified. Myra reached behind her and the hammer, coming from nowhere, cracked down hard on the back of Mel's right hand against the handrail, shattering the bones at the base of the fingers, and she screamed, then another blow, then another and with the agony searing, she lost her grip. She yanked her hair again. Mel took a steadying step but missed a stair at the top of the flight, spraining an ankle. She took another step, looking down the stairwell. The HR professional behind her higher, on the landing, still hanging onto her hair, the hammer raised high over her head. Mel was going to fall.

"No. No fucking way, you crazy bitch." Mel grabbed the handrail tight, steadied herself, confusion and fear giving way to defiance, she stood her ground, shielding her broken hand. She'd not be beaten.

Myra was still kicking wildly at Mel's legs, spitting gasps through gritted teeth. If the grip on her hair loosened, Mel could escape. That wasn't going to happen, but she couldn't reach Mel's hand gripping the banister. She waited to get a good, clear shot, then brought the hammer down hard on the back of Mel's head. It skimmed a glancing blow but had more of an impact where the neck meets the shoulder. Mel let go of the handrail, instinctively reaching for the back of her neck. She let go of her hair and Mel turned. She loomed in the landing half-light, steadying herself, hammer in hand. The crazy bitch had just hit her with a fucking hammer.

The stair carpeting was loose and dirty, the banister wobbly in the wall, the walls woodchip wallpapered, porridgey, painted a multitude of times in cream, eggshell emulsion. The things you notice when your line manager is trying to kill you. Myra pulled her leg back as far as it would go. Her eyes wide and wild, her mouth open, gritted teeth, bubbles of spittle, panting, growling, a wild raging face. She kicked Mel in the left breast. Her mouth fell open and her eyes rolled back with the sickening hot and deep agony. She kicked her again, full force in the tummy, to the left of her navel, and Mel let out a despairing cry, let go of the rail, her knee buckling, legs crumpling underneath and falling backwards down the stairs. Her legs flicked over her head. It happened so fast, her neck bending quickly by the weight and speed of her body backwards somersaulting; her chin was forced against her breastbone, biting her tongue. Falling backwards towards the cold, hard floor at the bottom, where she landed with a crumpled crack.

Tasting blood, Mel sobbed at the thought of her unborn baby and using her good hand, pulled herself across the floor of the archive room towards Trethendar's entrance. It was right there. Intense pain from her multiple injuries were nothing compared to the fear and grief she felt for her unborn child. Maybe she could pull her bum along the floor quicker than if she tried to stand and run for the door. Something had happened to her knee in the fall. Janice was running down the stairs. She could make it to the front door. It was within reach. She'd need to stand up to unlock it and hoped there'd be someone to help. Mike was on his way. She had to focus and get out and this could be her best chance, her only chance. She dragged her own dead bodyweight across the floor, her good leg pushing uselessly. Near the door, so nearly there, she could make it if she moved faster, dragging herself.

Myra reached the bottom of the stairs and scurried towards her. Mel rolled over and stood to make a run for it, hobbling in agony, staggering towards the door. Mel felt her hands grip her ankles and her feet tugged away from underneath, she bellyflopped against the floor, her chin cracking hard, blood and broken tooth fragments. Crying, she reached for the door again, but her palm weakly slapped against it, inches below the lock and handle. If she could just push herself up, she'd reach. She reached.

Myra tightened her hold on the ankles, lifted the legs and dragged her across the floor towards the basement. Mel's crumpled shirt rode up, showing the bruised base of her naked back as she helplessly watched her only way out, grow more distant. She threw open the basement door and pulled Mel down the first few steps. Trampling back up over the girl to reach the doorway, she tried to kick her down from there. Like kicking a sandbag. But she wouldn't go. She stamped her heel at the girl's shoulders and kicked at the side of her head, but she wouldn't budge. Precarious as it was, she squatted on the top step and lifted Mel as best she could, but Mel's bewildered arms flailed to shield herself. The pain was considerable, and she just sobbed, asking Janice to stop. "Please stop!" Broken, badly bruised and blood in her mouth. She hoisted Mel up by the armpits, then moved from her squatting position so the girl now knelt in front of her, teetering at the top of the basement stairs, reaching out from encroaching dark to steady herself but there was nothing to hold. Janice stood and drew her leg back to kick her again, swinging at speed, catching her under the chin, her jaw teeth snapping against her upper teeth. She still wouldn't fall so with her other leg, full force, she sideways-stamped on Mel's breastbone, and the girl she fell down the stairs backwards into the basement.

It was hard to tell if Mel was conscious as she stepped over her. She wasn't moving, her eyes half closed. Her breathing deep and raspy, sounding like she was still trying to talk or cry or beg. She took her by the ankles and pulled her along a little way, then stopped. She dropped the legs and disappeared behind the filing cabinets, looking to where Mike was going to install the new boiler. She ran back, Mel still not moving. She dragged her round the back of the cabinets. She dropped the legs and their deadweight and surveyed the site and the mess Mike had left and memorised the positions of the toolbox and other items lying about. He may be here soon. She'd move as little as possible and leave everything exactly as he'd left it.

There was a roll of silver tape, the thick, tough type plumbers use on leaky outside pipes. She tipped Mel onto her front. The end of the tape was stuck to the roll and hard to unpick with her Raynaud's gloves. About half the roll had already been used, she'd use it sparingly. She found the end, tore a two-foot length and taped Mel's wrists behind her back, tightly sticking a smaller strip over her mouth. She walked back to the old boiler's former position. No blood on the hammer in her hand. She checked the gloss-painted concrete floor, and the metal cover at the end with the cracked and dusty hole in the concrete to the side, about the width of Mike's finger. She needed a wee. She put the hammer back in his toolbox where she'd found it and took a wrench and the thickest, longest screwdriver. She levered the iron covering up – heavier than expected – and let it down. She levered it up again, enough to get the wrench in and hold the gap open. Soon she'd lifted the lid enough to slide it across and off. Taking the torch from a shelf, she shone a beam down the hole. It only had to be wide enough to get Mel's head and chest through, the rest would follow.

The torchlight illuminated part of the space below. It looked about four feet deep. She stuck her face in to see how far it went. The low, arched tunnel brickwork looked Victorian. No mice or rats or other nasties; just a few loose bricks and gritty rubble on the tunnel floor. Hard to tell how far it went. It was less than four feet wide. It was damp and there was a dark sludge-slick of grime. It could ruin her navy suit. She put another length of tape around Mel's legs at the knees, lifted her by the armpits again and dragged her the short distance to the open hole. Mel lay on her side, cheek against the cold floor, still breathing. She took a final length of tape, about four inches, and took Mel's face in her hands, the tape stuck to her thumb. Cradling her head, waiting till Mel breathed out she taped over the nostrils, adhering it permanently to the face. Mel's eyes opened wide in panic as she struggled desperately against the tape around her knees and wrists, over her mouth and nose, her hysterical screaming contained and muffled by the tape, her disabled legs writhing, thrashing breathless, immobilised, panicked in a final, wild death throe.

She'd positioned the girl so when she rolled her onto her stomach, her face would be over the hole, staring down. She stood up and took a step back, straining at the physical effort of it all. She lifted her hips as high as she could, high enough to drag Mel a couple of steps nearer the hole and gravity would take care of the rest. Eyes rolling in panic, her head and spine arched back to avoid the darkness with her muffled screams and desperate last moments. She strained, straightening. She arched, spasmed, then her body fell limp. Janice let go. Mel's head cracking against the concrete side before lolling into the darkness. She heaved the dead weight by the hips again and straddling, tugged her in short bursts closer to vanishment. Head, then neck, then shoulders, inch by inch, the girl disappeared into the dark and then, with one last tug, gravity took over and the floor swallowed her whole as she fell, face first, into the filthy tunnel.

Done. She'd done it.

But from the dank, a sudden gasp for breath echoed. The tape must've come loose. Mike would be here. She couldn't leave it like this. Mel softly cried, rasping, calling Janice's name, begging her to stop, to help. Then she screamed for help. It was too loud. She'd have to get in and finish it. There'd be loose bricks down there, she'd use one of them. She took off her jacket and hung it from a hook on the far wall, unzipped her skirt at the back and shimmied out, hanging it by the label. She unbuttoned her white blouse and hung it by the collar. Kicking off her shoes, being careful where she stepped, just in bra and knickers, she returned to the hole. The girl hurt, sobbing and bound, but still trying to move. She dangled her legs over the edge, took the torch and lowered herself in, steadied by putting a toe in a gap left by missing masonry. Mel saw the white, naked legs coming for her. She wriggled, dragging herself as far as she could from the dim shaft of light. There must be a way out.

Once down, Janice shone the torch in both directions. The torchlight lit perhaps twenty feet; she couldn't see further. Mel screamed, piercingly shrill. She shone the torch at her, seeing the tape loose, flap half off, Mel moving jerkily into the shadows almost out of torch range. Her eyes adjusted to the dark; there was other movement. Tiny dark shapes. They were moving, scurrying along the sides of the sludge on the tunnel floor, up the walls, everywhere, and she could hear them. Along the lines of the brickwork pointing, running through the silt. Their domain disturbed, the multitudinous rodents seethed around the walls of that ancient drain like loose leaves whirlpooling in a teacup. She picked up a fallen brick and, crouching slightly, darted towards Mel, scuttling like a cockroach. Mel screamed over and over; a last-ditch effort, maybe someone would hear, or Janice would stop.

She stepped over the broken administrator, put the brick under her arm and dragged her as far as she could. She pulled in the direction Mel had been heading, keeping a foot either side of the narrow, still river of thick, stagnant filth to avoid getting her bare feet too muddy. When about as far from the manhole cover to Trethendar's basement as she could easily get, and out of torch range, she stopped. She really needed a wee. She stepped over Mel so as not to get any on her and let it go, pissing like a pit pony. The urine spattered through her knickers and down her cellulite. The torchlight sparkled on her silver cross as she urinated and Mel sobbed, crying out.

Squeezing out the last drops she said, "We're so sorry you're leaving." Then she took the brick and beat Mel in the face to death with it.

She stood under the hole in the floor, exhausted. Silence. She pulled herself out using the same toe-hole and flicked off the worst of the dirt. She was just about to pull the cover back when she remembered the backpack by the door. So, still in her bra and wet panties she collected the backpack and dumped it in the hole next to the unrecognisable body.

She hoicked herself out again and sat with gnome-like legs dangling over the edge. This time her feet were filthy. She looked around to see what else she could use. There was nothing, so she worked off her wet knickers and wiped the muck from her feet with them.

Fully clothed now except for shoes and jacket, with knickers tucked in an impractical pocket, she replaced the manhole cover in its sealing position. She returned the screwdrivers and toolbox inner shelf layer just as they'd been, the tape and torch as well and anything that looked remotely like part of a bare footprint was erased with the ball of her foot.

One last look. With her shoes and jacket back on, she left the basement.

Mike came out of the tube station and headed towards Trethendar. He'd pick up a couple of buttered rolls with sausage on the way, brown sauce and a sweet tea, to set him up nicely for the day. He was early so in no rush. He'd be there in five or ten minutes, just like he said he would.

Upstairs in the office, all was quiet. The printing was gone, Mel must have it on her somewhere, in a pocket or something with the office keys she said she'd lost. Just Mel's personal mobile. She turned it off and took it. She left Mel's work phone in the desk drawer with her own, her own keys and snipped procurement card, all as she'd told Stuart it would be. She rolled off her gloves and popped them in her pocket, taking one final look around the office. All was just as it had been the night before.

As unlikely as it was that Mike would be in before 10am, she'd take no chances. She needed to leave. Mike would finish the boiler installation, in the basement directly over the cover to the tunnel, making it impossible to reopen and Mel would miss her flight. She bustled back downstairs and looked through the dusty windows to the still street. Not a soul. She reset the alarm, left, locked up and headed back to the hotel.

There was nothing she could do now, even if she had left some stone unturned, which she hadn't. She'd run it through her mind one final time. Best not ruminate or mull, she'd shower, change her clothes then maybe go to a gallery. The day was hers, after all. She concluded she'd covered everything, there was no box left unticked. She'd never need think about any of it again. Mike would arrive soon and let himself in. He'd get down to the basement and make good the tiny hole in the concrete by the manhole cover, sealing it with mastic, airtight, for good. He'd take the new boiler from its cellophane. He'd install it where the old one had been, over the manhole cover, entombing the missing mother-to-be for ever.

Strangely liberated, it was a first for her, to walk through London with no knickers on.

19

Just after 7:30am, the newest, biggest and most luxurious Princess cruise ship docked at Funchal, Madeira. She'd flown to Rome from Gatwick then spent half a day exploring before setting sail for Naples, then Tunisia, Casablanca and finally Lisbon.

She'd patronised the onboard spa for various treatments on an almost daily basis. She ate early and alone in her stateroom and managed, so far, to avoid speaking to any other passenger. Her only irritation, apart from the people obviously, was the constant photographing. Whenever they got on or off the ship, there'd be a pair of crew members dressed as centurions or pirates or explorers or the national dress of the country you'd arrived in. You'd be funnelled towards them, and they'd come at you from either side, grinning inanely while a picture was taken in the hope you'd purchase one from the gallery on deck seven that evening, while they ran around taking more pictures of you eating.

She'd avoided any pictures being taken but she didn't go unnoticed. She cut a lonely figure in the eyes of some. Hard not to notice the dowdy little woman in her navy suit with cream piping, traces of cat hair. Her straight, slate-grey bob; a style she'd not changed in decades and that tight, almost lipless, mouth pinched into what some refer to as a 'resting bitch face'.

Apart from attending the first of the two evening shows each night, regardless of what it was, she didn't participate in activities, bar one. There was a line dancing class, on Tuesdays, Thursdays and Sundays at 5pm. Sessions were forty-five minutes and she cut short her sightseeing not to miss them.

As the liner disembarked from Rome, she arranged her Fort Lauderdale accommodation at the agent's desk and transfers from there to her new home. It seemed a lifetime since Mike called to tell her he'd finished the boiler and that, once he'd tidied up, he'd be on his way. She'd been standing in the National Portrait Gallery, in front of a picture from 1908, *The Makers of British Music*.

"It'd been a doddle," he said. He'd locked up, reset the alarm. She thanked him for the update, he wished her well for her retirement and that was that.

The only other bit of business had been to tell Mr Savile she was going to visit Ben's house. She knew she'd probably never return to London or Whitstable again. She knew she may never speak to Mr Savile again, and so did he. Occasionally he'd do some work for a client like her and knew at the outset that they'd drop off the planet once the transaction was concluded.

He wished her well and told her to call him if she needed anything. She said she'd keep his number in the contacts of her new phone. His was the only number stored.

She'd already endured one sea day and was dreading the nine-day Atlantic crossing from Madeira to Florida; the last such trip of the season for this line and it could be choppy. Many ended their cruise in Funchal, and only a few new passengers joined it there.

All were issued with a card on day one the size of a credit card, which was scanned each time you left or boarded. Printed in gold with the relevant muster point, directions to get there from your cabin, the cruise dates and passenger name: Mrs Myra Westrell.

This would be the last time she'd see land for over a week. It was also the night she'd been looking forward to most. There was a Country 'n' Western night in the Emerald Room, with line dancing and impersonations of Grand Ole Opry greats, including Jim Reeves. The poster promised "…y'all a highfalutin, rootin' tootin' time" and she couldn't wait.

She didn't know if there was much in the way of shops at Funchal, but she took her card anyway. She needed at least one new outfit and hoped to pick up some bits and bobs to mix and match, arriving in America looking more like her passport photo and a less like Janice Mead. She left the ship with the A4 map she'd been issued and walked along the Avenida do Mar, towards the old part of Madeira's capital. She fancied a little sightseeing too before her hunt for new clothes, so as soon as it opened at 9am, she took the cable car into the mountains to the tropical gardens, ornamental ponds, paths, levadas and waterfalls. She pottered around the oriental-themed part, with black and scarlet bridges, pagoda and lion, dragon statuary, walking as far as the koi pond with its avant-garde spouting fountain, before turning back. She left refreshed after an hour's Zen meandering.

Outside the gates, a cab driver explained a deal for fifteen Euros. As the basket sledge took you only halfway down the mountain, he explained, you had to either walk the rest of the way or climb back up if you wanted to take the cable car down. Unless you went with him, in which case he'd either drive you the other half down or drive you back up so you could get the cable car. Sledge ride and cab was all included. She thanked him but said she'd skip it. She didn't want the sledge ride; she'd go the way she'd come.

She had a sticky slice of almond tart in town and a milky coffee at Opan before browsing boutiques and more familiar chain stores along the Avenida Arriaga. It caught her eye almost immediately. In the window of Senhora Maria was a leather-look cowgirl hat – cork treated to emulate leather. There were bags, wallets and even shoes made of the same material. The hat was covered in tiny rhinestones that curled and spiralled over the entire surface. She bought it with a matching belt and bag. She'd never bought anything like it before and didn't know if she had the courage to wear it, but it would be perfect for her evening in the Emerald Room if others were dressing up. She could afford to splash out now and a little collateral wastage was neither here nor there. Janice Mead would never wear this stuff, but Myra might. With a swelling, diamanté-delivered confidence, she got directions to the most expensive dress shop in Funchal that stocked age-appropriate garments.

Shopping done, she luxuriated at a table outside The Ritz, by the theatre and spectacular Jardin Municipal, with a glass of pinot grigio and plate of black scabbard fish and grilled banana. Delicious, with the texture of Dover sole but a delicate, distinctly meaty flavour. Custard-yellow cabs glinted in the sunlight, shadows lengthening and flowers blooming in abundance. She'd return to Funchal one day, she thought, and spend more time. There were seven boutique shopping bags under her table. All new underwear, two evening looks, a sort of workwear outfit of skirt and jacket if she needed to attend anything dressy, some slacks and a selection of blouses to go with them. She'd bought three pairs of shoes, various odds and sods to accessorise with and either ensemble up or dress down in countless casual outfits.

The shop girls helped her with dressing up and making over. The language barrier and fact she'd never see them again, made the experience an enjoyable respite from her lifetime's sense of intimidation in such stores. They nodded enthusiastically at most things, but occasionally grimaced and shook their heads, leading her to believe they really did have her best interests at heart and weren't simply using her to get rid of any old shit no one else would buy. They saw her as a challenge that desperately needed to be risen to. Sure, they made money that day, but they had fun too. Apparently, her name, 'Myra', was an acronym in Spain or Portugal that roughly translated as 'scheduling arrangement' or 'multiyear debt'. It couldn't be described as 'a whole new wardrobe', but it was a substantial start and would help her arrive in Florida looking the part. She'd never have worn these flamboyant cuts, colours or styles at home. Maybe she'd have a ceremonial burial at sea for her old clothes and the aged make-up dogends she'd replaced that afternoon. She checked the time. Just four hours till she'd need to be back on board.

She'd asked at a couple of salons, and they couldn't fit her in, but the last place suggested she try Renata's in the shopping centre back towards the dock, so she headed there. After the girl washed her hair, she was handed over to a woman of about forty, working under the watchful eye of a short, square-jawed harridan wearing too much make-up, possibly Renata. None spoke any English and the three generations stood behind her, staring at the brownfield site in the mirror in front of them, like the Fates. The old one spoke quickly and loudly and, with a hand gesture indicating something along the lines of, 'what the fuck are we meant to do with this?', turned her back. As the hair-washer pulled up the violet nylon and tucked tissue into her collar, Myra showed the middle Fate tasked with the work, her passport photo. Pointing at the picture, then at her lank, wet, grey hair, the Fate took the passport looked closer in disbelief, then back at Myra in the mirror. She pointed at the picture and said something in Portuguese. Myra nodded. She rolled her eyes – 'well if you're sure' – then got to work.

Her hair was coloured, cut and set within a few hours, all under the watchful eye of the youngest; obviously there to learn a trade but with little real interest in hairdressing. She asked Myra if she could see the make-up she'd bought. She was clearly impressed and as the finishing touches were being applied to her hair, the girl asked, in Portuguese again, if she'd like her to do her make-up before she left. Why not? Make-up was obviously more the girl's forte and as well as completing the makeover, managed to sell the transformed client some additional pieces to complete her set; some more daring autumnal tones. She'd never looked like this before, not even when her passport picture was taken. She looked at herself, the three generations standing behind admiring their handiwork; even Renata was impressed, begrudgingly. With the tip, it cost just over one hundred euros. She suspected they'd overcharged. She looked like she had money with her numerous shopping bags from Funchal's finest, but she still added an extra fiver each for the middle and youngest, then left for her liner, transformed.

After dressing for dinner, she sat on the edge of her stateroom bed to watch the end of an episode of *The Love Boat*. It always seemed to be on, day or night. Her overnight bag, so old and tatty. There was a shop on board where she could buy some modern luggage, in keeping with her spanking look. She'd leave the old bag behind in her room for the cute Filipino steward to deal with at the end of her trip. She'd tip him extra for the trouble. She placed it, empty, in a wardrobe compartment, deciding she'd not open it again.

A sated horn sounded a farewell to Funchal.

She drifted to the lowest deck, the back of the ship where the engines were louder, in full evening wear, with a Grace Kelly scarf keeping her hair unruffled by the wind, and dark glasses. She held a stuffed Tesco bag, the handles knotted, and the contents drenched to ensure it would sink. She watched the lights of Madeira and Europe grow distant. It would be over a week before she saw land again. She stood for a moment, mesmerised by the engine hum and seawater churn.

"Goodbye," she said quietly, dropping all she had left of her former life over the side, without hesitation or second thought. Her shoes, her underwear, her make-up, her blouses, her navy suit and her Raynaud's gloves. From her new handbag she took the mobile phone she needed to dispose of and dropped that into the ocean too, along with the keys to Trethendar that she'd had cut. Everything of Janice Mead was lost to the strong currents, all but the old overnight bag, abandoned in a corner of her stateroom. All she'd kept was a memory stick from work, the tiny silver cross she'd die wearing and the beaten-up notebook her former colleagues had given her, every page now filled with recipes. There was nothing else left of that woman who'd hidden for so long behind leylandii. The bag bobbed about for a bit before sinking, little by little, in the distance. Sinking with the memories she had pushed down or squeezed out, making room for the new.

Dear Ben. Mother. Martin. Baby Bimbo, bless his cotton paws. That dreadful Margie what's-her-name, the vicious Irene gone and deservedly so; and not forgetting the others from before, from much longer ago. She pictured Mike installing the hefty new appliance in position, masking the fact there'd ever been a manhole there. All material trace of that past gone, and any possible immaterial traces fading.

The Country 'n' Western theme had splurged over into the atrium, where a fiddler and banjo played. Heads turned as Mrs Myra Westrell descended the staircase of the grand atrium for the Raphael Restaurant. A slight woman stepping daintily down the spiralling stairs; reborn and resplendent in a white satin, bolero-jacketed trouser suit, with silver filigree embroidery. A huge rhinestone belt buckle spangled at her waist, glittering shoes fizzed and popped and the jazzy, dazzling cowgirl hat perched jauntily on top of a mass of Harpo-blonde permed curls, looking more like the entertainment.

All that the beaming Floridian wanted now was to have her dinner, hear some lovely Gentleman Jim and line dance the night away, dreaming of the blessed life she was embarking on in her adopted country and new home, Casa Cariño.

20

The person in the next seat opened the blind, letting the dawn sunshine in. It woke her, burning her eyes. She stretched, checking out the map graphic on the back of the seat in front. She'd endured two crappy movies and had all the usual interruptions for food and nibbles. It seemed like an age now since she'd finished her beer at Scotty 'n' Mal's on Cuba Street, before shooting to the airport.

"Landing soon," said the man who'd blinded her.

Glancing up the aisle, apart from a small queue outside the toilet, people were still asleep. She took her toothbrush and paste from her bag and squeezed out of her seat. Not designed for a woman with hips.

"How long? Do we know?" she asked him.

"An hour maybe."

She made her way down the aisle to join the queue. It felt good to stretch her legs. A small zit was forming by her mouth. She leaned her backside against a partition and looked across the sleepy people sea. Next time she'd pay the extra to go by the emergency exit, for the legroom and window. Bright sunlight emblazoned the clouds.

She had a pee and washed her face in the diminutive basin. She brushed her teeth and began to feel human again. Conscious she was holding others up, she quickly checked where the zit was forming. Not a problem. It would be concealed by part of the scrolling tattoo that swirled femininely down from the corners of her mouth to her chin. She had a full face, almond, with dark brown eyes and short hair, lacquered flat, black and glossy in gentle waves. She quickly gave her pits a wipe with a damp paper hand towel before binning it and applying a fresh coat of underarm.

Unlike her countrymen, travel wasn't something she'd ever felt compelled to do. Especially not Europe, especially not London; small, wet, dark and overcrowded. Back at her seat, just as they were coming round with breakfast, she'd resigned herself to the misery of it all. Ever since arriving at the airport she'd been shunted about.

Being a Taurean, she could be stubborn and measured, but she always ended up where she needed to be. She didn't suffer fools gladly and to the uninitiated, came across as serious, almost fierce, but she was a pussy cat. A great ally, she always had the backs of her friends in a crisis. Injustice was not tolerated. She had been a fighter too, figuratively and literally.

She hadn't really slept, just dozed. Knackered, but not incapacitated.

Within twenty minutes of breakfast being cleared, she'd landed at Heathrow and, after being shepherded through arrivals, passport control, and whatever other sheep-dip processes they'd herd her through in England, she'd head to the hostel she'd booked for the first week, till she found something better.

She was impressed by how sunny London looked considering it was October. After a ridiculously long walk down tunnels and walkways, she waited by the carousels with the rest of her herd. Her large, red, hardbacked case on wheels rolled round and she lifted it off as if it were empty. She wheeled it down a slope to UK Border Control. The non-EEA line she'd joined snaked, moving quicker than expected, and before long she was standing, the image of compliance, behind the green marker, waiting to be called next. The surly young guard ushered her forward, and she handed him her virgin passport. He looked at her picture, then at her face, then at her passport and then at her face again. Same tattoo, same face.

"I'm going to have to take your prints. Please put your index finger on the plate first." She complied. "Thank you. Now please look straight ahead." She complied. "Thank you. May I see your itinerary, please?"

"My what?"

"Your travel itinerary?"

"I don't have one. I'm staying in London."

"You're on a Youth Mobility Visa?"

"Yes."

"How old are you?"

"Twenty-eight."

She qualified up to the age of thirty. She knew it. He knew it. What was she? A student? There was no record of her having entered the UK before or outstaying a visa but there was always a first time. He needed to dig deeper to cover his back. Sandip was still fairly new. It's what he'd been told in training.

"This is you? Kamana? Christine Kamana?"

"Yes."

"Is that Italian?"

"It's Maori."

"How long are you staying in London?"

"Six months." She was beginning to sound irritated. Was this grilling normal?

"Did you pack your bag yourself?"

"Yes."

"And you're travelling from...?" He looked at her quizzically. Was he taking the piss? He had her passport in his hand.

"Wellington. I've come from New Zealand." She glanced at his name badge. "Is there a problem... Sandip."

Macho mask slipping. "I'm sorry, Ms Kamana, I have to ask these questions. Sorry." He reached for his stamp.

"That's alright, mate. I'm a bit tired and fucked off too. Long bloody flight, you know? Sorry to snap. Are we good? Can you stamp my thing or is there something else?" She looked over her shoulder at the new arrival behind the green line, in mounting embarrassment.

"Just one more question," he remembered.

"Shoot."

"What's the purpose of your visit?"

"What?"

She seemed suddenly floored, genuinely confused, but there was something else, as if she didn't know where to start. She blinked slowly, exhausted, defeated. Her pinkening eyes starting to fill. Was she going to cry? He suddenly felt bad. He'd upset this stunning, tough-looking woman. He'd hoped this would be the career for him, after eighteen months of drifting in and out of retail and unsuccessful interviews for crappy jobs, but in his heart, he wasn't a Border Forces officer.

"I asked what the purpose of your visit is."

She took a deep breath and wiped an exhausted, angry tear from her eye. She'd say it as calmly and concisely as she could, sticking to the facts. She'd never been forced to tell a stranger she was gay before and her lip quivered.

"My girlfriend and baby, our unborn baby, should've got home three months ago, but she never arrived. She's missing. No one has heard from her, not even her mum and it makes no sense. Technically she outstayed the terms of her visa, but she wouldn't do that. She is a total goody-two-shoes. Something's very wrong here, but no one will do anything. I love her to the fucking moon and back, so... I just..." She was exhausted and couldn't finish. He quickly stamped her passport, sorry he'd asked, and passed it to her, but she needed to finish. "I'm here to take her home," she said. "To find her, find out what happened and to take her home."